T0128854

THE EVERYDAY HOUSEWIFE

Murder, Drugs, and Ironing

Bryan Foreman

iUniverse, Inc.
Bloomington

The Everyday Housewife
Murder, Drugs, and Ironing

This is a work of fiction. All of the characters, names, incidents, organizations, and dialogue in this novel are either the products of the author's imagination or are used fictitiously.

iUniverse books may be ordered through booksellers or by contacting:

iUniverse
1663 Liberty Drive
Bloomington, IN 47403
www.iuniverse.com
1-800-Authors (1-800-288-4677)

ISBN: 978-1-4502-3472-6 (pbk)
ISBN: 978-1-4502-3473-3 (cloth)
ISBN: 978-1-4502-3474-0 (ebook)

Library of Congress Control Number: 2010908279

Printed in the United States of America

iUniverse rev. date: 2/6/12

For my mom and dad

Chapter 1: A Woman's Work is Never Done

The alarm clock went off at 6:45 AM, as it did every weekday morning, and woke Frank and Katharine Beaumont from deep sleep. Frank reached over the nightstand to shut it off and then rolled slowly out of bed in his blue pajamas.

"Oh shit," Katharine grumbled and gradually opened her eyes. "Where am I?"

"You're in Oklahoma City, my dear," her husband answered as he walked up to the dresser and turned on the lamp.

"Great," Katharine said. "And it's Monday ... isn't it?"

"Afraid so," he replied. "The date is May the third, two thousand and ten. And it is currently six forty-seven in the AM."

"I was having such a wonderful dream," she said. "We were having cocktails on the beach ... Cancun I think. Or was it Rio?"

"You don't have to get up just yet," Frank said. "Go back to sleep. Maybe you can pick up where you left off."

"Yeah, right," she scoffed, knowing it was her job to wake the kids and see them off to school. She pulled the covers aside and rolled out on her side of the bed. "I'll go fix breakfast."

Before she headed off to the kitchen, she stumbled to the bedroom closet, slipped out of her nightgown, and donned a pair of blue jeans and an orange blouse. Then she walked into the adjoining bathroom and stood in front of the mirror next to her husband, who was busy brushing his teeth. She grabbed a comb from the counter and drew a heavy sigh.

1

"Oh God … is this me?" she muttered, noticing her puffy cheeks and the lines on her face. Only her beautiful blue eyes reminded her of the hottie she had once been. Though it seemed like a lifetime ago, she had been elected homecoming queen two years in a row at the University of Oklahoma; she still had the photographs to prove it.

Her husband looked at her in the mirror and smiled. "You're still a knockout," he said. Toothpaste dribbled down his chin.

"Shut up." She laughed, realizing he was just trying to make her feel better.

He still looked the same as when they'd first met—tall, dark, and handsome, with a thirty-two-inch waistline. *Life can be so unfair,* she thought.

She ran the comb through her hair a few times, but it didn't seem to help much. Finally, she gave up and slapped it back down on the counter.

"I'll go fix breakfast," she grumbled.

She walked out of her room and stopped in front of the staircase, which led to the upstairs bedrooms. "Billy, Maggie! Time to get up!" she shouted.

Next she headed off to the kitchen, threw some bacon into a frying pan, and turned on the stove.

"Mama!" her daughter shouted from her bedroom about a minute later.

"Here we go." Katharine laughed and shook her head, quickly turning off the front burner and walking out of the kitchen.

"I lost a button, Mama," Maggie whined as Katharine entered the room. The girl was thirteen years old and looked almost as pretty as her mom even though she had a chubby face and was thirty pounds overweight.

"Can you fix it?" Maggie asked with a helpless look on her face. She held up a pink shirt.

"Jesus, Maggie. Can't you find another one?" Katharine said.

"I want to wear this," Maggie whined.

"Oh all right." Katharine sighed as she walked over to her and grabbed the shirt. She rushed downstairs to her sewing room. Three minutes later, she returned and handed Maggie back her shirt; its brand-new button was sewn firmly in place.

"Thanks, Mama," said Maggie, breathing a sigh of relief.

"If you expect that button to stay on, you're gonna have to lose some weight," Katharine replied sternly.

The girl huffed and immediately turned away.

"I know you don't like to hear it, but it's for your own good," Katharine said.

"You're stomach's gettin' bigger, and nobody's nagging at you," her daughter blurted out foolishly.

Completely shell-shocked, Katharine just looked at Maggie. *How could she?* she thought. *After all that I've done for her, day in and day out.* Though she felt like slapping her daughter, Katharine quickly came to her senses and said, "You're right. Who am I to talk?" Then with a smile, she added, "I'll tell you what, tomorrow we'll start dieting together. What do you say? I hear that South Beach Diet's pretty good."

"Whatever," the girl scowled and started to take off her pajamas.

Katharine stormed bitterly out of the room. "Billy, I said get up!" she exclaimed. She walked to his bedroom and opened the door. Her fourteen-year-old son lay in bed, breathing heavily; his hand frantically bobbed up and down underneath the sheets.

"Jesus! Do you ever stop?" she scolded him. "Put that thing away and get your butt out of bed!"

She went back to the kitchen and finished frying the bacon. Then she started the eggs as she toasted two slices of bread and prepared the orange juice. The meal was all waiting on the table for Frank when he finally walked into the kitchen. She felt him sneak up behind her as she stood over the counter making the children's breakfast.

"Oh, Kat, you're too much," he said, putting his arms around her and kissing her cheek. "I don't deserve you."

"I know," she jokingly replied. Then she let out a sigh and said, "When are we gonna get this kitchen remodeled once and for all? I can barely move around in here."

"When we can afford it," he answered.

"Which means never." She laughed.

"Are you sure you want to put up with a bunch of noisy construction workers for three to six months?" he asked.

"If the outcome is more working space and brand new appliances, then yes," she replied.

"Someday," he said. "As far as breakfast is concerned, I'm afraid I'm gonna have to skip it. The boss wanted me to come in a little early this morning. Sorry. Guess I should've told you." He kissed her one more time and then immediately stepped away. "Why don't you eat it for me?" he said as he rushed out of the room, dressed in his suit and tie. "You could probably use a good breakfast." He stuck his head back in for a second and added, "You need a break from all of this anyway. I'll bring home a pizza tonight. How does that sound?"

"Don't bother," she replied. "I don't mind cooking."

"Nope. Dinner's on me," he insisted as he hurriedly walked away.

After she heard him leave the house, she shouted, "Billy!"

"I'm up!" her eldest child shouted back at her from his bedroom.

Suddenly the doorbell rang. Katharine set the extra food down on the table and went to answer the door. Not surprisingly, it was her next door neighbor, Mrs. Guzman, who was always bugging her about something. The large woman had a dark complexion and wore a yellow muumuu. She held her toy schnauzer with her left arm. The dog had a Band-Aid on her little nose, and both she and her owner looked very upset.

"What can I do for you, Mrs. Guzman?" Katharine asked.

"Look what your stupid gato done to my lil' Poopsi," said the distraught old woman.

"Are you sure it was our cat?" Katharine asked, glancing over at their gray tabby laying at the foot of the stairs with a devil-may-care look about him.

"Yes, Mrs. Beaumont," the woman sneered. "He keeps jumpin' the fence at night and tries to … well, you know." She disgustedly shook her head. "Didn't you hear them fighting earlier this morning?" she asked.

"No, I'm afraid we're all sound sleepers around here," Katharine replied.

"Well, you better keep your animal out of my backyard from now on or I don't know what," the woman warned her. "I don't keep guns in the house, but I hear antifreeze will do the trick."

"All right, Mrs. Guzman. I understand," Katharine said and immediately shut the door on her before things really got ugly. She turned around and glared at Mugsy the cat, who remained indifferent. "I'll deal with you later," she said.

Finally both kids came downstairs fully clothed, ate their Pop-Tarts, and then hurried out the front door to catch their bus. Katharine breathed a huge sigh of relief as she watched them leave. At last she had the house all to herself. She thought about going back to bed but decided to clean up the kitchen instead. After that, she tackled the bathrooms—both upstairs and down—and the children's bedrooms. Then she vacuumed every inch of carpet in the house and ironed all of her husband's shirts that she pulled out of the dryer.

Catching her second wind, she stepped out into the backyard to water the plants and hose down Dusty, their family's golden retriever, who was long overdue for a bath. Next she dragged the cat outside and gave him a good soaking as well. He angrily scrambled away and headed for the doghouse.

"Jump that fence again and you'll get more of the same!" she warned him.

Her best friend, Norma dropped by just before lunch and did her best to distract Katharine from her duties. Norma had always been a big, robust woman, even back in college when they were roommates. She was the strong, feisty one while Katharine was extremely shy and reserved. It had been Norma who helped Katharine come out of her shell back then, which had led to her becoming homecoming queen. And it had been Norma who helped her discover her dark side, by introducing her to the off-campus party scene. Katharine's ambition to become a serious journalist was suddenly replaced with a desire to have fun and become a serious party animal, going out to the local pub almost every night and bringing home strange men. She also acquired a taste for cheap vodka, marijuana, and cocaine.

Then, she met Frank in English class and it all came to an abrupt end as she quickly fell in love. It was as if that side of her never even existed… just a bad dream, perhaps. She devoted herself and her time completely to him, accompanying him to the movies, hanging out with him and his frat buddies at the pool hall, helping him study for the big exam, etc. Before long, they were discussing marriage and children and planning to spend the rest of their lives together. It was already decided that he would be the traditional breadwinner, making loads of money in the advertising game, while she would stay at home to take care of the children. They played out their roles admirably. And thanks to their hard work and dedication, it appeared that they were now living the American dream.

Norma wasted very little time trying to sway Katharine to the dark side once again. As they sat next to each other on the living room couch, Norma reached into her purse and pulled out a big bag of weed, placing it directly in between them.

"What's this?" Katharine asked, completely taken aback.

"What does it look like?" Norma said. "I found it in my son's underwear drawer, this morning. I told him that the next time I found pot in his room that I would confiscate it. I was going to wring his neck when he gets home from school, but I think I'll just smoke it all instead. That should be punishment enough for him."

"Okay," Katharine said. "But, what's it doing here?"

Norma just looked at her with a fiendish grin as she reached back into her purse and pulled out some rolling papers, along with a cigarette lighter.

"Absolutely not," Katharine said, laughing nervously and shaking her head. "We'll have this whole house smelling like marijuana and then how am I going to explain that one to Frank and the kids?"

"Oh c'mon, Kat," Norma begged her. "It'll be fun… just like old times."

"Nope, put it away," Katharine insisted. "I don't do that stuff anymore."

"Okay," Norma sighed and put all the items back into her purse. "You're just no fun at all… now that you're all grown up. You put all of us housewives to shame, the way you keep this place in such immaculate condition. Is Frank paying you, at least?"

"I don't mind it, really," Katharine said.

"It's slave labor, I'm tellin' ya," Norma blurted out. "You should give yourself a break and live a little."

Katharine just looked at her and smiled.

"How's that book comin' along, anyway?" Norma then asked.

"It's not a book," Katharine corrected her. "It's not much of anything, actually—just scribbling in a notebook."

"Well, let's see it," Norma said excitedly.

"Oh no," Katharine replied, embarrassed.

"Come on," Norma said, nudging her in the arm. "You can show me. We're friends."

"No." Katharine laughed.

"Forget it, Kat. I ain't takin' no for an answer, this time," Norma said. We never do anything together because you're always too busy writing. So, let me see it. Or was it just a ruse to avoid spending time with me?"

"Oh very well," Katharine huffed. "If it will save our friendship."

She got up and headed for the bedroom. Seconds later, she returned with a large notebook in hand. It was about three inches thick, and the majority of its pages were curled along the edges and filled with ink. She immediately gave it to her friend, who began to thumb through it with a look of childlike excitement.

"Good lord, you *have* been busy," said Norma. "There must be over four hundred pages here. So what's it all about?"

"Well, it's two stories, actually," Katharine explained. "The first one's about a nurse who slowly goes insane and starts killing off her patients one by one. It took me almost two years to write it."

"A nurse turned serial killer." Norma smiled. "I like it. So does Frank know about this?"

"No, no one does. Except for you," Katharine answered.

"It's a shame. How they all take you for granted and have no idea just how talented you are," Norma said. "What's this other story about?"

"Oh, it's just a spy thriller," said Katharine. "I'm not quite finished with it yet."

"And what's it called?"

"*The Amazing Adventures of Kitty Everhart—Volume One: Lost on Devil's Island.*"

"Ah, a female spy," Norma said. "Is it you?"

"Of course," Katharine replied. "I try to put a little of myself into all my characters. That's why I enjoy writing so much. I get to be all these different people at once and travel all over the world without ever leaving the couch."

"Well, you need to hurry up and finish so you can get this thing published," Norma declared.

"I don't care about that," Katharine said.

"Oh really?" her friend scoffed. "You're not interested in seeing your published work in all the bookstores, with your name on it? Or making millions of dollars and buying a second home in Santa Barbara?"

"No, it doesn't interest me at all," she replied, unflinching.

"Come on." Norma laughed. "You can bullshit yourself all you want. But this is your best friend you're talking to."

"I'm serious," Katharine said. "My place is here with my family. I've got a husband who adores me and two kids that really need me. Boy, do they need me." She sighed and shook her head. "It might not sound like much to you, but it's the life I've chosen. And I'm willing to stick it out to the bitter end."

"I'm sure that you can hang on to all of this and still become a published writer," Norma scoffed.

Katharine laughed. "Yeah, but you know how that kind of success changes people," she said.

"Nonsense," Norma said. "Why do the work if you have no desire to show it to the world?"

"I don't know. It fills the time. And it beats working a crossword puzzle," Katharine joked.

"Who's that famous romance writer you're always talking about?" Norma asked.

"Elaine Cook," she answered.

"Yeah, that's the one," said her friend. "I read an article about her somewhere. Get this: she has a house in the Hamptons with twelve bedrooms, over a dozen servants, a private gym, and even her own personal trainer. I bet she's fucking him."

"Who in the hell needs twelve bedrooms?" Katharine laughed. "It's just more to clean."

"Anyway"—Norma scowled at her—"what I thought I'd do is go home, get on the Internet, and find out who her agent is. Then I'll write down all of her contact information and bring it back to you."

"Why would you want to do that?" Katharine sighed.

"To get you published, dear. What else?" Norma said, gently bopping Katharine on the head.

Katharine knew there was no point in arguing with Norma once she had made her mind up, so she kept silent.

"If you had a computer in the house like most people, we could do it here," Norma continued. "Plus you wouldn't have to be workin' out of this crappy notebook."

"Billy had one in his room," Katharine replied, "but we had to get rid of it when we discovered that he was using it for other things besides his homework."

"I don't know who's worse, your kid or mine?" Norma laughed and shook her head. She got up, tossed the notebook in Katharine's lap, and rushed to the front door. "I'll be back later with that information," she said. "Meanwhile, you keep writing. It's not going to get finished on its own."

As Katharine watched her friend leave, she imagined what it must be like to be a best-selling novelist, waited on hand and foot by her beautiful manservants while her lover and personal trainer—the wonderful George Clooney—gave her a massage. *Maybe Norm's got the right idea,* she thought with a huge smile on her face.

She grabbed her pen from the coffee table and started to write, just as Norma had suggested. Suddenly it was April 5, 1938, and Katharine's sexy young spy, Kitty Everhart, and Kitty's field commander, Alan Stone, were on board a cargo ship headed for an uncharted island somewhere in the South Pacific. Their mission—to kidnap Swedish billionaire, Mikael Ljungberg, who lived on the island with his mother and sister. The forty-three-year-old Swede was a shrewd businessman, banker, and financier. Through fellow spies in Nazi Germany, the two secret agents had learned he was about to join forces with Adolf Hitler by becoming the primary financier for Hitler's war against Poland. Once they kidnapped him, they would take him back to British Intelligence in London, England, to be brainwashed and held captive there until Hitler's demise, which they felt certain was very near.

At the moment, a violent storm raged at sea. The fate of the ship and its inhabitants remained uncertain as thirty-foot waves violently rocked the ship back and forth.

"Where in the hell is my chief officer?" Captain O'Hara said as he stood on the bridge with a third of his crew. The silver-haired captain was smartly dressed in his old naval uniform and matching white cap. "Go find Fielding, and get him up here immediately," he said to his gofer, who was standing next to him.

"Yes, sir," said Omar, a young Egyptian boy who had no other home or family to speak of. He lived aboard ship with his beloved captain. He quickly saluted the captain and rushed below deck.

"You don't need him here to tell you what to do," Commander Stone of British Intelligence said sternly to Captain O'Hara. "Just get us to that island. That's your job."

The big, burly fifty-year-old man stood just a few feet away from the captain and studied his every move, as did everyone else on the bridge. For someone so wise and experienced, the old captain seemed a little unsure of himself this time, as if he had suddenly lost his touch. And if ever there was a time that he needed his first mate by his side to give him guidance ... Unfortunately, Fielding would rather be playing cards with the men down below or romancing a beautiful woman, when there happened to be one on board.

"Sir, if we're going to turn away from this thing, we have to do it now," said the young, curly-haired navigator sitting at his station.

He listened to weather reports through the headphones he wore. "That waterspout's headed right for us."

"That's not a waterspout, you twit," Stone scoffed as he stared out into the darkness. "Believe me, I've seen worse." He turned to the captain again and said, "We can't afford to turn around at this point. There's been too many delays already. The Germans probably know exactly what we're up to by now."

"In just a matter of seconds, this ship's either going to capsize or break apart, and we're all going to drown," the young navigator warned them.

"Where in the hell is Fielding?" the captain grumbled.

"Oh, forget him!" Stone exclaimed and angrily turned away. "He's somewhere down below shagging my apprentice. She's a hell of a spy. But seducing men is more than just a job to her, I'm afraid; it's a religion."

Finally the captain looked over at his helmsman named Kamau Osei-Owusu—Jones for short—who stood behind the wheel. "All right, steady as she goes," he told Jones.

The large muscular man gave him a quick nod and forged ahead, undaunted. He was dressed very sparingly because he had grown up in the African jungle as a Maasai warrior. He wore short pants, sandals, a brown leather vest, and a colorful set of beads over his massive neck. He also wore a little stocking cap on his shiny bald head and had a long knife hanging from his hip. His fellow crewman and best friend, Barkesdale, stood just outside of the wheelhouse in his raincoat, preparing the lifeboat. Barksdale looked in for a moment, and the two men exchanged glances of pure dread.

A minute later, the young navigator looked up at gray-suited Commander Stone and said, "Do you want the good news? There it is." He pointed straight ahead.

Stone's eyes suddenly lit up as he noticed the dark cluster of trees off in the distance.

"I see it," he said.

"The bad news is we're all about to die," the young man added and scowled at the agent as the vision of the island quickly faded, replaced

by the sight of a two-hundred-foot wave headed right for them at an alarming speed.

"Jesus!" Stone blurted out, his eyes growing even wider, this time full of fear.

"My God, what have I done?" Captain O'Hara muttered, staring at the monstrosity.

Suddenly the telephone rang. Katharine immediately put down her pen and notebook, got up, and ran into the kitchen to answer it.

"Hello?"

"Mrs. Beaumont, this is Mrs. Prichard—student principal from Highland West Middle School."

Oh shit. Not again, Katharine thought and let out a heavy sigh.

"You need to come pick up your son," the woman continued in a curt manner. "I'm afraid he's gotten himself into more trouble."

"I'll be right there," Katharine said and immediately hung up the phone.

She arrived at her son's school about ten minutes later and walked up to the principal's office, filled with dread. *What did he do this time?* she thought. *Burn down the school cafeteria? Poke someone's eye out with a number two pencil?*

"Mrs. Beaumont, we caught your son Billy masturbating in the girls' restroom," the school principal said as Katharine opened the door and stepped in.

The middle-aged woman sat behind her desk and had a stern look on her face. Billy sat in the chair in front of her, dressed in faded jeans and a Radiohead T-shirt. The young dark-haired teen stared down at his shoes and appeared to be mad at the world, as always.

"Actually, it was our science teacher, Mrs. Cruddle, who found him." She continued. "He was sitting in one of the stalls and making strange noises. The poor woman almost had a heart attack when she kicked open the door and saw him sitting there. We also found *this* in his locker." She held up the latest issue of *Hustler* magazine with two naked lesbians on the cover. "Do you know where he might have gotten ahold of it?"

"No," Katharine gasped. "We don't subscribe to that particular magazine."

The woman slapped it back down on the desk and looked up at Katharine disapprovingly, as if she was the one in trouble.

"This isn't the first time your son's been in here, Mrs. Beaumont, as you and I both know," she said. "Three weeks ago, he was caught hiding in a broom closet inside the cheerleaders' dressing room."

"Yes, I remember it well." Katharine blushed.

"Such unacceptable behavior won't be tolerated at this school, Mrs. Beaumont," the principal said. "That's why I'm sending him home with one week of suspension. I'm sorry, but we've tried everything—counseling, detention. It's up to you now. Perhaps you should consider a psychotherapist."

"A psychiatrist?" Katharine smiled. "But aren't they a little expensive?"

"Take control of your son, Mrs. Beaumont," the woman said sternly. "Talk to him. Make him listen. And hopefully when he comes back in one week, he'll have a whole new attitude."

"Yes, Mrs. Prichard, whatever you say," Katharine said. She looked over at her son and said, "Well, Billy, are you proud of yourself?"

The young boy smirked and continued to stare at the ground with his angry expression.

"Go home with your mother now, Billy," the principal ordered him.

He quickly jumped up from the chair and marched out of the room without acknowledging either of them. His mother turned and started to walk out behind him.

"Mrs. Beaumont," the principal said.

She slowly turned back around to catch another glimpse of the woman's abusive stare.

"If this sort of thing happens again, I'm going to have to expel him."

"Sure, I understand."

The drive home was extremely awkward. She didn't know how to handle the situation or what to say to him as she kept glancing at him in the passenger seat.

"Well, you really outdid yourself this time," she finally blurted out. "Wait 'til your father hears about it."

He just smirked again and kept looking out his window.

"So where did you get the *Hustler* magazine?" she asked him.

"I bought it," he grumbled.

"You bought it?" She gasped. "Where?"

"The Quickie Mart by our house," he snapped. "They never ask for your ID."

"Well, I guess we'll just have to talk to the manager about that," she said. "What else have you been gettin' there? Beer, cigarettes? Please tell me you haven't been smoking."

"Jesus, Mom," he huffed and suddenly turned to look at her. "Let's all jump to conclusions, why don't we?"

"If you don't straighten up, they're going to expel you," she said. "Did you know that?"

He immediately turned toward his window again.

"What are we supposed to do, then?" she continued. "Spend thousands of dollars to put you in a private school? Your poor father works hard enough as it is to make ends meet." She could tell by the permanent scowl on her son's face that she wasn't getting through to him. So she tried a softer approach with a little more kindness and understanding. "You know, if you need to talk about anything, anything at all," she said, "I'm here to listen." She noticed him laughing at her. "What's so funny?" she said a bit defensively. "I was your age once, believe it or not. I know exactly what it's like. Your voice changes, body's changin'. And all of a sudden you find yourself drawn to the opposite sex. It's all a part of becoming an adult."

"Please, Mom. I'm not a retard," he grumbled.

"Sorry. I'm just trying to help," she said. "You should probably talk to your father, though. He's much wiser, and he always knows just what to say." She thought about it for a second and added, "Or maybe you'd rather talk to a professional. I don't know how we'll be able to afford it, but we'll figure something out."

"I don't need a goddamn shrink, if that's what you're drivin' at!" he exclaimed. "So why don't you just drop it? Okay?"

"First of all, don't swear, and don't yell at your mother," she said, trying to stay calm. "And, no, it's not okay. Do you know how embarrassing it is to walk into the principal's office and hear that your son's been pleasuring himself in a public restroom—a women's restroom, for that matter—when he's supposed to be learning something in class with all the other boys and girls?" She lost her composure. "It's sick, Billy!" she exclaimed. "I'm sorry, but there's no other word for it! It's just … sick!"

"Okay, I'm sorry, and I won't do it again!" he shouted back at her. "Now just leave me alone!"

He turned away from her once more as if he wanted to shut her out for good. His rude and insensitive behavior hurt Katharine deeply. They didn't say another word to each other until the SUV was parked in the garage and they were walking into the house.

"Go to your room," she demanded. "And don't come out 'til I tell you to."

"Yes, mein Führer," he jeered and began goose-stepping toward the stairs.

An hour later her daughter came home and confronted her with more school troubles.

"What's the matter?" Katharine asked as Maggie walked into the living room, bawling like a baby.

Katharine immediately jumped up from the couch and threw her arms around her.

"The boys all made fun of me at school," Maggie cried. "They called me Miss Piggy and snorted at me."

"Well, you shouldn't have worn that tight shirt," Katharine pointed out to her. "Look at it. The button's startin' to pop off again."

"But I love this shirt," she cried. "And what does *that* have to do with it? They had no right to say those things."

"Yes, I know," Katharine consoled her. "But boys will be boys. They're cruel and obnoxious. I'm sorry, but that's just the way it is. You either got to be thick-skinned and not let them get to you, or you can show them up by losing those extra pounds that I keep tellin' you about."

"Jeez, Mom! You're just as bad as they are!" Maggie shouted and quickly broke away from her. "Why can't you all just accept me for who I am?"

Katharine looked at her daughter, completely dumbstruck once again and wondering how she had become the villain all of a sudden. As the child frantically ran upstairs, the doorbell rang.

"Oh, what now?" Katharine huffed and went to answer it.

It was Norma returning with a sheet of paper in her hand. The big woman barged right on in as Katharine opened the door. "Well, here you are. She lives in New York City, so you'll have to correspond through the mail or by telephone ... or email if you ever get that computer."

"What on earth are you talking about?" said Katharine, finally managing to interrupt.

"Elaine Cook's literary agent!" Norma exclaimed. "It's all here— her address, phone number. For Christ's sakes, woman! Where's your head?"

"I really don't have time for this." Katharine stepped away as her friend attempted to hand over the sheet of paper.

"Is everything all right?" Norma asked in a concerned tone.

"Everything will be fine once this day's over with," Katharine huffed.

"Well, I'll just leave this with you then," her friend said. She turned around and placed the sheet of paper down on the windowsill next to the door. Before she walked out, she added, "Don't lose sight of your goal! We've gotta get you published!"

"It's your goal. Not mine!" Katharine shouted back a second too late.

Her husband came home at 6:00 PM; he walked straight to the kitchen counter to look through the mail. Katharine was in the dining room, putting supper on the table. After she told him what Billy had done, he simply shook his head and said, "Boy, that's a new one. I suppose you had a talk with him."

"No, you talk to him," she replied sternly. "If he was flunking algebra or something normal like that, I could deal with it. But masturbation—that's your department. Besides, he won't listen to me."

"Well, *I* don't know what to say to him," Frank blurted out and shrugged his shoulders, making himself completely useless to her.

"And that's why you're treated like a saint around here and I'm the Wicked Witch of the West," she snapped and started to walk off.

She felt his hand grab the back of her belt and came to a sudden stop.

"All right, I'll do it," he said. Yet he continued to look at the utility bill.

"Now, Frank!" she yelled at him.

He slapped the mail back down on the counter and walked out of the room. He returned within a couple of minutes and started to thumb through it again.

"Well? Did you talk to him?" she asked and got right back in his face.

"Yeah, I talked to him," he said very curtly.

"And did you punish him?"

"Yes, I did," he said. "I grounded him for a couple of days. It'll give him something to think about."

"Oh, that oughta do it," she scoffed. "Did I mention that they're going to expel him next time?"

"What was I supposed to do, Katharine?" he exclaimed. "Bend him over my knee and beat the livin' tar out of him?"

"Yeah, for starters!" she shouted back at him. "Our boy's a sex offender, Frank! We're lucky if the school doesn't press charges!" Then she stormed out of the kitchen mumbling, "I swear, I have to do everything 'round here."

She rushed upstairs and burst into her son's room. She didn't even bother to knock first.

"You're grounded for six weeks, mister. With no allowance!" she swiftly announced to him. "No TV either!"

He looked up at her, completely stunned as he lay there on the edge of his bed with his pants down and one hand on his member. His other hand held up a *Penthouse* magazine.

"And for the love of God, would you stop playing with yourself!" Katharine added, suddenly on the verge of tears.

"Damn it, Billy, don't you make me come up there again!" Katharine heard her husband shout.

She immediately slammed the door on Billy and rushed back downstairs. Frank was now seated on the living room couch with the television remote in his hand. She glared at him and walked straight back into the kitchen.

Chapter 2: Midnight Confession

Katharine fell right asleep that night, only to be awakened by her husband about two hours later.

"Honey, are you awake?" he asked and gave her a gentle nudge on the shoulder. She lay with her back turned to him.

"Not tonight, dear. I'm very tired," she said in a faint voice, thinking that he wanted to make love. "Just go to sleep."

"I can't," he replied. "There's something I have to get off my chest." Then he hesitated and drew a heavy sigh. "I guess I'll just come right out with it," he said finally. "I've been seeing someone else."

Her eyes popped open, and she was suddenly wide awake.

"You're kidding, right?" she replied, keeping her back turned to him.

"No," he answered plainly.

"Who is she, and how long has it been going on?" she asked, still doubting him.

"About six months," he replied. "She works at the company, but I don't think you've met her. Her name's Bernice. She's Albert's secretary."

Bernice, Bernice, Katharine thought to herself, trying to put a face to the name. *Oh yeah, Bernice.* "Didn't I see her at the Christmas party?" she asked him. "Kinda tall and awkward-looking? Like a female Lurch?"

"Yeah, that's her." He sighed.

"But she isn't even all that pretty," she said.

"No, you're much more beautiful," he swiftly replied.

"Well, that doesn't make much sense," she said skeptically. "Why would you want to be with someone who isn't as pretty?"

"I don't know," he answered, sounding deeply frustrated. "I tried to resist her at first, but she just kept coming on to me."

"Coming on to you how?" she asked.

"Grabbing my tush, telling me I'm sexy … Do we really need to go into specifics?" he snapped. "Just stuff you'd never do."

"I would, if you asked," she said.

"It doesn't matter," he replied. "The point is it happened, and I feel bad about it. The last thing I wanted to do was to hurt you."

There was a long silence as Katharine lay there, totally flabbergasted.

"Don't you have anything to say?" he asked her finally.

"I don't know what to say," she answered.

"You're not mad?"

"I'm surprised more than anything," she said. "I mean, you … having an affair? Who would've thought?"

"Why is it so hard to believe?" he snapped. "I'm quite capable of being with other women, you know."

"I know," she replied. "It's just that you've always seemed so … faithful. I thought you loved me."

"I *do* love you," he assured her. "Don't you even doubt that for a second. It was a mistake, that's all. Just a huge mistake."

"Still, I don't see how you managed to pull it off," she said, remaining skeptical to the end. "You're always home by six and here on the weekends."

"Jesus," he muttered. "If you really must know, it all happened at work—long lunch breaks, pretend meetings. Do you remember that meeting I had with the General Mills executive, a couple of weeks ago? It never happened. It was all a lie."

"I remember," she said. "You called me up just before it."

"Actually I was calling you from the Hyatt Regency," he confessed. "We were just about to get a room—me and her."

"I was wondering why you bothered to call me at work just to tell me about some silly old meeting," she said. "But I guess you had to—guilty conscience and all."

"For God's sake, Katharine. Don't try to analyze it," he begged her. "It's over. I swear to you, it's over." Again there was a long silence. "So do you think we'll be able to get past this or not?" he asked.

"I don't know, Frank," she sighed. "First the kids … now this? I've had enough for one day. Please, let's just get some sleep, and we'll deal with it in the morning."

"All right," he muttered. "But I won't be able to sleep unless you forgive me. Guess I'll just lay here and keep staring up at the ceiling."

"I forgive you," she said just to shut him up.

"You mean it?" he asked excitedly. Then he immediately began praising her as he turned over on his side. "Oh, baby, you're one in a million," he said. "How could I have been so stupid? I know one thing for sure. It'll never happen again."

Katharine pretended to be asleep at that point, but her eyes remained wide open as she wondered what to do next now that her whole world was going up in flames. *It's bad enough that the kids treat me disrespectfully, but him too?* she thought. *I guess I have to show them that I'm not someone they can just push around.* She suddenly grew very fearful as she contemplated leaving her safe environment and venturing out into the unknown. *Goddamn it, why is he making me do this?* she thought.

The next morning, she had breakfast waiting for him on the table, as always. But this time it was his favorite—a stack of blueberry pancakes topped with a slice of butter and hot maple syrup. Standing next to it was a tall glass of milk. *Surely he'll stick around for this one,* she thought as she sat at the other end of the table in a pretty blue dress, drinking a cup of coffee.

"You are something else," he said to her as he walked into the dining room in his suit and tie. "You did all of this for me?"

She nodded and smiled.

"I'm so lucky to have you," he said. Then he looked down at his watch. "I did promise the boss that I'd come in early again," he said. "But he can wait. I'm going to sit down and eat this while it's hot."

He sat in the chair and stuck his nose over the plate.

"It smells delicious," he said.

He grabbed his eating utensils and began shoveling the food into his mouth while she nibbled on a piece of sausage.

"Mmm, this is so good," he said to her.

After he finished his plate and put down the knife and fork, she said, "I'm leaving you, Frank. I just didn't want to tell you on an empty stomach."

"Well, I appreciate that ... I guess," he replied with a belch and a confused look on his face. "What? You're leaving?"

"I've thought about it all night, and it's just something I have to do," she said.

"So you *are* mad at me." He sighed.

"No, not really," she said, surprising herself. "It's just that there's things I've always wanted to do with my life. I was perfectly willing to give 'em up as long as I knew that you loved me and were being faithful. But now I'm thinking, what's the point in stickin' around if you're not going to meet me halfway?"

"I told you I'm sorry, and it won't happen again," he said.

"I'm sorry, too," she replied, resolute in the matter.

"What do you mean there's things you wanted to do with your life?" he asked. "What things?"

"Well, for one ... I want to go to New York to become a writer," she replied a bit hesitantly at first, but she ended the statement with a look of sheer enthusiasm.

"Oh, sweetheart, have you lost your mind?" he said, affectionately shaking his head at her. "They'll eat you alive in New York City. And you've never been out of Oklahoma."

"I know," she replied. "But I think I can do this. I know I can."

"What about the kids?" he said. "You can punish me all you want, throw me out of the house even, but don't do this to them. They're innocent."

"Innocent?" she scoffed, suddenly losing her temper. "Don't even try to lay that shit on me! For fourteen years I've put up with all their crap, cooked and cleaned for them! And what do I get for it? Go away and leave me alone, Mom! Just drop dead, why don't you, Mom? Well, now it's your turn, Frank! You take care of 'em! Maybe you can get Bernice to help you!" With that, she jumped up from the chair and started to walk off.

"Where are you going?" he asked.

"I'm packin' my things," she said. "Don't try to talk me out of it!"

"For better or for worse, Katharine!" he exclaimed as he jumped up and ran after her. "Do you remember those vows?"

She rushed into the living room without saying a word, heading straight for her bedroom. When she reached it, she slammed the door in his face.

"You can't just run away from this!" she heard him shouting through the door. "We can work it out!"

She pulled her enormous gray suitcase out of the closet, lifted it onto the bed, and started packing. She hurriedly stuffed about a fourth of her clothes, an extra pair of shoes, and a few toiletry items into it. When she finished, she grabbed the phone from the nightstand and called a cab. She walked out of the room about twenty minutes later, carrying the heavy suitcase in her hand and her purse over her shoulder. She noticed Frank standing in the living room with a doleful expression. She stopped for a moment.

"Kids! Better come down here!" he shouted. "Your mother's leaving!"

Maggie came running down the stairs while Billy stood at the very top.

"You're leaving, Mama?" her daughter whined.

"Yes," Katharine replied.

"Is it because of us?" she asked.

"No, of course not," said Katharine, patting her daughter on the head. "You two be good, and do what your father tells you." She turned and headed toward the door before she started to cry.

"Where are you going?" Maggie shouted at her frantically.

"Your mother's going to New York to become a writer," Frank answered for Katharine.

"Will you be coming back?" Maggie shouted.

Katharine didn't know what to tell her, so she just kept walking and pretended not to hear her. She could imagine the looks of betrayal on her children's faces as she stepped out the door, and for once she felt they had every reason to hate her guts. The worst thing a mother could do was leave her own children, she realized. But she couldn't stand another minute inside that house, knowing her husband had been unfaithful.

She hopped into the taxi that waited for her in the driveway and had the driver take her to the bank, where she promptly withdrew all of the money from her account. Then she had him drop her off at the bus station downtown and bought a one-way ticket to New York City. While she waited for her bus to arrive, she stepped into a phone booth just outside of the building and called Norma to let her know that she was leaving, starting with the why.

"Well, you did the right thing by leaving him, the cheating bastard," Norma said after she received the news. "Frank, having an affair? Who would've thought?"

"That's what I said," Katharine replied.

"Only you should've made him leave instead of the other way around," said Norma. "Of course if Harold cheated on me, I'd have cut his balls off, and they'd be hauling me off to jail. But that's just me."

Katharine laughed to herself.

"So now you're headed off to New York," said Norma. "Are you sure you want to do this? You don't have to travel all the way to Manhattan to find an agent, you know."

"I know," said Katharine. "Like I told Frank, it's just something I've gotta do. I feel like I've been shut in my whole life, and now I have to see what's out there." She laughed. "Maybe I won't like what I see and come hightailing it back here," she said. "Who knows?"

"Well, all I can say is I'm proud of you, girl," said Norma. "It takes a lot of guts to leave your hometown. I know I could never do it. Do you need money? I've got a couple of hundred I can let you borrow."

"No. I had two thousand dollars saved up from garage sales and selling Avon that one year," Katharine said. "I'll be all right."

"Well, keep both hands on your purse," Norma warned her. "I hear they let the criminals run wild there, and you're liable to get mugged. Oh, and stay off the subways."

"Don't worry. I'll be careful," Katharine assured her.

The conversation paused for a brief moment. Then Norma asked, "So do you think you'll ever be coming back?"

"Not until I've seen this thing through," Katharine replied.

"All right." She sighed. "Knock 'em dead, Kat."

"Thanks, Norm," Katharine said.

Soon after she hung up, her bus arrived. She immediately boarded along with a handful of other people, handed the driver her ticket, and took a seat up front next to a window. A few minutes later, the old driver pulled away from the station and drove them through downtown Oklahoma City. They swiftly got on the interstate and headed east. *I can't believe I'm actually doing this*, she thought as they approached the state line. The last time she left the state, she had been twelve years old and going on family vacation.

People continued to board at every stop until the bus was completely full. She had never seen so many strange, interesting faces, and she wasn't even in New York yet. An elderly woman sat next to her for the first thirty minutes or so, replaced by a Jewish rabbi a couple of stops later. Then finally, a young teenage boy who wasn't much older than Billy took the aisle seat next to Katharine. It was like a scene out of her favorite movie, *Midnight Cowboy*, where people kept coming and going. And she was like Jon Voight's character—in it for the long haul and going all the way to the Big Apple to reinvent himself. The thought was so exciting that she wanted to jump up and holler, just like Joe Buck.

The driver pulled into a Burger King in Jefferson City, Missouri, and they all got off the bus to eat lunch. Suddenly it seemed a bit strange to her that she had never actually stepped inside a Burger King before, even though there was one right next to her house. Her only explanation for it was that she had always been a McDonalds person.

After she received her meal, she sat down at a little table opposite an elderly man wearing a John Deere cap and overalls and bit into her first Whopper with cheese, minus the pickles. *Hey, this is pretty darn good,* she thought, wiping the mayonnaise off her cheek with her napkin. *Why haven't I ever tried it before?* As she took another bite, she started to think of all the other things that she never tried even though they had always been there for the taking. *What a miserable waste of life. Thirty-eight years under lock and key. And the key was always in my possession.*

She noticed the old man staring at her as if she was some alien creature, and she started to get a little annoyed. Finally, he raised his half-eaten sandwich and said in his gruff voice, "They make a hell of a burger, don't you think?" She simply smiled at him and nodded.

After they got back on the bus, she removed the pen and notebook from her purse and started writing.

April 6

As the storm intensified, Kitty Everhart was "ravaged" by the ship's first mate inside his little cabin. The tall, handsome man ripped off his shirt and stripped her down to her undergarments. Then he threw her into his bed, jumped on top of her, and started to kiss her from head to toe. All the while plates flew off the shelves, and water seeped in underneath the cabin door. Yet they were completely oblivious to it all and unaware of the massive freak wave headed straight for their boat. Suddenly there was a knock on the door, which finally managed to break their concentration.

"What do you want?" First Officer Fielding grumbled, reluctantly tearing his lips away from Kitty's.

"The captain needs you up on deck!" young Omar shouted through the door.

"Tell him I'm busy," Fielding snapped.

"He says it's urgent!" the boy persisted. "The storm's getting much worse!"

"Oh very well," Fielding replied. "I'll be there in a minute."

"Really?" Kitty sighed as she heard the boy stomp away.

"No, not really," Fielding smiled. *"If this is my last minute on earth, I want to spend it here with you, not up on deck with some smelly old captain."*

"Oh, Miles, you're so loyal," she joked.

"Aren't I though?" he smiled, and they started kissing again.

All of a sudden, the walls of the cabin began to shake violently. He reluctantly tore his lips away from hers again and looked around the room.

"Maybe we should start heading for the lifeboat," he said just as water ripped through the ceiling like a buzz saw. He forced one last smile and gazed directly into her eyes. *"It was good to know you, Miss Kitty Everhart,"* he said.

"Likewise," she replied, forcing a smile of her own.

They kissed for the last time, both determined to go out with a *"bang."* Seconds later the bed broke loose from the wall, and the two young lovers flew across the room as the ship turned over on its side. They shot through the enormous crack in the ceiling and were hurled out into the ocean, bed and all. The two were separated at that point. Kitty instinctively swam to the ocean's surface, gasping for breath and dog paddling to stay afloat. Violent waves and heavy rain made it very difficult for her to keep her head above water.

"Miles!" she shouted and swam around in a small circle, looking for him. She soon gave up the search, however, realizing he must have perished.

The giant vessel floated just twenty feet in front of her, nearly turned upside down and sinking very rapidly. She hurriedly swam away from it and was shocked to discover the large mountainous island off in the distance. My God, there it is, *she thought and continued to swim toward it as hard and fast as she could. She finally reached shallow water about a mile and a half later. She crawled up to the shoreline and passed out from exhaustion right there in the cold, wet sand.*

When she woke up a couple of hours later, the storm had passed. She lay in the grass, wearing a long raincoat over her scantily clad body. Four familiar faces stared down at her. There was the ship's doctor, Dr. Faraday; the cook, Jenkins; and two seamen, Jones and Barkesdale.

"Hello, luv. We thought you'd never come to," Barkesdale said to her in his heavy Cockney accent. He was a young fair-haired brute with a scar down his neck and calluses all over his enormous hands.

Kitty looked down at the raincoat she wore.

"That's mine," he said. "You were wearing next to nothin' when we found you."

"Thanks," she said. "No one else made it out alive?"

"Thirty-four men were killed, including the captain," said Dr. Faraday with a grave expression. The old man had short-cropped gray hair and was thin and wiry. He also happened to be in perfect physical condition for a man in his early sixties.

"I tried to get him to jump overboard," said the big man, Jones, referring to the captain. "But he refused to leave the ship."

"Wise decision if you ask me," Barkesdale sneered. "How could you live with yourself, knowing that you were responsible for so many deaths? The poor lads never knew what hit 'em."

"What about Commander Stone?" Kitty blurted out.

They all looked at each other. No one answered.

"Can someone please tell me what happened to Commander Stone?" she snapped and quickly got up from the ground.

"He made it out on the lifeboat," the doctor said with an encouraging smile. "But then the boat was ripped apart by a waterspout, I believe, and a huge chunk of it ended up inside him."

"So he didn't make it." She sighed.

"No, we got him here—barely—on half a lifeboat," the doctor said.

"I want to see him," she demanded. "Where is he?"

The doctor grimly shook his head while the other three men looked at her rather contemptuously.

Finally Barkesdale said, "You'll find your beloved commander over there," and pointed toward a bush and some trees behind them.

"Follow me." Jones suddenly turned to lead the way.

She walked behind him, filled with dread, and found Commander Stone on the other side of the bush. He was sitting up against a huge rock with a chunk of wood protruding from his belly like a giant splinter. His white long-sleeved shirt was soaked with blood from his chest down to his navel, and his gray jacket covered his legs, which were shivering.

"Come closer, dear. Don't be frightened," he said to Kitty.

Jones chose to keep his distance.

"We made it," said Commander Stone in a weak, gravelly voice once she stood directly over him. He even managed a smile over his painful expression. "The captain got us here—the beautiful bastard. It's not the way we planned it, of course. But we're here. I'll be sure to thank him when I see him."

"Don't talk like that," Kitty scolded him. "You're going to live."

"Oh sure. This should heal up in no time," he jested and looked down at his mutilated body. "Let's face it, Kit. The old man's a goner. I'm afraid it's up to you now. You have to see this thing through."

She fearfully shook her head.

"Don't worry, you'll do fine," he assured her.

"No, I can't do it without you," she muttered.

"How many missions have we completed … you and I?" he asked. "Twenty-five, twenty-six? Believe me, you're ready. There's nothing more I can teach you." He smiled at her affectionately and added, "You know, I've always been very proud of you. You've been like a daughter to me."

She started to cry.

"Save those tears," he said. "All good things must come to an end eventually."

Then he motioned her to come even closer. She knelt down beside him, and he began to speak to her in a much lower voice.

"It's a good thirty miles from here to the other side of the island," he said. "And that's where you'll find Ljungberg. Forget about kidnapping him … unless you can find a way to get him off of here. You'll have to get close enough to kill him. I'd lend you my gun, but I'm afraid it's ruined." He pointed toward his water-soaked pistol and its holster, which hung from a tree branch above their heads. "You'll just have to be resourceful, as always," he said. "And remember, his place might be heavily guarded by German soldiers. So be careful." He suddenly let out a painful moan. "Go now," he ordered her. "I don't want you to watch me die."

She slowly rose to her feet and started to walk away. Jones walked out ahead of her.

Rejoining the others, she turned to the doctor and asked, "Isn't there anything you can do for him?"

"I've been giving him morphine to help stop the pain," he answered grimly. "But other than that, no. If we try to remove that thing from his belly, it'll just end up killing him. Either way, he's finished. I'm sorry."

"Well, I'm not," Barkesdale callously remarked. "The way I see it, we wouldn't be in this mess if it wasn't for her and old stone-face over there."

"Right," the little beady-eyed cook agreed. Both men looked at Kitty hatefully.

"Now, now, gentlemen, we mustn't talk like that," said the good doctor. "We all have to get along while we're stuck here in this godforsaken place."

"Sure, Doc. Whatever you say." Barkesdale smirked. He walked over to his friend, Jonesy, as he often referred to him, and they had a good laugh.

The doctor went back to check on Commander Stone a few minutes later and saw that he was dead. Jones and Barkesdale buried him in the sand and put a cross made of tree branches to mark the spot. Then they all stood over him while Kitty delivered the eulogy.

"He was the strongest, bravest man I ever met," she began, desperately trying to hold back her tears. "A man who so loved his country that he would gladly give his life for it. And he did. He will be missed."

"Not by me!" Barkesdale exclaimed as he turned and walked off.

The other three men were at least decent enough to remain standing with her for a bit longer.

That same evening while Kitty was searching for food and water, she heard Jenkins cry out, "Friends, come quick! Another survivor!"

She ran out to the beach to join the others and was thrilled to see First Officer Fielding staggering onto shore with Jenkins at his side. The taller man had nothing on but his boxer shorts. Directly behind him was the sheet of wood that he had apparently floated in on. It appeared to be the headboard from his cabin's bed.

"Well, hello, Fielding," Barkesdale said to him as he fell to the ground directly in front of the whole group and tried to catch his breath. "Glad to see you made it. Too bad you weren't on deck when we needed you. You could've stopped the captain from doing something stupid … thus saving us from this terrible predicament."

Miles and Kitty exchanged warm glances as Barksdale spoke.

"But you had other things on your mind, didn't you, pretty boy?" Barkesdale added.

"What are you implying, Barkesdale?" Fielding said, suddenly rising up to face him.

"I could probably spell it out for you," Barksdale brazenly replied. "But the fact that you and little missy here were washed ashore in your knickers speaks volumes, don't you think? Not that I blame you, of course. I'd like to get a piece of that myself … if you don't mind."

The other man was so infuriated by the remark that he lunged and started to throw a punch.

"Stop it, you two!" the doctor shouted and swiftly jumped between them and separated them.

"What, old man?" Barkesdale said. "Are you going to give us another speech about how we all need to get along?"

"No. No more speeches," the doctor replied bitterly. "Go ahead and kill each other if that's what you want."

They suddenly heard the sound of someone crying for help; the noise came from the direction of the woods.

"It's coming from over there," Jones said, pointing to the west.

They all darted off in that direction and ran for almost a quarter of a mile until they found the little Egyptian boy, Omar, about twenty feet in the air, clinging to a coconut tree. At the base of the tree was the wild boar that had chased him there. Broken coconut shells littered the ground all around the angry beast. The boy was just about to drop the last one on him when he noticed his fellow shipmates staring at him from a short distance.

"Hello, friends!" he shouted. "Would you mind getting this nasty creature away from me?"

"Hey there, boy!" *Jenkins shouted back at him with a huge grin.* "*I thought you were dead for sure!*" *He and Omar had become good friends while working together on the ship.* "*Hold on a minute!*" *he shouted.*

He bent down to pick up a long, thick branch and headed toward the tree.

"*Where do you think you're going?*" *Jones asked, immediately stepping in front of him.*

"*I'm gonna shoo it away,*" *Jenkins replied.*

"*Don't be foolish,*" *the black man said in his thick Maasai accent.* "*You're looking at our next meal.*"

"*Well, I'll be glad to cook it for ya,*" *the little man replied,* "*but how do you propose getting it into the pot?*"

"*Watch and learn.*" *Jones pulled his long knife out of its sheath and swiftly walked away.*

The others stood there and watched in disgust as the beast charged at him, and he whacked off its front limb. The boar's mighty roar turned into a terrible squeal. Jones then stabbed the beast repeatedly through its neck and jawbone.

"*Don't look at it, Kitty,*" *Fielding said, forgetting she was a deadly spy who had seen it all.*

She simply rolled her eyes at him and continued to admire Jones's warrior mentality and amazing skills with a bolo knife.

"Excuse me!" someone exclaimed, which forced Katharine to put down her pen.

She looked up and saw it was the young woman seated directly in front of her who had spoken. One of the woman's children sat next to her while the other one was seated next to Katharine.

"Do you mind if my daughter trades places with you?" the woman asked. "She wants to look out the window."

"No, of course not," Katharine said.

She immediately got up and switched seats with the little one.

"Thank you." The woman smiled. Glancing down at her notebook, she added, "What are you writing, if you don't mind me asking?"

"Oh, it's just a novel," Katharine replied. "I'm going to New York to become a writer."

The woman nodded and smiled. She immediately turned around in her seat and slapped her little boy, who was picking his nose. The three got off at the next stop, and Katharine had the window seat all to herself again. She tried to write more, but she couldn't focus. Not only was she tired, but she kept thinking back to that horrific night. She could hear her husband say to her, over and over again, "I've been seeing someone else." Plus she started to feel a little guilty. *Am I really all that courageous?* she wondered. *Or am I just a coward, choosing to run away at the first sign of trouble in my otherwise spotless marriage?*

She thought very seriously about getting off at the next stop in Morgantown, West Virginia, and going back home, but she fell asleep before they got there. When she woke up, it was dark outside, and a very clean-cut young man sat next to her, dressed in a fancy blue suit and wearing glasses. His sudden appearance felt almost surreal, as if she was still dreaming.

"Howdy," he said as he looked at her and smiled.

"Hello," she groggily replied and smiled back at him. "Where are we?"

"Williamsport, Pennsylvania," he answered. "Are you going the whole way?"

"Yes," she said. "How 'bout you?"

"Absolutely," he answered with an excited grin. "We should be there by sunup. I just graduated from Ohio State, and I've been accepted into one of the biggest law firms in Manhattan—Wilcombe, Bumgardner and Associates. Ever heard of them?"

"No, but congratulations." She smiled.

"They offered me a plane ticket," he said, "but my parents didn't want me to fly because of 9/11 and all. Are you afraid of flying?"

"No," said Katharine. "I just thought the bus would be cheaper."

"So is this your first time to New York?" he then asked.

"Yes," she said.

"There to stay or just visiting?"

"There to stay, I guess. I'm going to be a writer."

"Well, good luck to you." He smiled.

"You too," she said as she laid her head back against the seat and closed her eyes.

"I could use a little shut-eye myself," he added, "but I'm too excited. I'll wake you when we get there."

"Thanks," she said.

It seemed like very little time had passed when he nudged her shoulder. She woke to a beautiful spring day and the famous New York City skyline just up ahead.

"There it is." The young man pointed and grinned excitedly as they approached the Hudson River. "Ain't it grand? We must be the two luckiest people in the world."

"Yes, I believe so," she said with the same look of wonder in her eyes; it was as if his adventurous spirit had suddenly transformed her.

Yesterday she might have had her doubts, but now she was utterly convinced she was doing the right thing.

Chapter 3: Alone in the Big Apple

The bus made its last stop at the Port Authority Bus Terminal in Midtown Manhattan. Katharine immediately stepped off and found herself in a giant metropolis that more than exceeded her expectations. It wasn't the dirty, smog-filled city that she had seen in so many movies. The air was clean and crisp, and the giant skyscrapers were a wondrous sight to behold. She had also assumed that all New Yorkers were mean-spirited people. But as she walked down Eighth Avenue during the morning rush, she saw a lot of friendly, multicolored faces. It was as if people from all over the globe had come to this beautiful, exciting place to find happiness and to pursue the American dream. Having traveled there for those very same reasons, she felt at home as she walked among them.

She had already memorized the address to the Miriam Levi Literary Agency; now, all she needed was a cab to take her there. She noticed one parked against the curb and swiftly headed to the edge of the sidewalk, still wearing her high heels. As she reached the back door of the vehicle, however, a well-dressed man with a briefcase jumped in front of her and quickly let himself in. He smiled at her through the window as the driver pulled away.

"Jerk," she muttered.

She stepped up to the curb and waited for another taxi to come along. Three of them zoomed right past her even though she waved at them to stop. When she saw a fourth coming, she boldly stepped into the street and waved, forcing it to come to a sudden halt. The driver turned around and glared at her as she opened the back door and threw her suitcase in. He looked like Ernest Borgnine in his prime, with his stocky build, chubby cheeks, and piercing blue eyes.

"Could you take me to One Hundred Twenty-Two East Seventh Street in the East Village?" she asked him nicely. "I'm new here, and I'm afraid I'm lost."

"Ma'am, you don't have to tell me the whole story," he snapped. "Just get in, will ya?"

"Sorry," she said, quickly sliding in and shutting the door.

The silence was uncomfortable as he drove off; she felt embarrassed and humiliated. It was even more awkward when he glanced at her through the rearview mirror every few seconds.

"Look, I didn't mean to be so rough on you back there," he said to her, finally. He had a heavy New York accent. "It's been a lousy week. First my girlfriend left me. And I've got the boss on my ass all the time. He's a real prick. I shouldn't take it out on you, though."

"That's okay." She smiled.

"Where are you from anyway?" He grinned excitedly. As she was about to answer, he said, "Wait, let me guess. Utah?"

"Oklahoma," she corrected him.

"No, that's not it," he said.

"Yes, I'm from Oklahoma," she assured him.

"Huh," he replied, looking a little disappointed. "I thought for sure that you were from Utah. My sister owns a ranch there—her and that no 'count husband of hers. She has a beautiful, white horse named Jasmine. Prettiest damn filly you ever saw. She won't let me ride her, though."

Katharine noticed his cheery expression suddenly turn bitter.

"Okay, so I've got a weight problem," he continued. "Sure, I admit it. But this is a two thousand pound animal we're talkin' about. How big does she think I am?" He sent Katharine another glance in the rearview mirror. "So what brings you here, if you don't mind me askin'?" he said.

"I'm a writer," she said. "And right now I'm looking for an agent."

"What do you write? Books?" he asked.

"Yeah," she answered.

"I don't read all that much," he said. "But I like to see a good movie now and then. You go to the movies?"

"Yeah, I go to the movies," she answered.

"I like the ones with Anthony Quinn," he said, grinning excitedly again. "Now there's a real man for ya. I've seen just about everything he's done. Haven't seen him in anything lately though. I guess he's slowed down a little since he's gotten older."

"He's dead," she blurted out.

"What?"

"I believe he's dead."

"You're shittin' me," he said.

"No, I think he's been dead for several years now," she replied.

"Well, I'll be damned," he said, appearing crushed by the news.

"I hear he played here on Broadway once," she said in an effort to cheer him up again. "They say his Stanley Kowalski was even better than Brando's."

"Eh, I don't care for the theater," he sighed. Then he looked at her long and hard through the rearview mirror. "You know, you seem like a really nice gal," he said. "Give us a smile, will ya?"

She just shook her head at him, suddenly feeling very uncomfortable.

"Come on, let me see those pearly whites," he urged her, his eyes shifting back and forth from the road to the mirror.

Finally, she gave in and flashed him a big phony smile.

"That a girl," he grinned. "Do me a favor and promise me you won't become an asshole, like everyone else 'round here. Most of these people would sell their own mothers to get ahead."

"I promise." She laughed.

"I mean it," he said. "This city will wear you down and take away your soul if you're not careful. I'd hate to see it happen to someone like you."

"Thanks," she muttered. "You're very kind."

"What you need to do is find yourself a man," he said. "You know, someone to warm the bedsheets at night."

"Oh really?" she scoffed.

"So, do you like bowling?" he asked.

She felt relieved when they finally drove up to the ten-story building on Seventh Street. He parked directly in front of it, and she handed him his money. As she rushed out of the car with her purse and suitcase, he said, "I'm cookin' some steaks out on the grill tonight if you want to come over."

"I'm married," she replied, showing him her ring through his window before she hurried away.

Thank God I decided to keep it on, she thought as she entered the building. She took the elevator up to the second floor and found suite 219 at the end of the hall. Quickly stepping inside, she set her suitcase down by the door and walked up to the front desk with her purse and oversized notebook in hand. A young blonde receptionist sat behind the desk and continued talking on the phone for another minute or two before she finally looked up at Katharine.

She placed her hand over the receiver. "May I help you?" she asked, looking extremely irritated.

"I'm here to see Mrs. Levi," Katharine replied.

"Do you have an appointment?" she then asked. "I'm sorry, but you need to have an appointment."

"Could you make an exception just this once?" Katharine pleaded. "I've come all this way, and I really need to see her right now."

"Just a second," the woman huffed and got back on the phone. "Kim, I'll have to call you back."

She quickly hung up. Then she got up from the chair and walked into the agent's office. She walked back out a few seconds later and said, "Mrs. Levi will see you now."

"Thank you." Katharine smiled and swiftly headed toward the door.

Mrs. Levi—a little old woman in her late sixties or early seventies—was barely visible behind her enormous desk. Massive bookshelves stood all around her, filled with hundreds of books. The desk itself was cluttered with them. She was cutting a cheese bagel with a plastic knife and fork when Katharine stepped into the room.

"Hello, young lady ... I'm Miriam Levi," she said. "I'm afraid you caught me during breakfast. Who referred you to me, if you don't mind me asking?"

"Norma Jean Kruger," Katharine answered.

"That name doesn't ring a bell," Mrs. Levi said and started thumbing through her Rolodex.

"I'm sorry. She's a friend of mine," Katharine explained to her. "She got your name off of the computer, seeing that you represent Elaine Cook."

"I used to represent that ... woman," Mrs. Levi said bitterly. "She dumped me just as her career was taking off."

"I see," Katharine muttered.

"It doesn't matter," the old woman said. "Water under the bridge. And you are?"

"Katharine Beaumont," Katharine answered.

"Where are you from, my dear?" she then asked very curiously.

"Oklahoma City," Katharine replied.

"Of course you are," Mrs. Levi said. "Now, what can I do for you?"

"I want you to help me get published," said Katharine.

"That's my job." The old woman smiled. "Why don't you go ahead and grab a seat?"

Katharine immediately sat down in the chair directly in front of the desk.

"Do you have your manuscript with you?" Mrs. Levi asked.

"I have this," Katharine replied and handed her the notebook. "It's a mystery thriller," she explained as the old woman opened it and started skimming through the pages.

"Hmm," Mrs. Levi said, seeming unimpressed. "Is your main character a woman?"

"Yes," Katharine answered.

"That's good," Mrs. Levi said, "seeing that most of the publishers that I deal with cater to the female audience. And does she have a love interest and a sex scene or two?"

"Mmm hmm," Katharine nodded.

"That's always a plus," Mrs. Levi said. Suddenly she looked very puzzled when she reached about three quarters of the way through the notebook.

"Oh, I forgot. There's another story," Katharine explained. "But I'm not quite finished with it yet."

"My, you have been busy," Mrs. Levi said. "So what's this one about?"

"It's a spy thriller," Katharine replied.

"A female spy?" Mrs. Levi asked, starting to show some interest.

"Yes," Katharine answered.

"This is the kind of stuff we've been lookin' for—a female James Bond," the old woman muttered as she continued reading.

"Like I said, I'm not quite finished with it yet," Katharine said.

"How will it end?" Mrs. Levi asked. "Is it worth the read?"

"I believe so," Katharine answered very confidently. "It's where she finally comes into her own ... becomes her own woman, so to speak."

"Well, it all sounds very interesting." Mrs. Levi suddenly closed the notebook. "But unfortunately I'm not seeking new clients at the moment. I barely have enough energy to handle the ones I've already got. You'd be better off to find someone younger to represent you."

"Please, Mrs. Levi, don't make me look for agents all day," Katharine begged her. "I came here to find you."

"Oh very well." The old woman sighed. "My commission is fifteen percent ... if I'm able to land you a publisher. Otherwise, I get nothing." She let out another sigh. "I'm probably crazy for doing this," she said. "But your work seems to have a lot of potential ... and I like your face. "Sometimes, you can just look at a person and tell if they're gonna make it or not in this town. You're a Scorpio, aren't you?"

"How did you know?" Katharine asked, surprised.

"I know a Scorpio when I see one," Mrs. Levi said with a shrewd nod. "Just send me the manuscript for the completed story, and I'll see what I can do. Meanwhile you can keep working on the other one."

"But this is all I have," Katharine said.

"You're kidding. No manuscript?" she replied. "I'm sorry, but no one will even look at this. It has to be typewritten and double-spaced ... preferably on a PC. Publishers require electronic submissions these days."

"Oh, I see." Katharine sighed. "But I don't even own a computer. And I never learned how to type."

"I could get someone to type your manuscript for you, but those services don't come cheap," Mrs. Levi said. "It usually costs five dollars a page ... or more."

"I guess I don't have much of a choice," Katharine replied.

"I might even get my daughter to do it," Mrs. Levi said as if the idea had just popped into her head. "She's looking for a job ... and this is right up her alley. She types ninety words per minute. I used to be pretty good myself before the arthritis set in." She lifted her hands to show her decrepit little fingers. Then she pushed a little button on her desk and spoke into the intercom. "Mrs. Carmichael, would you come in here please?" she said. There was no response. "Get off the phone, young lady, and come in here please," she said a little more sternly. Still no response. "*Mrs. Carmichael!*" she shouted at the top of her lungs.

Finally the young woman stomped into the room in her high heels and headed straight for Mrs. Levi's desk.

"I need you to print a copy of the standard form contract and bring it back to me," Mrs. Levi said to her. "Then I want you to get a hold of my daughter and tell her that I need to talk to her. I've got a job for her."

"Yes, ma'am," the young woman muttered and immediately stomped out of the room.

"You just can't find quality help these days," Mrs. Levi said, shaking her head as she watched the woman go back to her desk.

"What if your daughter can't read my handwriting?" Katharine fretted.

"Don't worry about it," said Mrs. Levi. "If I can read it, I'm sure she can." She grabbed a pen and a sheet of paper and said, "Now, I need to get a little information from you—your address and a phone number where you can be reached."

"I don't have either of those just yet," Katharine said. "I just got here."

"Just got here?" Mrs. Levi exclaimed.

"Yes. I arrived here about thirty minutes ago," she said, looking up at the clock on the wall. "I traveled all the way from Oklahoma—on a Greyhound bus."

"You didn't have to do that!" The old woman laughed. "We've could've done this over the phone. Or through the mail."

"No, I had to come here," Katharine replied. "How can you be a serious writer if you're stuck in Oklahoma your whole life?"

"Well, the first thing *you* need to do is find an apartment," Mrs. Levi said. "Finding a decent and affordable place in New York City isn't as easy as you think." She opened her desk drawer and took something out of it. "Here's my brother's card," she said as she slowly reached over her desk and handed it to Katharine.

Katharine looked the card over very carefully: *Manchester Apartments, Oscar Levi—Superintendent.* Underneath that was the address.

"He's a real easygoing guy. You'll like him," the old woman assured her. "Tell him I sent you, and he might even give you a discount."

"Thank you," Katharine replied.

Mrs. Carmichael returned with the contract and handed it to her employer.

"Let me go over this thing with you really quickly," Mrs. Levi said to Katharine. "Then you can be on your way."

After Katharine signed the contract and said good-bye, she took a cab to the Manchester Apartments on Second Avenue, where she met Oscar Levi inside his office. He was a little old man about the same height and age as his sister. They both had the same facial features—big blue eyes and pointy chins.

"So, how is the ol' shyster?" he joked after Katharine told him that his sister had recommended him. "Is she still up to no good?"

Though Katharine pretended to find his words amusing, it actually made her wonder if she was putting her trust in the right people. He showed her a one-bedroom apartment, and she absolutely loved it until he told her the price—two thousand dollars a month. And that was after the discount.

"I think I'll just look around for a little bit," Katharine said to him very politely.

"Mrs. Beaumont, I guarantee you that you're not going to find anything cheaper in this town," he assured her. "What can I say? It's Manhattan."

"Still, I think I should look around." She smiled.

"Suit yourself," he said, shrugging his shoulders.

Katharine went back to his office, grabbed her purse and her suitcase, and promptly left the building. She looked at other brownstones in the vicinity and soon discovered that the old man was right. There simply wasn't anything available for under two thousand dollars a month, which meant she would be completely broke after the first month's rent. *How stupid of me to think that I could make it in New York City on two grand*, she thought as she walked down Second Avenue with a discouraged look on her face. *Everyone knows about the high cost of living here. That's probably why there's so many people living on the streets.*

She had already spotted seven or eight homeless people thus far. At least they had appeared to be homeless. They all wore raggedy clothes and were covered in filth. Some lay in front of the buildings, while others walked along the sidewalk with the rest of the crowd. One old man walked very slow and talked very loudly as people passed him. He wasn't asking them for money, though. He was merely quoting from the Bible. It seemed that all he really wanted was to make a connection with somebody. Perhaps a friendly pat on the back would suffice. Yet everyone acted as though they couldn't see or hear him. He was like a ghost. *How can these people be so mean?* she thought to herself. But then *she* walked right past him without even looking at him because she felt a bit intimidated by him. *That's it. They're afraid of him … and everything that he represents,* she thought, *hunger, destitution, insanity, even death.*

She was just about to give up the search and look for a cheap hotel somewhere when she came upon a little four-story apartment building that stood out from the others because it was smaller and built with gray bricks. It was so old and deteriorated that the bricks were starting to decay; they even had vegetation growing out of them. The red neon sign on top of the building read, "The Greystone," but only the first six letters were lit up. *This one's got to be in my price range,* she thought as she walked up the concrete steps and entered through the glass doors.

The inside was even less appealing. The lobby was filled with antique furniture from the 1950s. The walls and ceiling were cracked, the fluorescent lights kept flickering on and off, and the ceiling fans made terrible squeaking noises. But worst of all, there were cobwebs everywhere—never a good sign for an arachnophobic like Katharine. She slowly walked past the stairwell and the elevator and stepped inside the main office. A handsome middle-aged man in a blue suit and brown shoes lay back in his chair with his feet on the desk.

"Sorry. It's been a slow morning." He laughed and immediately sat up. "Welcome to the Greystone. I'm Mr. Brown, the superintendant. How can I help you?"

"I need a place to stay," she said.

"One or two bedrooms?"

"One … with a bed, preferably."

"Ah, so you're looking for a furnished apartment," he said. "We just happen to have one of those available. It's twelve hundred dollars a month, with the first month paid in advance and a hundred-dollar deposit. And I'll need references, of course."

"That's the best offer I've heard all day." She smiled.

"Great! Let's go take a look at it, shall we?" he exclaimed. He stood up and grabbed a key from the wall behind him. "Go ahead and set your luggage down and come with me." He stepped out in front of her and cheerfully led the way.

An old man dressed in a janitor's uniform and wearing a silly-looking toupee had just stepped out of his closet and was busy mopping the marble floor when they bumped into him in the lobby.

"This is Juan Martinez, our handyman," Mr. Brown said. "If you had any problems with your plumbing, electricity, or what have you, he'd be the man to see."

The old man looked at her and grinned excitedly. "You rent apartment?" he asked.

"We're gonna go take a look at it," Mr. Brown explained to him.

"Oh, you like it here, miss," Juan said. "Very quiet. No one bother you."

"That's good." Katharine smiled. "I don't like to be disturbed while I'm writing."

"So, you're a writer, huh?" Mr. Brown said.

Katharine nodded.

"Well, great. Maybe you can write your next bestseller here," he joked. "Let's go check it out and see what you think."

"Nice to meet you, Mr. Martinez," Katharine said as they swiftly walked away.

"Work, work, work." The old man laughed and started mopping again. "Keep the place nice and clean for you."

They rushed right past the old-fashioned elevator with a sliding metal grate and a sign over the handle that read *Temporarily Out of Service*.

"I hope you don't mind taking the stairs," Mr. Brown said. "The elevator's on the blink."

"No problem," Katharine said as they headed for the stairwell.

They proceeded up the old marble steps. He stopped once they reached the second floor.

"Mrs. Poindexter is the assistant manager," he explained. "She lives right there in apartment 201." He pointed to the first door on the left overlooking the stairwell. "So she's here all the time if I'm not available."

They walked up one more flight of stairs, and by the time they stepped into the third floor hallway, both were breathing heavily.

"Well, looks like I'll be gettin' plenty of exercise," she joked.

"We'll have the elevator up and running by the end of the week," he assured her.

As they walked past the room closest to the stairs, an elderly woman opened the door and poked her head out.

"Everything's all right, Mrs. Chang," he smiled. "Have a good day now."

The old woman immediately shut the door.

"Don't mind her," he said to Katharine. "She just likes to know what's going on around here, which ain't always a bad thing."

They continued walking down the hall until they came upon room 311. He unlocked the door and immediately stepped inside to switch on the lights. She walked in behind him, looked around the room, and was thoroughly disgusted. It was small, dank, and in complete disrepair, just like the rest of the building. But on the plus side, it had an old leather couch that looked nice and cozy and a TV directly in front of it. In the bedroom, there was a double bed with covers and two fluffy pillows, which was all she really needed at the moment.

"I know it doesn't look like much," Mr. Brown said after he gave her the tour. "But you've got all the modern conveniences—running water, central heat, and air. And it's furnished, of course."

"I'll take it," Katharine blurted out.

"Well, alrighty then," he smiled and shook her hand. "Welcome aboard, young lady. Let's go back down to my office and take care of business. Then I'll hand you over these keys and leave you alone."

"Great," she replied.

When they returned to the main office, they sat down at a little table in the corner of the room. He asked her for four references, two from previous landlords.

"Mr. Brown, I have to be perfectly honest with you," said Katharine. "I've never rented an apartment before."

"Never?" he replied, looking a little surprised.

She shook her head, embarrassed.

"Okay," he said. "Then my next question is, are you currently employed?"

"No," she answered.

"Hmmm." He sighed. "Well, Mrs. Beaumont, I suppose I don't have to worry about you trashin' the place. But how can I trust that you're going to make your payments on time when you don't even hold a job?"

"I have more than enough money here to pay the first month in advance and the hundred-dollar deposit," said Katharine, taking her purse out of her lap and setting it on the table. "And my novel's going to be published soon, probably in the next day or two. Then hopefully the money will start pouring in."

"I'll tell you what I'm gonna do," Mr. Brown said, suddenly looking very enthusiastic again. "I'm gonna have you sign on a month-to-month basis. And, seeing that it's already May the fifth, you'll only have to pay a thousand dollars up front. Then twenty-four days from now, we'll see if that book of yours is a major success. Maybe you should consider getting a job, just to be on the safe side."

"I came here to write," Katharine said a bit defensively. "That's what I'll be doing from now on. Don't worry, Mr. Brown. I'll make sure that you get your money."

"Okey-dokey." He smiled.

He got up, walked over to his desk, and then came back with the contract for her to sign. After she signed it, she dug the cash out of her purse and handed it to him.

"It's all yours," he said and gave her the key.

By the time she made it to her room, she felt completely worn out. She walked straight into the bedroom, put down the suitcase, and threw herself onto the bed. Just as she was about to close her eyes, she heard two people yelling and objects crashing to the floor in the room directly above her. It sounded like they were trying to kill each other.

When she looked up at the ceiling, she noticed a big brown spider staring right back at her, or so it seemed. Her unnatural fear of them led her to believe he had something sinister in mind. All of a sudden, a smaller spider crawled up next to it, which caused her even more anxiety. *Great, there's two of them,* she thought as she lay very still, trying not to make any sudden moves. *What have I gotten myself into?*

Chapter 4: Bug Trouble

Katharine hardly ever stepped out of the apartment during the first week, except to buy food and other necessities, which were all right there on Second Avenue. A convenience store and a fruit stand were less than a quarter of a mile away. There was a small bakery directly across the street, next to the pawnshop. Every morning she could open her living room window and smell the fresh bread being pulled out of the ovens.

She often thought about visiting Times Square or the Empire State Building, but she chose to keep working instead. She did most of her writing on the living room couch and sometimes in her bed, when she wasn't too distracted by the spiders on the ceiling. She felt like getting up on the mattress and crushing them with her brand new five-hundred-page notebook, but she was afraid one might get away and tell the others. *I'd really have trouble sleeping then,* she thought.

She didn't realize the enormity of the situation until the middle of the second week when, on May 14, she hopped out of bed in her pajamas and went into the kitchen to fix herself a bowl of cereal. As she reached up and opened the cupboard, an enormous cockroach scrambled out of it and ran behind the refrigerator.

"*Ah!*" she shrieked, nearly jumping out of her skin.

She slowly reached up again and grabbed the box of cornflakes on the top shelf, wondering what would pop out next. She pulled it away and was relieved to find nothing behind it. Yet she knew there had to be more of them hiding away somewhere. She poured some cornflakes into a bowl, along with a little milk and sugar, and sat down at the dining room table, placing the opened cereal box directly in front of her. As she started eating, she noticed a pair of antennas slowly working their way up to the top of the lid of the box. She immediately spat out her food and slapped the box with the back of her hand, which caused it to tip over and half of its contents to spill out all over the table. Four more cockroaches scrambled out of the container as she sat there completely horrified. *The whole kitchen must be infested,* she thought.

She immediately put on her clothes and went downstairs to see Mr. Brown, but he wasn't in his office. So she walked back up to the second floor to talk to the assistant manager, Mrs. Poindexter. She knocked on the door, and the woman quickly answered, opening it ever so slightly. All that Katharine could see of her was her big nose sticking out over the chain. She heard opera music playing in the background.

"Mrs. Poindexter?" she said.

"Yes?" the woman replied in a high-pitched voice.

"I'm Katharine Beaumont from room 311," she said. "I was wondering if there was any way I could get a hold of Mr. Brown. I haven't seen him around here lately."

"No, he's away on business," the woman explained. "And I'm not allowed to give out his cell phone number. Is it urgent?"

"Yes it is," Katharine answered firmly.

"Well, maybe I can help you."

"Actually, what I need is an exterminator," said Katharine. "I've got bugs running all through my apartment."

"Bugs?"

"Yes, bugs … lots of them."

"Then you need to talk to our maintenance man, Mr. Martinez," Mrs. Poindexter said. "He does all the exterminating in this building. You'll find his office down in the basement."

"Thank you, Mrs. Poindexter," Katharine said.

"You're welcome, child," the woman replied and immediately shut the door.

Katharine took the stairs all the way down to the basement, which seemed a bit too dark and eerie to be walking through all alone. The weak fluorescent lights kept flickering on and off, just like they did in the lobby. Mr. Martinez's office was directly across from the laundry room and was actually the boiler room. There was an eight-foot chainlink fence in front of it, and a sign that read "Maintenance Only" hung over the gate. She opened it and boldly stepped through. Then she hurried past the giant boilers, which produced a lot of heat and made a terrible noise. In the very back was a little, six-by-eight room, but he wasn't there. Nor was he anywhere else to be found. After searching every floor, she finally gave up and went back to her apartment, angrily slamming the door behind her.

By the end of the week, she had pretty much decided to live and let live. She even began to talk to the spiders on her ceiling when she felt particularly lonely. *Now if I could only get them to help out with the rent,* she thought.

Sunday night came around, and it was time for her bath. She stepped into the bathroom, stripped off all of her clothing, and pulled back the shower curtain to reveal the most hideous creature that she had ever encountered. It looked like a centipede, with its long slender body, a pair of venomous claws, and brown and red markings on its back. It was larger and meaner-looking than those typically found in the Midwest, possessing at least a dozen more legs and body segments. *Maybe it's one of those South American centipedes,* she thought, *the kind that eats rats and small children.* Franz Kafka couldn't have imagined anything more frightening. And, like all the other insects in the apartment, it wasn't the least bit intimidated by her. It remained perfectly still in the middle of the tub and just kept smiling at her as if it was saying, "Come and get me if you dare."

"That's it," she said, once again choosing not to be a victim in her own house. "One of us is going down."

She immediately armed herself with the closest things she could find—a toilet plunger and a hair dryer—and charged at the poor creature, trapping it inside the rubber cup while she turned on the hair dryer and waited for it to heat up. She was hoping to set the damned thing on fire after she lifted the plunger, but all she did was sweep it off its legs for a few seconds. It quickly gained control of its body and scrambled away, ultimately crawling up the spout.

How am I gonna be able to take a bath now? she asked herself.

Then she came up with an idea, quickly plugging the drain and turning the water on full blast. The insect shot back into the tub and was held underwater by the constant pressure until it drowned.

"Gotcha, you son of a bitch!" she exclaimed, watching its lifeless corpse float around in circles.

Both Mr. Brown and his maintenance man showed up the very next day.

"Mrs. Poindexter told me you've been having some bug trouble," the manager said as he walked into her room in his blue suit and tie.

Mr. Martinez stood next to him, holding an insect sprayer with a three-gallon tank.

"You might say that," she replied.

The old man turned to his employer and said something in Spanish. Mr. Brown just nodded and smiled.

"He's just sayin' that it's very unlikely," he explained to Katharine. "He sprayed in here a few weeks ago … just before you moved in."

"No, no bugs," Mr. Martinez added.

"Why don't you come and look for yourself if you don't believe me," she sneered and led them into the kitchen.

Then she stood back and watched as they opened all the upper cabinet doors and started removing everything from the shelves. After they were emptied, the maintenance man stood on his tiptoes and took a quick peek inside.

"Nada," he said to Mr. Brown and shook his head.

"They're in there, I assure you," Katharine huffed.

"Of course they are," Mr. Brown said, being very diplomatic. "They're just hiding in the woodworks somewhere." Then he looked at his employee and said, "Spray it, Juan."

Mr. Martinez sprayed the entire kitchen, and then Katharine took them into the bedroom to show them the spiders on her ceiling. It appeared that they had gone into hiding as well. The two men began to search the entire room—behind the dresser, inside the closet, and even underneath the bed. Finally, Juan Martinez looked above the bedroom door and said, "There's one," pointing at a little, black spider, hiding on top of the air vent. They all three huddled together and looked up at it in awe. Juan stepped up a little closer, lifted his trusty spray nozzle and pulled the trigger. The insect instantly fell to the ground, and he bent down to pick it up while Katharine and Mr. Brown leaned in to examine his handiwork.

"He dead," Juan said, showing it to them.

They both nodded in agreement.

"Good job," Mr. Brown smiled and gave the man a quick pat on the back. "Now spray everything else, will ya? And let's get it right this time."

The old man swiftly sprayed the rest of the apartment. Then he rejoined them in the kitchen.

"Well, you can rest easy now," Mr. Brown said to Katharine with a confident smile. "No more bugs. Is there anything else we can do for you, Mrs. Beaumont?" he asked.

"Actually, there is," she said. "Are you familiar with the people living directly above us?"

"Yes, a young black couple, I believe," he replied. "I forget their names. What about them?"

"Well, I hear them fighting all the time," she said. "It's not that I mind the noise so much. I'm just afraid that they might end up killing each other from the sound of it."

"I appreciate your concern, and I'll definitely look into it," he assured her.

"Thank you." She smiled, feeling very relieved.

That night, her creative juices began to flow again as she lay in bed with her pen and notebook, occasionally looking up to make sure she was all alone.

April 7

It was late at night and the seven castaways were sleeping around the fire pit. The half-eaten roasted boar still hung on a skewer over the dying embers. Barkesdale suddenly woke up screaming after he felt a sharp pain on the back of his foot.

"Ah! Son of a bitch!" he cried out and quickly jumped up to see a big hairy spider crawl away into the bushes.

"What is it, man?" Jones said, who lay next to him.

"A bleedin' spider just bit me!" Barksdale exclaimed. "The damn thing got away from me before I could kill it!" He got back down on the ground and rubbed his foot. "Goddamn this wretched island," he whined.

"Oh, don't be such a baby," Fielding said from where he lay next to Kitty. "It's just a little spider."

"Little, my ass!" Barkesdale exclaimed. "It was the biggest one I've ever seen!"

Fielding laughed along with several of the others.

"Was it light brown with black and yellow spots?" the doctor asked.

"I don't know … I suppose," Barkesdale grumbled. "I didn't get a very good look."

"Well, should we form a search party and go after it?" Fielding gibed.

"Very clever, Fielding," Barkesdale sneered and raised his foot. "Come over here and kiss it for me, why don't you?"

"No thanks," Fielding smiled. "I'm happy right where I'm at."

Then he lay back down and cuddled up next to Kitty again. The rest of them went right back to sleep as well. They woke up early that morning. Jones carved up the rest of the boar for their breakfast. While they ate, Dr. Faraday kicked down the skewer made of tree branches and threw another bundle of twigs onto the fire pit. But as he knelt down to light the match, Jones stepped in his way.

"What is it, Jones?" the doctor asked. "I was just gonna start another fire to knock the chill off."

"No more fires," the big man said. "After we finish eating, we'll start moving farther inland. That'll warm you up."

"Are you mad?" the doctor asked. "God knows what's waitin' for us inside that jungle. Our only hope is out there." He looked out toward the ocean. "If we stay here and keep our eyes peeled, we may see a ship or a plane in a day or two."

"Even if there is a ship, it'll be miles away," Jones scoffed. "It'll never see us, no matter how big of a fire you build."

"Right," Barkesdale said as he walked up to stand next to his friend. "And planes don't fly through here. We're out in the middle of nowhere, in case you've forgotten. Hell, we're not even on the map."

"Then we'll build a raft," said the optimistic doctor, "and send a couple of guys out on it to find help."

"A raft?" Barkesdale exclaimed with a crazy laugh that caught everyone by surprise. "Sounds like a suicide mission to me, Doc. Don't expect me to volunteer for it."

"I won't," the doctor replied.

"The doctor's right. We should stay here," Fielding said. "What's the point of moving farther inland?"

"Yeah, Jonesy, I'm kind of wondering that myself," said Barkesdale, looking very puzzled. "We could die of thirst or exhaustion. That is, if the animals don't get us first."

Jones looked over at Kitty, who stood off by herself, being very quiet, as usual.

"Are you going to tell them, or shall I?" he asked.

"Tell us what?" Barkesdale exclaimed, quickly walking toward her with a rabid look in his eyes. "Are you hiding something from us, little missy? Better come clean or we'll beat it out of you."

"That's enough, Barkesdale," Fielding said, jumping directly in front of him.

"All right!" she exclaimed before they started fighting again. "There's someone else on this island. He owns it, in fact. We were supposed to kidnap him and take him back to headquarters."

"Who is he?" Fielding snapped.

"The Swedish billionaire—Mikael Ljungberg," she answered. "He's been loaning money to Hitler to build his army."

"So he's a Nazi." Fielding nodded with a look of disgust.

"No, not quite," she said. "But he has to be stopped."

"I'll say," he muttered. "How do you plan to do it?"

"I was going to sneak out of here and go after him myself ... when the time was right," she answered.

"Well, if that don't beat all," Barkesdale said and laughed crazily again. "Here we are, stranded, dying of thirst, and she thinks she's still on the job."

"You'll never make it on your own," Fielding said to her.

"Yes, I will," she assured him. "I've had over a hundred hours of survival training, and I've killed at least a dozen men. I'm perfectly capable of taking care of myself, believe me."

"Look, I don't care if the guy's Jack the Ripper," Barkesdale said. "She ain't gonna lay a finger on him if he's our only chance to get off this island. Right, Jonesy?"

Jones looked at him disapprovingly. "Jack the Ripper just killed a few whores," he said. "If Hitler invades Poland, there will be a great war, and millions will die. And what will become of the Jews and my own people once he has taken over all of Eastern Europe?" He patted Barkesdale on the shoulder. "Don't worry, my friend," he said. "I still intend to get off the island. But if I see this man who has befriended that monster, I will definitely kill him."

"What do you say now, Doc?" Barkesdale said, turning to the doctor. "You still want to stay here and wait for a ship?"

"No, of course not," he replied. "If this guy's loaded like she says, surely he has a way to get us out of here. I say we kill him and steal his yacht. That way, everyone's happy."

"There's just one problem," said Kitty. "We believe his house is heavily guarded by German soldiers. Hitler knew we would try something like this, and he wants to make sure his bank is well secured."

"Wonderful," Barkesdale scoffed. "Let's all fight the good fight and win one for ol' King George, why don't we? They've got submachine guns. What do we have ... one rifle? I suppose when we run out of bullets, we can throw rocks at 'em."

"I'm not afraid to fight," little Omar said, standing proudly.

"Of course not. You're just a boy," Barkesdale replied as he walked up to Omar and patted him on the head. "I'm sure this is all just one great big adventure to you."

Omar looked up at him angrily.

"But you've never seen a real battle, have you, son?" he asked. "It isn't pretty, I promise you." He looked at Jenkins, who stood beside the young boy. "I suppose you're ready for combat as well?" he scoffed.

"Me?" The little man gulped. "I know this Hitler's a real nasty fellow and all, but I'm just a cook. All I want to do is go back to my home in Liverpool to be with my family and continue doing what I do best."

"Well, it's good to see that someone hasn't completely lost their marbles!" Barkesdale exclaimed. "I say when we meet this chap, we should be on our best behavior and keep our politics to ourselves. Then maybe we can all leave here in one piece."

"At least we're all agreed on one thing," Jones said. "It's time to move out. So let's get started."

He grabbed the rifle and strapped it to his back while Dr. Faraday gathered up all of his medical supplies. Just a few minutes later, they were stomping through the woods and climbing up steep hills in single file. The big man led the way, followed by Kitty, Fielding, and the good doctor. Kitty looked back for a second and noticed Jenkins and Omar lagging a little farther behind. Barkesdale brought up the rear. When she looked back again just a few minutes later, Barkesdale was nowhere in sight.

"We have to go back," she said as she stopped and turned around. "I think we lost Barkesdale."

The others turned and followed her back down the hill, except for Jones, who was several yards ahead of them. He continued to press on.

"Goddamn it!" Kitty heard him shout.

They found Barkesdale at the bottom of the hill, hunched over on the ground and appearing to be in great pain.

"I'm all right," he groaned as they walked up to him. "Just give me a minute."

"Who are you trying to kid, Barkesdale?" Fielding said. "You look like you just went fifteen rounds with Joe Louis. And your face is all red and covered in sweat."

"He's probably dehydrated," Kitty said.

"But we have no water," Omar reminded her.

"Let's at least get him out of the sun," she said.

"Help me grab him," Fielding said to the doctor.

The two men picked him up by the shoulders and carried him over to the nearest oak tree. He let out a painful moan and cursed them the entire way. They were all sitting under that same tree when Jones caught up with them about five minutes later.

"What is this?" The big man scowled.

"It's time for a break," Fielding said, pulling rank on him. "We've been walking for a whole hour without any water."

"We're not on board a ship anymore," Jones reminded him. "If you want out of here, you'll listen to me. Tonight we rest. Right now we need to take advantage of the daylight."

"Look at your friend," Fielding said and pointed over at Barkesdale, who sat in the middle of the group with his back against the tree. "Can't you see he's sick?"

"I'm all right ... just a few more minutes," Barkesdale grumbled, barely able to hold his head up.

"Very well," Jones sighed. "We'll rest here for five minutes."

Five minutes turned into an hour, however, as Barkesdale's condition worsened. He shook uncontrollably and kept laughing to himself. It was the same crazy laugh they had all heard earlier that morning, but this time it was nonstop. They dragged him behind a large, four-foot-tall boulder to give him some privacy, at which point he began talking crazily as well.

"Here Kitty, Kitty, Kitty," he said in a high-pitched voice. "I've got something for you, my little pussycat."

Kitty and Miles stood just on the other side of the boulder. He immediately stepped closer to her and put his hands over her ears.

"Oh stop it, Miles," she snapped and pushed him away. "It's nothing I haven't heard before." She rolled her eyes at him. "Fucking men," she muttered.

"Don't you have something to quiet him down?" Fielding asked the doctor, who stood next to Jones and the other two castaways.

"Yes, of course," Dr. Faraday said.

He picked up his medical bag and rushed back behind the boulder.

"Go away, Doc!" Barkesdale shouted at him furiously. "I don't need to be drugged up or knocked out! I'll take my pain like a man! Get the hell out and bring me back the girl, you dirty, old bastard!"

The doctor swiftly rejoined the group, shrugging his shoulders.

"What the hell is wrong with him, Doc?" Jones asked as his friend continued to spout obscenities.

"I can't say for sure," Dr. Faraday replied, "but I think he might have been bitten by a Banana Spider—the most deadly spider there is in these parts. He has all the classic symptoms—dementia, foaming at the mouth. If I'm right, he's in for a very slow and painful death."

"So there's nothing you can do for him?" Jones asked.

"I wish there was," the doctor said very grimly. "But without the antivenom, I'm afraid there's no hope."

"Very well," Jones replied and slowly walked around the boulder.

"Hello, Jonesy, my friend!" Barkesdale exclaimed as Jones stood before him and withdrew his blade. "Jonesy?"

The big man quickly dropped to his knees out of sight of the rest of the castaways. Kitty heard him apologize to Barkesdale, and the latter put up a bit of a struggle. Then Barkesdale made a hideous, gurgling sound. That was the last they heard of him. Everyone stood silent as Jones stood up, put his knife away, and stepped out from behind the boulder.

"What are you all looking at?" he sneered. "Was I supposed to just leave him here to suffer?"

"So he's—" Dr. Faraday began.

"Yes, Doctor," Jones interrupted him. "I slit his throat. You all would've done the same if he was your friend."

"It's all right, Jones," the doctor said and put his hand on his arm. "Nobody's judging you."

"We should go ahead and bury him," Fielding said. "Come on, Jenkins."

"I'll go, to," the doctor said.

"No," Jones snapped just as they started to leave. "I'll do it. Alone."

"Sure, Jones. If that's what you want." Dr. Faraday nodded.

After he buried Barkesdale, Jones walked up to where the entire group was sitting and said, "Okay, let's go."

"We've had enough for one day, and it's getting late," Fielding said as he stood up to face him. "We're camping here for tonight."

"Here is death," Jones pointed out to him. "Food and water are waiting for us on the other side of the island."

"You don't know that for sure," Fielding said. "I say we get some rest and head out in the morning."

"Rest—that's all you people have being doing," Jones grumbled.

They stared each other down like two ornery bulls.

"I'll leave you the gun," Jones said to them all finally. "I won't need it." Then he turned around and walked out on them.

"Where are you going, Jonesy?" the doctor asked as they all stood up and took notice.

"I've gotta keep going while there's still some daylight left," Jones said, not looking back.

The doctor immediately rushed after him. "So you're just gonna walk off and leave us here, huh?" he asked, walking alongside the big man.

"That's right," Jones said. "I'll make better time that way."

"Don't do this," the doctor urged him. "We have to stick together. That's the only way we're gonna make it."

"You keep sayin' that, but it isn't true," Jones said. "I always tend to do better on my own. Don't worry, Doctor. When I get there, I'll let 'em know that you're still out here. But one of us has to get through. And you people are just holdin' me back."

"Let him go, Doctor. We don't need him!" Fielding shouted. Kitty appeared a little more apprehensive.

Her plan had been to sneak out in the middle of the night when everyone was asleep; she hadn't seen the job at hand as a team effort. But now with Jones out of the picture, she was the group's only hope for survival.

All of a sudden, Katharine heard the couple upstairs screaming at each other again. Then there was a thunderous crash directly above her head, followed by a constant pounding against the rafter beams. It sounded as if someone had just fallen to the floor and was now getting punched in the face repeatedly. She quickly jumped out of bed and ran out of her apartment. As she rushed through the hallway, Mrs. Chang in room 306 opened her door and poked her head out, trying to figure out where all the noise was coming from.

"Where you going?" the old woman asked fearfully.

"Can't you hear them?" Katharine exclaimed.

"Please don't go up there, miss," the woman begged her as Katharine walked past her door and headed straight for the stairs. "It's not safe."

"I'm not going up there," Katharine assured her. "I'm going to talk to the assistant manager."

She quickly disappeared down the stairwell as Mrs. Chang shut her door and locked herself in. Katharine walked down to Mrs. Poindexter's apartment on the second floor and banged on the door. The woman opened it very slightly like before and stuck her nose out. Once again, opera music played in the background.

"Yes, Mrs. Beaumont? How may I help you?" she asked in her shrill voice.

"You should do something about those people on the top floor before someone gets hurt," Katharine said vehemently as the noise continued to fill the halls.

"Are those two at it again?" the woman replied, showing very little concern.

"Just listen to them!" Katharine exclaimed.

"I'd prefer not to," Mrs. Poindexter said. "That's why I play my music so loud."

"So you're just going to let them kill each other?" Katharine asked.

"My, you *do* have quite an imagination, don't you, my dear?" She laughed. "Mr. Brown told me you were a writer."

Katharine just looked at her sternly.

"You really shouldn't worry yourself," Mrs. Poindexter said. "They're just a couple of kids. I guarantee you, they'll be kissing and making up before you know it."

"Mrs. Poindexter, if you're not going to do anything about this, then I guess I'll just have to go to the police," Katharine said.

"Now that's just plain silly," she replied. "You don't want to do that."

"You're right, I don't," Katharine said. "But one of us has to do something."

"Mrs. Beaumont, my advice to you is not to get involved," the woman warned her. "You're new here, and the people are a lot different than what you're used to. You should leave them be and let them work this thing out on their own. In the meantime, you could check out one of our wonderful parks or maybe catch a Broadway show. I hear *Cats* is back in town."

"Goodnight, Mrs. Poindexter," Katharine huffed.

She quickly turned around and stomped down the hall. She headed back up the stairs. But instead of going to her room to call the police, she got very bold all of a sudden and took one more flight up, following the sound of angry voices, which grew louder and more violent with every step she took. She slowly crept up to room 411, took a deep breath, and knocked on the door. Suddenly the noise ceased, and there was total silence. No one ever answered. After standing there for a whole minute, she finally turned and walked away, thinking she had just solved the problem.

She hopped back into her bed and tried to pick up where she left off. But as soon as she grabbed her pen, the couple started fighting again.

"Oh for crying out loud," she said and glared at the ceiling.

That's when she discovered the spiders were back and looking for payback, no doubt.

The phone rang about five minutes later. She got up and ran into the kitchen to answer it. It was Norma, who was in the habit of calling her almost every night just before bedtime. After Katharine brought her up-to-date on her latest ordeal, she asked her about Frank and the children.

"How are they?" she asked. "Have you seen them lately?"

"Yes, I have," Norma answered. "And they're still a little shook up, as you can imagine."

"I've been wanting to call them—the kids, I mean," Katharine said. "But I don't know what to say to them."

"You should at least let them know that they're not to blame for your leavin'," Norma said. "They're beatin' themselves up over it."

"Are they?" Katharine gasped. "Could you please tell them that it wasn't their fault?"

"I've tried," Norma said. "They need to hear it from you, Kat."

"I know," Katharine sighed. "It's about eight o'clock there, isn't it?"

"Eight thirty-five," Norma replied.

"All right, I'm gonna call them," Katharine said. "Talk to you later."

She hung up and dialed the number to her own house.

"Hello?" Billy answered.

Katharine couldn't find the words to say. Just hearing his voice moved her to tears.

"Hello!" Billy repeated more loudly. "Is this a crank call? You better watch your step. You're fuckin' with the wrong family, buddy."

He immediately hung up, and Katharine started bawling uncontrollably.

Chapter 5: Adventures in the Food Service Industry

Katharine woke up early the next morning, put on a dress, and quickly headed out to see her agent, Mrs. Levi. As she entered the stairwell, she bumped into someone from the upper floor—a tall, slender black man with long sideburns and a Jheri curl. He wore a flashy yellow suit. He stood there and gave her the evil eye, and right away, she knew that it was him—the man from 411. He just seemed like the kind of man who'd beat his poor wife to death while the whole world listened in. And now it looked like he wanted to slap Katharine around a bit.

"Excuse me." She smiled and immediately stepped back so he could continue on his way.

He just kept looking at her, however. Finally, he turned away and headed down the stairwell. She felt relieved to watch him go; it was as if the Devil, himself, had just left her presence. *Damn that Mrs. Poindexter,* she thought. *She must have told him everything.*

She waited until he was completely out of the building. Then she proceeded down the steps, rushed through the lobby and the front exit, and walked over a mile to her destination; she was on a budget now and could no longer afford a cab.

"May I help you?" said the blonde receptionist, Mrs. Carmichael, as Katharine stepped into the room.

"I'm here to see Mrs. Levi," Katharine replied.

"Do you have an appointment?" the young woman asked.

"No," Katharine said.

"Go ahead," she huffed.

"Thank you," Katharine said as she walked up to her agent's door and quickly stepped in.

The old woman sat at her desk, dressed in a lavish fur coat even though it was the tail end of May. She sipped a cup of cappuccino through a straw.

"Well, hello, stranger. Long time no see," she remarked. "Oh, don't mind this. I just had the air conditioner fixed. And now I'm freezing my butt off." She slowly got up from her chair and asked, "What can I do for you, young lady? Do you have the rest of that story for me?"

"No," Katharine said.

"Well, you better get a move on, child," the old woman scolded her. "We've got to get this thing out there."

"What about the other story I gave you?" Katharine said. "Have you showed it to anybody?"

"I most certainly have," she replied. "But the truth is no one's all that interested. It's just too dark for most people's taste. I mean, the whole idea of a nurse killing her patients ..."

"But that's what makes it so compelling," Katharine argued. "Who would ever suspect a nurse of committing such terrible acts? The one person you trust the most after dear old Mom?"

"I'm not saying it isn't good," said Mrs. Levi. She walked up to Katharine and grabbed her hand. "I love it. Otherwise, I wouldn't have taken you on. But the simple fact of the matter is it won't sell, and I was wrong to think that it would."

Katharine was shocked at her words.

"The one you're working on now is our best bet by far," the old woman continued. "My daughter tells me that it's fun and exciting and that it should be a hit. She's got a lot of it typed already."

"Wow, she *is* fast," Katharine replied.

"That's my Linda," the woman said proudly. "She's a chip off the old block." She paused for a second and added, "By the way, you owe her five hundred dollars for the last ten chapters of *Nurse Nancy: A.K.A. The Syringe Killer*. She sent you a bill. But I figured that you could just give the money to me since you're here, and I'll see that she gets it."

"But I already paid you five hundred dollars last week," said Katharine.

"That was for the first ten chapters, dear," Mrs. Levi explained to her. "A hundred typed pages at five dollars a page comes to five hundred dollars. She also corrected a few spelling and punctuation mistakes, which comes free of charge."

Katharine dug into her purse and pulled out three hundred dollars.

"Here. This is all I have," she said and handed it to her.

"That's fine," Mrs. Levi replied. "You can pay her the rest later. I know you're good for it." She walked back over to her desk. "I'll write you a receipt," she said.

"I was really counting on that story," Katharine muttered. "Now I don't know how I'm gonna be able to pay next month's rent."

"Oh heavens, child." The old woman laughed as she sat down at her desk and filled out the receipt. "Did you actually think that I could make you a star overnight?""

"No, of course not." Katharine sighed. "I was just hoping that the money would've lasted longer. I guess it's time to start looking for a job."

"Do you have any other skills besides writing?" Mrs. Levi asked her.

"Not really." She sighed again.

"My ex-husband knows a couple of guys in the restaurant business," Mrs. Levi said. "They're brothers, and they own the place. I met 'em once or twice. One's a real standup guy. The other one's an asshole. I'll get their number from my ex here shortly. Then you can call them and set up an appointment."

"Thank you," Katharine said as she walked up to her desk. Mrs. Levi handed her the receipt.

"I trust you've waited on tables before," Mrs. Levi said.

"No, never," Katharine replied.

"Well, I'm sure you'll get the hang of it," she said. "The restaurant's in Queens, so you'll have to take the subway."

"I see," Katharine said, suddenly looking a little apprehensive.

"What's the matter, dear?" Mrs. Levi asked.

"Oh, nothing." She laughed. "I was told to stay off the subway 'cause it's too dangerous."

"Who told you that?"

"My best friend, Norma."

"Has she ever been on the subway?" Mrs. Levi asked.

"No," Katharine replied.

"Then don't listen to her," she said. "I've been riding it my whole life and never had any problems whatsoever."

Katharine nodded, though she still felt a little uneasy.

"It's affordable public transportation, dear." The old woman smiled. "Take advantage of it."

That same morning, Katharine got on the phone and made an appointment to see the two brothers. Then late in the afternoon, she walked down the steps of the MTA New York City Transit, bought a two-dollar MetroCard at the station booth, and joined the twenty or thirty people on the waiting platform. The crowd grew larger by the second, and Katharine felt increasingly nervous. She kept both hands on her purse, as her friend had suggested. Finally, a train whizzed down the tracks. It stopped directly in front of the crowd, and everyone pushed and shoved their way toward the opening doors. She avoided being crushed and slid inside. She grabbed a seat between a white-faced man in gothic attire and a young pregnant woman.

A bunch of people stood over Katharine as the train started to roll. They kept giving her dirty looks, if only for the simple fact that she managed to secure a seat before they did. She even noticed a young man staring at her from the other end of the car. His look was far more intense than the others, as if he had something sinister on his mind. He appeared to be Spanish or Puerto Rican. He had dark, frizzy hair and wore blue jeans and a sports jacket. She quickly averted her eyes from him and moved her purse from one hip to the other so that it was no longer in his view.

Then all of a sudden, she stared back at him, full of spite. He immediately looked away. She laughed to herself, thinking that she had just beaten him at his own game. But then she noticed his eyes slowly moving toward her again until he was once again looking straight at her. He wore a smile that chilled her to the bone. When the train finally came to a stop, she quickly jumped up and was one of the first people out the door. She exited the subway station as fast as she could, blended in with the crowd, and swiftly headed down Queens Boulevard. It seemed very unlikely he would chase after her, especially in a crowd full of witnesses. But she looked back for a split second, and there he was, quickly gaining on her. She began to walk even faster, though she could already feel him on her back.

"Miss?" he shouted as he reached out and grabbed her shoulder.

She immediately turned around and swung her purse at him. Then she slapped him in the face with it repeatedly.

"Is this what you want?" she exclaimed. "Here, take it!"

"What? Are you crazy?" he shouted back at her, putting his hands over his face. "I don't want your goddamn purse! I thought we had a moment back there! I was just gonna ask you out!"

She suddenly lowered her "weapon" and backed off.

"I'm so sorry," she said with an embarrassed look on her face. "I thought you were trying to rob me."

"Do I look like a mugger to you?" he exclaimed. "I'm a fucking stockbroker for crying out loud! I bet I make more money in one day than you do in an entire week!"

"I'm sorry. I really am," she continued to apologize. "I'm new here and ..."

"Oh, you're a newbie, huh?" he interrupted her. "One word of advice, newbie! Don't go making assumptions based on the color of one's skin! You're not in Crackerville, Kansas, anymore!"

"Actually, I'm from Oklahoma," she said as he angrily walked away. She watched him walk a little farther and shouted, "I'm not a racist!"

Then and there she decided not to be so fearful and naïve from that point on. That way people wouldn't get the wrong impression. *If you want to hang with New Yorkers, you got to be tough like them,* she thought.

A police officer showed her the way to Cardenelli's Italian Eatery, and before long, she was sitting inside an office and being interviewed by both owners. Manny Cardenelli sat directly in front of her, conducting the interview while his older brother, Sal, stood behind him and hardly said a word. She assumed he was the "asshole" her agent had referred to because of his curtly manner and the fact that he never smiled. He was a thin bald man and looked very prim and proper in his white dress shirt and blue neck tie. His brother Manny, on the other hand, was overweight and looked like a slob. His shirt hung out and he had a big food stain on *his* tie. It seemed like the only thing the two men had in common was that they were both bald and wore spectacles.

"So have you ever been a waitress?" asked the younger brother.

"No," she answered.

"Thirty-eight years old, no resume, zero references …" He sighed. "Do you have any work experience at all?"

"Nearly fifteen years of being a housewife," she answered. "Surely that must count for something."

"It says here that you're from Oklahoma," he said, looking at the application in his hand. "So you and your husband relocated?"

"No, I left him," she answered. "I'm here by myself."

"You left him?" he said curiously. "I know it's none of my business, but why?"

"I found out that he was cheatin' on me," she replied bluntly.

"I see." He nodded. "Well, we need someone with experience for our waitress position." He looked disappointed at first. Then, he smiled at her and said, "We can use another cook. Can you cook?"

"I learned from the very best—my mama," she answered.

"Oh." He smiled again. "And what are your specialties?"

"I cook a mean casserole." She laughed. "My meatloaf's pretty good, too."

"Well, we only serve Italian food here," he said. "But right now we're looking for someone who can bake cakes, bread—that sort of thing."

"I'm afraid I'll have to pass," she swiftly replied. "I'm tired of cookin' for other people."

"Okay," he said, looking a little stymied. "The only other position I have open is for a dishwasher."

"I've had enough of that, too," she replied.

"Well, I don't know," he said and scratched his bald head. "I guess we could work something out."

At that point, Sal stepped in and said to him, "Can I see you outside for a minute?"

"Be right back." He smiled as he got up and followed his brother out the door.

"She has no experience whatsoever," Sal grumbled as they stepped into the hallway. "And we don't have time to teach her the basics. This isn't waitressing 101."

Katharine overheard every word; they were standing right outside the door.

"I'll do it," Manny said very enthusiastically. "I'll take her under my wing. She'll have it all down in no time."

"All right," his brother grumbled. "But she's your responsibility. And, *you're* gonna fire her if it doesn't work out. I'm tired of cleaning up after your messes."

Manny rushed back into his office with a huge smile. "Congratulations," he said to Katharine. "You got the job."

"Great," she replied, even though she wasn't all that excited about having to go to work.

When Katharine stepped back into her apartment building, she heard jazz music playing and people partying upstairs. She even noticed them hanging out on the stairwell as she walked up to her floor. A young couple made out on the steps directly above her. To their left a huge, black man in a black leather jacket leaned against the hand railing, smoking a joint. Sitting next to him was the man from 411. He wore tan-colored slacks and a blue silk shirt that perfectly accented his lean muscular frame. He quickly jumped to his feet and walked up to greet Katharine, holding a bottle of Colt 45 in one hand.

"Well, hello, neighbor," he said with a look of disdain. He stood directly over her so she couldn't get away.

"Hi," she said, desperately trying to control her fear.

"Someone told me that you threatened to call the cops on us last night," he sneered.

She just looked at him with wide eyes.

"That wasn't very nice," he said.

"I was just trying to help," she muttered. "I didn't want anyone to get hurt."

"And how would that be helpful to either of us if the police were to come and haul me off to jail?" he said. "I'd have to come down and pay you a little visit as soon as I got out." He lifted his hand to her face, and she cringed as he proceeded to run his fingers through her hair. "I know you meant well," he said with a sudden eerie smile. "You're a real sweetheart, I can tell." He looked over at his enormous friend, still leaning against the hand railing. "Isn't she a real sweetie?" he asked him.

"Yeah, she's sweet all right," his friend answered in a deep voice.

"I think it would be better for all of us if you just minded your own business next time," the man from 411 said to her, continuing to stroke her hair. "Don't you agree?"

"Yes," she muttered under her shaky breath.

"Sorry, I couldn't hear you," he said. "Was that a yes?"

"Yes," she blurted out.

He laughed, exposing his pearly white teeth once again. Then he removed his hand from her hair and grabbed her by the arm.

"Why don't you come upstairs with me and I'll fix you a drink?" he said.

At that point, Katharine looked up and noticed a young black woman standing at the top of the stairs with her hand on her hip. He had no idea that she was looking right at him the whole time; his eyes were focused on Katharine.

"Leon, what do you think you're doing?" the woman said to him angrily.

She was very slim and petite, but she had a fierce voice. Plus Katharine noticed the fresh bruise on her left cheek.

"Nothin', woman," he answered very sternly. Yet he did not dare to look up at her. "I'm just welcoming our new neighbor to the building."

"Yeah, I can see that," she snapped. "Now take your hands off of her so she can be on her way."

"Sure, baby. Whatever you say," he smoothly replied, slowly removing his hand from Katharine and stepping back.

Katharine just stood there and gawked at the young woman, concerned about the wound on her cheek.

"What do you think *you're* looking at?" the woman scolded her. "Go on. Get out of here."

Katharine turned and walked away, feeling deeply humiliated.

The next day she waited tables in her new uniform—a sexy red dress—under the tutelage of Manny Cardenelli. He taught her everything, such as how to write in shorthand when taking orders and how to carry a tray full of food and drinks without spilling a drop. But most importantly, he told her to always treat her customers with a smile, even when she felt like strangling them. Some customers showed patience and understanding when they saw it was her first week on the job. One well-dressed elderly couple never complained when she left their cups half empty or when she accidentally spilled coffee on the table. They left her a huge tip, in fact. And as they were leaving, the old man turned to her and said, "Hang in there, kid. You'll be all right."

Now, why can't all my customers be like that? she thought. The majority of her customers were crude, insensitive, and downright hostile. And her co-workers were just as bad, especially Annabella and Suling—a pair of dark-haired beauties and the two youngest waitresses on her shift. It seemed like they were always watching her, and they loved to see her screw up someone's order or overfill a glass. They had also made bets with the other waitresses on how long she would last, or at least that was what she was told.

Only her boss seemed to be on her side, always trying to build up her confidence with a quick pep talk and a pat on the back. Yet she noticed his hand moving lower and lower on her back after each talk. The first time he slapped her tush, she was completely stunned to the point that she didn't say anything. When he tried it again a couple of days later, she immediately grabbed his hand and warned him never to touch her again.

"You like it though, don't ya?" he said with a look that both frightened her and completely shattered her image of him.

"Are you nuts?" she exclaimed. "Go fuck yourself!"

She immediately walked away and went right back to work, trying to forget it ever happened. It was Friday, the busiest day of the week, and her station was almost full. Insurance salesman Fred Burnham sat at table three. He was a regular— a "regular asshole" as far as the other waitresses were concerned. So naturally, they pawned him off on the new girl. They enjoyed watching her sweat every time he asked her how much longer his pasta primavera was going to take.

"I could've just gone to Eddy's across the street and had a steak for lunch," he said to Katharine at one point.

She secretly thought to herself, *I wished you had.* But on the surface, she merely pasted on smile and said, "Your food will be out here shortly."

"I certainly hope so," he grumbled before she managed to get away. "I'm a busy man. I can't afford to be sittin' here all day."

Four beautiful young actresses from the Broadway circuit sat at table six; they gave Katharine the silent treatment whenever she came around to refill their glasses. They laughed hysterically as soon as she left, however. It almost seemed as if they were laughing at her. The rest of her tables were filled with art dealers, poets, lawyers, and politicians—all of them snobs and terrible tippers. They kept her on her feet the whole time, but none were quite as bad as the insurance salesman, who once he received his meal, wondered what happened to the extra roll he had ordered.

"It's coming," she assured him while Annabella and Suling continued to snicker at her from a distance.

And just when she thought that things couldn't get any worse, her husband walked through the door and was seated at one of her empty tables. He looked thin and pale, and he was unshaven and wearing a wrinkled suit. *I don't believe this,* she thought as she watched it all from her station. She took a deep breath and tried to remain calm. Then she grabbed a menu and walked straight up to him.

"What are you doing here, Frank?" she said in a low voice.

"So what's today's specials?" he asked and snatched the menu right out of her hand.

"You're supposed to be taking care of the kids," she scolded him as he started to read through it.

"The kids are fine," he assured her. "My mother's taking care of 'em. You'd be proud of our little Maggie. She's turned out to be a real Martha Stewart in the kitchen. Plus she does all the laundry and keeps the house clean."

"What about Billy?" Katharine asked.

"That's another story." He sighed, suddenly putting down the menu and looking up at her. "I honestly don't know what to do with the kid. He's way out of control. For one thing, his grades are slipping. He just received two Ds and an F on his final report card before the summer break. And the other day I had to pick him up at the police station."

"Huh?" She gasped.

"He was caught stealing a *Girls Gone Wild* tape inside a video store," said Frank. "The manager wanted to throw the book at him just to set an example, but I somehow managed to talk him out of pressing charges. The police sergeant let us off with a warning." He laughed nervously and measured an inch with his thumb and forefinger. "Our fourteen-year-old son came this close to having a criminal record," he said.

Katharine shook her head. "Maybe he'll grow out of it," she replied.

"Well, I've got a feeling that things are going to get much worse with just one of us there," he said, looking very desperate all of a sudden. "And you were much better with him than I am, obviously. He needs his mother."

"How did you find me?" she huffed.

"Norma. Who else?" he replied. "She's the only one you've been keeping in touch with the whole time."

Katharine just stared at him blankly, feeling betrayed by her best friend. "So what do you want?" she asked him finally.

"I just wanted to see you," he said defensively. "You're still my wife. I told you that it's over between me and Bernice, didn't I? I don't remember if I did or not."

"Yes, you did," she replied.

"I don't know why I screwed things up," he said, his voice filled with remorse. "I guess we've been together for so long that I forgot how much I loved you. If you'd give me a second chance and come home with me, I promise that I'll never take you for granted ever again." His eyes began to tear as he gazed into hers. "Please come home with me, Kat," he begged her.

"Don't do this," she huffed. "I've already started over, and I'm beginning to get the hang of things."

"This?" he scoffed and looked around the room. "This is what you want? I thought you were all about becoming a writer. I didn't expect to see you waiting on tables when I got here. If that's your ambition, there's plenty of restaurants in Oklahoma City, you know."

"You don't become a published writer overnight," Katharine said, paraphrasing her agent's words. "It takes months, even years. In the meantime, I've got to work to pay the bills."

"Yeah, but here?" he remarked with a look of disgust. "You're too old for this line of work."

"Shut up, Frank," she sneered.

"Sorry," he muttered. "All I meant was you don't belong here. You're too good for these people. If anything, they should be serving you."

"It's a little late to be putting me on a pedestal, don't you think?" Katharine said.

"Yes, it is," he said regretfully. "I should've been doing it every day for the last fifteen years." He paused for a moment. Then he asked, "What will it take to make you come back with me? Do I have to get on my hands and knees and beg?"

"Please don't," she said.

"But I miss you so much," he blurted out and started to cry uncontrollably.

"Come on, Frank, get a grip," she whispered, worried he was causing a scene.

Looking around the room, she noticed Annabella and Suling eyeballing her as usual. But this time they weren't laughing. They appeared to be in shock.

"Come home with me, Katharine," Frank continued sobbing. "Give me just one more chance. I swear to you I'm a changed man."

He suddenly got out of his chair and grabbed her leg.

"Stop it," she snapped. "You're gonna get me fired." Finally she jerked away from him and said, "I don't have time for this. I've got other customers to tend to."

She swiftly walked away and headed back to her station.

"Waitress, where's my roll?" Mr. Burnham shouted at her as she passed his table.

"It's coming," she shouted back at him, keeping a swift pace.

A minute later, she returned with the roll and placed it on the table in front of him.

"What is this?" he asked, picking it up from the saucer and staring at it.

"It's a roll," she answered.

Then she watched him strike the table with it repeatedly.

"I can't eat this," he said. "It's overcooked and as hard as a rock." He placed it back on the saucer and shoved it away. "Get it out of here," he demanded.

Just as she was about to let him have it, her husband stepped in.

"Hey, that's my wife you're talkin' to," Frank said as he jumped out of his chair again and raised his fist to the insurance salesman.

"That's it!" Katharine exclaimed, rushing up to her husband's table and forcefully pushing him toward the exit. "Get out of here! Get out!"

"Okay, I'm leaving," he said. Then he turned around and walked out on his own.

Embarrassed and upset, she turned and headed for the break room. She immediately ran into her boss, who stood right in her way.

"Everything's all right, folks!" he said to the customers with a huge smile, while he placed his hand on Katharine's shoulder. "It's all over!" Then he looked at Katharine and whispered, "What the hell just happened here? Is this how we treat our customers now … by throwing them out on the street?"

She suddenly snapped and punched him right in the gut.

"Uhh!" he groaned and grabbed his belly.

"I told you not to touch me ever again!" she exclaimed and then continued on her way while the other waitresses applauded her.

She rushed into the break room in back of the restaurant, sat down at an empty table, and put her hands over her face. She heard someone storming through the hallway just a few seconds later. *Oh boy, here he comes,* she thought, suddenly filled with dread.

"Hold on there, little brother," she heard Sal say to him right outside the door.

"Let go of me, Sal." Manny growled.

"Where are you going?" his brother asked.

"I'm going to fire that little cunt," Manny answered.

"Do you really think that's wise?" Sal said. "I saw you puttin' the moves on her earlier." There was a slight pause. "Maybe you better let me handle this one, Hoss," he said. "Before we end up with a major lawsuit on our hands."

"All right, Sal," Manny replied in a much calmer voice.

Sal stepped into the break room and walked up next to Katharine.

"So I guess you heard all of that?" he asked her.

She looked up at him and nodded.

"I have to apologize for my brother," he said. "He still has a lot of growing up to do. It's pathetic, actually. He's a fifty-two-year-old man."

She laughed to herself.

"You're thinking about leaving us, aren't you?" he asked.

"Honestly, the thought *did* cross my mind," she replied.

"Please don't," he said. "I've had my eye on you the last three days. You're a real go-getter, and I'd sure hate to lose you." He placed his hand on her shoulder and smiled. "It gets a hell of a lot easier after the first week, I promise you," he said.

Definitely not the asshole, she thought as she smiled back at him.

"So what do you say?" he asked. "Will you give us another chance?"

"All right," she replied.

"Good," he said. "And don't worry about Manny. I don't think he's gonna bother you anymore. If he does, you have my permission to hit him again."

She laughed. Then she stood up and checked to see that her hair and scrunchie were in place.

"Guess I better go tend to my customers," she said and hurriedly walked out of the room.

As she went back to her station, she wondered how she could've been so wrong about the Cardenelli brothers. *I've been closed off and shut in for so long that it's made me a poor judge of character,* she concluded. *I've spent too many years living inside my head. I guess I better brush up on my people skills now that I'm out in the real world.*

Chapter 6: A Wild Night on the Town

Katharine finally rolled out of bed around 11 AM on her day off, gathered up all of her dirty clothes, and took them to the laundry room down in the basement. She always dreaded going down there because it was so dark and eerie. It also reminded her of Leon, as she had heard his wife or girlfriend refer to him. Since it was the creepiest place in the whole building, she realized she was bound to run into him there sooner or later. But that day, she ran into his "better half" instead. The woman was busy removing her clothes from one of the washing machines when Katharine boldly stepped into the room and sat her laundry basket on the washer directly across from her. She opened the lid and began filling it full of clothes, occasionally looking up at the young woman until their eyes met. Katharine blushed and smiled. Then she looked down again.

"I didn't mean to be such a bitch the other night," the woman said in a stern voice. "Leon always puts me in one of those moods, where you just want to kill him and everyone else in the room."

"It's okay." Katharine smiled again, noting the bruise on her left cheek was much smaller and a little less visible. She pointed at her own cheek and asked, "Did he do that to you?"

The woman just looked at her very harshly.

"I'm sorry. It's none of my business." Katharine blushed.

"It's nothing," the woman assured her. "He just got the edge on me, that's all. You should take a look at his face sometimes."

Katharine laughed and said, "My name is Katharine Beaumont. What's yours?"

"Bree Withers," the woman answered. She studied Katharine very curiously. "Where's you from?" she asked. "You ain't from New York City, that's for sure."

"Oklahoma," Katharine replied.

"Oklahoma?" she exclaimed. "Girl, what you doing all the way out here?"

Katharine then proceeded to tell her all about the cheating husband, which didn't seem the least bit surprising to Bree.

She simply nodded and said, "My man's cheated on me a bunch of times. He thinks he's got me fooled, but I know when he's been with other women. I can just smell it on him."

"Why don't you leave him?" Katharine asked her.

"Now why would I want to do that?" she said very sternly. "First of all, if anyone leaves, it's gonna be him. It's my apartment. And frankly, I don't see how a person could ever leave someone if they really love 'em. I don't mean you, of course."

Katharine thought about it for a second and said, "I guess I'm not in love with Frank the way I use to be. We married straight out of college, and that seems like ages ago."

"Well, at least now you'll be able to find someone new to fall in love with," Bree said. "I'm just not quite sure that you should've come all the way out here for it. This place is hell on earth."

"I'm not looking for love," Katharine quickly pointed out to her. "The last thing I need right now is another man in my life. I came here because I'm a writer, and this is where they all come to be inspired."

"You're a writer, huh?" said Bree. "Perhaps you could show me your work sometime."

"Sure," Katharine smiled.

"How did you find out about your husband?" Bree asked her very curiously.

"He told me everything," Katharine replied.

"He told you?" she said with a surprised look on her face. "Has he ever cheated on you before?

"No," Katharine said, wondering what she was driving at. "All in all, he's a good man. He even told me that he was sorry and that it would never happen again."

Bree just looked at her and nodded.

"What?" Katharine said.

"Nothing," she replied. "It's just that most men would never admit to something like that. They're habitual liars. Maybe yours deserves a second chance."

"Maybe," Katharine said. Then suddenly, she smiled and became excited. "You could come over now if you like," she said. "If you really want to see my work. I'll make us some hot tea."

"Not today. Next time, perhaps." Bree laughed. She quickly grabbed her basket full of wet clothes and walked over to the dryers.

Katharine walked back into her lonely apartment and breathed a heavy sigh. *It's twelve noon on a Sunday,* she thought as she looked up at the clock on the living room wall. *That means it's eleven o'clock in Oklahoma. I wonder if Frank's mom took the kids to church this morning.* She walked over to the phone on the kitchen counter and considered giving them a call. But this time she couldn't even pick up the receiver. *To hell with it,* she thought and grabbed her pen and notebook from the counter.

There were places throughout the apartment where she loved to write, not just on the couch or in bed. She also liked to write on the kitchen floor or inside an empty bathtub with all of her clothes on. But her most favorite spot was the little old rocking chair in front of the living room window. She just loved to sit there and watch people come and go as she made stuff up. The distraction seemed to help her creativity rather than hinder it. It was like her own little four-by-four window to the world. She sat down in the chair and gazed through it for several minutes before she opened the notebook and picked up where she'd left off.

April 10

 Kitty and her fellow survivors continued to plow through the jungle during the light of day, stopping every once in a while to rest and share a coconut—their most readily available source of food and water. The only problem was that the coconut milk contained a lot of sugary substances that made them even thirstier, so they could only drink it in very small doses. Kitty and Miles left the camp early in the morning while the others were still sleeping and went deeper into the woods to gather up more coconuts and hopefully find a freshwater spring along the way.

Kitty now wore Barkesdale's clothes, minus the raincoat, and carried a pointed spear made from a long, thick branch. Miles had on the dead man's vest and still wore his own boxer shorts. It was the first time Kitty had been alone with him since they were aboard the ship. As they walked, the sexual tension slowly mounted until she could no longer stand it. She sensed he felt the same as they suddenly turned to face each other. She threw herself on him and took him to the ground. They fervently removed each other's clothing and rolled around in the grass until he was on top. He entered her swiftly and kept pushing deep inside her.

"Yes, yes," she moaned and dug her fingernails into his hairy chest, feeling a surge of euphoria.

She could always count on Miles to push the right buttons in only a matter of seconds. But this time it ended much too quickly, and he left her wanting more as he got up and started looking for his shorts.

"Well, that was fun," she said. She slowly lifted herself off the ground and slid back into her oversized pants.

"We better go find us a coconut tree before they all get suspicious," Miles said as he pulled up his shorts and put on the vest.

"Right," she agreed, buttoning her shirt.

As they headed off again, they heard something growling in the trees up ahead. The sound alone was so fierce and menacing that it stopped them dead in their tracks. They both gasped as a beautiful white tiger suddenly came into view. It carefully eyeballed them and slowly inched its way forward.

"Can there actually be tigers on this island?" Miles whispered.

"Apparently so," Kitty replied. They started inching their way backward. "Whatever you do, don't take your eyes off of him. And no sudden movements," she said.

The tiger let out a mighty roar and bared his fangs, forcing them to a standstill once again.

"Now what?" Kitty muttered to herself, at which point Miles jumped out in front of her. "No, Miles. Don't try to be a hero."

"Get out of here, Kit," he said. "Go back to the camp and warn the others."

"Please don't do this," she begged him.

"Go!" he shouted and shot off into the trees to the left of them.

The tiger immediately chased after him. Kitty headed in the same direction, with her spear in hand. The tiger's angry roar kept her on his path. She heard her lover cry out as if he was being attacked.

"Ah!" he screamed.

She saw the beast's tail sticking up in the tall grass ahead, aimed her spear, and charged full speed ahead. The weapon landed in the tiger's thigh. She pulled it out as the cat slid off his victim and suddenly turned on her. The only thing keeping them apart was the eight feet of sharpened branch pointed directly at its face. Furious, the wounded animal stood up on his hind legs and swatted at the spear with his enormous paws, but she held firm and jabbed him in the nose.

"Get the hell away from him, you son of a bitch!" she shouted with such determination that the cat got down on all fours and started to back off.

She breathed a heavy sigh of relief and threw down her weapon as the tiger turned around and hobbled away. She looked down at Miles to assess the damage. His left leg was a bloody pulp from his thigh all the way down to his ankle. He was still conscious, however. He lay helplessly on his back with a painful look on his face, breathing very heavily and groaning occasionally.

"Damn it, Miles. You shouldn't have run," she scolded him.

"I thought at least one of us would have a chance." He smiled.

She knelt down beside him, ripped off the bottom half of her shirt, and wrapped it tightly around his leg to stop the bleeding.

"Uh!" he groaned.

"There. All done," she said, patting him on the shoulder. She got up and stood over him again. "Now we've got to get you back to camp," she said. "I'm afraid I'm gonna have to drag you."

"*To hell with that!*" *he exclaimed.* "*I'm not going to let you drag me all the way back to camp. Help me up. I'm gonna try to walk.*"

"*No, absolutely not,*" *she said.*

"*Damn it, Kit, don't argue with me,*" *he groaned as he tried to lift himself off the ground.*

"*Oh, you're so pigheaded,*" *she said, grabbing his arm and helping him to his feet.*

Though his pain must have been excruciating, he tried not to show it. He closed his eyes and grit his teeth until he finally stood erect and took several steps forward, using Kitty as a crutch.

"*Where have you two been?*" *Dr. Faraday shouted at them as they walked into camp about an hour later.* "*We've got to get a move on!*"

Kitty was practically dragging Miles on her shoulder by that point. They both looked extremely exhausted.

"*Good lord, what happened?*" *the doctor asked as they got a little closer. He and the others rushed up to them.*

"*We had a run-in with a tiger,*" *Kitty groaned.*

"*There's tigers on the island?*" *Jenkins gasped.*

"*Well, that's odd,*" *the doctor said.* "*Are you sure it was a tiger?*"

Kitty and Miles just looked at him. He and Jenkins grabbed a hold of Miles, carried him over to the campfire, and sat him down with his back against a tree. The doctor removed Kitty's blood-soaked shirt from Miles's leg to observe the wound. The other three stood behind them and winced. A huge chunk of his thigh was missing, exposing muscle and bone. The doctor bandaged the leg as best he could and then gave Miles shots of morphine and penicillin.

"*Am I going to lose the leg, Doc?*" *Miles asked, looking even more woozy than before.*

"*Perhaps,*" *the doctor said.* "*Don't worry about that right now.*"

"*What are we supposed to do now?*" *Jenkins asked.* "*It's obvious he can't walk.*"

Everyone had liked Jenkins before because he hardly ever spoke. But now that Barkesdale was gone, he seemed to have taken his place; he constantly bickered and thought only of himself.

"*Don't worry about it,*" *Kitty said.* "*I'll carry him the rest of the way.*"

"*You'll do no such thing,*" the doctor snapped. "*The two of you barely made it back to camp. What we'll do is make him a stretcher. Then two people can carry him.*"

"*Not me,*" Jenkins said. "*And what the bloody hell are you gonna make it out of? Fig leaves?*"

"*I don't mind carrying him,*" Omar said very proudly.

"*Ain't nobody gonna carry me anywhere,*" Miles finally butted in. He turned to the doctor and asked, "*How many miles do you think we've come so far?*"

"*I don't know. Fifteen ... twenty, maybe,*" he answered.

"*Would you say we're over halfway there?*"

"*Easily.*"

"*Then leave me here,*" Miles insisted. "*I don't want to slow you guys up. And after you get there, you can send someone back for me.*"

"*No, forget it,*" Kitty said. "*We're not leaving anyone behind.*"

"*He's making a lot of sense, Kitty,*" the doctor said. "*I'm sure this Ljungberg fellow has a plane or a jeep—some way to get from one side of the island to the other. We can get there in a couple of days. And it won't take long at all for us to get back here.*"

"*There won't be anything left of him in a couple of days,*" she argued. "*There's a bloody tiger out there, probably more than one, and with that open wound of his, I bet they're gettin' a good whiff of us already.*"

"*I'm staying here, Kit,*" Miles said. "*It's my decision to make, and I've made it.*"

"*All right,*" she huffed. "*But the gun stays here with you.*"

"*To hell with that!*" Jenkins shouted. He happened to be wearing it over his shoulder at that moment. "*We need it!*"

She immediately rushed up behind the little man and jerked it right off his back.

"*No, we don't,*" she said, making sure it was fully loaded and then tossing it down to Miles. The box of ammo was already close by.

"*Now you all move on out of here,*" Miles said. "*I'll be all right.*"

Kitty knelt down beside him and kissed him on the lips. Then she whispered in his ear, "*I'll come back for you. I promise.*"

He just looked at her and smiled as she slowly rose to her feet and walked out of the camp behind the others. Three of them carried spears. They had walked for almost a mile when they heard a gunshot.

"Miles," Kitty gasped, quickly turning around and heading back to the camp.

"Kitty, wait!" the doctor shouted as he turned and went after her.

"What! Are you both mad?" Jenkins exclaimed. "We've come too far to turn back now!" Then he and Jenkins turned and ran as well.

When they got back to the camp, they found Miles just as they had left him, sitting against the tree with the rifle in his lap. But now it appeared that he had killed himself with a bullet through the chin. He was surrounded by five boars, two of which were chewing on his wounded leg. Kitty picked up a huge rock and charged at them, while the other three ran at them with their spears and shouted to the top of their lungs like fierce warriors. The entire pack immediately shot off into the woods.

"Damn you, Miles," she said as she stood over his body. Tears streamed down her face.

"It doesn't make any sense," said Dr. Faraday. "He had plenty of cartridges to shoot 'em with. Why would he take his own life instead?"

"Miles was all about pleasing the ladies ... more than most men are, in fact," Kitty replied. "And I imagine the thought of losing the leg was just too much to bear."

She dropped to her knees, threw her arms around him, and clung tightly to his grossly disfigured face.

"Oh Miles, you beautiful fool," she muttered. "Wasn't it enough that I loved you?"

Suddenly the phone rang on the kitchen counter. Katharine jumped up to answer it.

"Hello," she said.

There was no response, but she could hear someone sniffling. On a hunch, she immediately put down the receiver, rushed over to the window, and opened the blinds. Sure enough, her husband stood in the phone booth directly across the street. He looked up and caught a glimpse of her before she went back to the phone and hung up.

"Damn it, Norma," she huffed.

She picked up the receiver again and made a long-distance call.

"Kruger residence," Norma answered.

"Jesus, Norm. It's bad enough that you told him where I worked," she began. "But did you have to give him my address and phone number as well?"

"I'm sorry, hon, but he kept hounding me for it, and he wouldn't let up," Norma replied. "And you should've seen his face. You can tell that he's really torn up over this mess. The man loves you, Kat."

"So now you're taking *his* side?" Katharine said.

"No, no, of course not," Norma awkwardly replied. "He made a huge mistake. There's no doubt about it. But how long are you going to make him pay for it? We all miss you, and we want you to come home."

"I've been gone for what? Less than a month?" said Katharine. "Why can't you people just give me some space and let me do what I have to do?"

"You people?" Norma replied.

"I've gotta go now," Katharine said. "I still got a lot of work to do."

She quickly hung up the phone. It rang about a second later, and she picked it up again.

"Katharine?" her husband said, sounding a little shook up.

She didn't respond.

"Please don't hang up," he said. "I need to talk to you face-to-face. I could've just knocked on your door, but I knew you wouldn't want that. Will you let me come up?"

All of a sudden she got scared and hung up on him again. *What am I so afraid of?* she asked herself. *Why can't I talk to my own family anymore?*

You know why, said her conscience. *What you're doing is wrong, and you know it. There's no defending it. A mother doesn't leave her children, no matter what. Just look at you ... so racked with guilt that you can't even face them.*

Don't listen to her, said her heart. *You're going on this journey because you have to. And you should be commended for it. Frank has always had his way with you. You shouldn't let him or anyone try to talk you into going back to that awful situation. He's weak and unfaithful.*

Oh, why don't you both just shut the hell up? she said to herself finally. Then she went back to her writing.

At the workplace on the following day, everyone appeared much friendlier. Sal was more like a big brother to her than a boss. The other waitresses talked to her more. Even her worst customer, Mr. Burnham, showed a gentler side to him that no one even knew existed. What surprised her the most, however, was when Annabella and Suling sat with her at break time and actually struck up a conversation as if they were her new best friends.

"It was really neat what you did to Manny the other day," Annabella said. "You should have punched him in the nads, though. That really would've been cool."

"Yeah, get him where he lives," Suling added. "He asked me if he could touch my boobs once. I told him to fuck off."

"Who was that other guy you threw out of here?" Annabella asked.

"That was my husband," Katharine answered. "We're separated."

"What did he do? Cheat on you?" Suling asked.

"Yeah," Katharine replied.

"I thought so." She nodded. "And now he expects you to forgive him and take him back."

"Men are pigs," Annabella sneered. They both nodded.

Then Suling asked, "You wanna hang out with us after work? There's this really cool nightclub, and tonight's ladies' night."

"Which means free beer," her friend added.

"Sure, why not?" Katharine replied.

That night, the two girls picked Katharine up in their '93 Dodge Neon and introduced her to the New York club scene, starting with a couple of lesbian bars and then The Diamond, one of the hottest new dance clubs in Midtown Manhattan. Both girls were dressed like Vampira in their matching black miniskirts while Katharine was her sweet, wholesome self, wearing her same old blue dress.

She mostly sat alone at their little table, sipping margaritas through a straw and watching the other two bounce all over the place. When they weren't dancing with each other out on the dance floor, she could usually spot them talking to somebody at the bar. Everyone seemed to be having the time of their lives except for her. She much preferred the gay bars, where ninety percent of the customers were women going through menopause. Here it was noisy, overcrowded, and full of men and women half her age. It was extremely uncomfortable for her, to say the least. Finally the girls came back to the table with their beers and Jagermeisters. They looked concerned.

"What's the matter?" Annabella asked. "You look really tense."

"It's no wonder," Suling said. "She's been milking that same drink since we got here."

"Do you want me to get you another one?" Annabella asked.

"No thanks," Katharine said rather stiffly.

"C'mon, Katharine. Tell us what's wrong?" Suling begged her.

"I feel old," she blurted out.

"You're not old," Annabella said.

"Thirty-eight isn't old," Suling concurred. "I just hope I look as good as you when I'm that age."

"Really," Annabella said. "All you need is a makeover—lots of makeup, maybe a little rouge, and some eyeliner. We should be able to smooth those lines right out."

"Yeah, but first we gotta do something about that dress," Suling added. "Maybe tomorrow we'll go shopping for some new clothes."

"Other than that, you're fine, girl," Annabella concluded. "In fact, you're better than all of these people."

"Yeah," Suling agreed. "We saw how you handle men. You're the shit."

Katharine laughed.

"Maybe we better find Steve," Annabella said to Suling.

"Right," the latter nodded, quickly getting up from the chair and walking off.

She returned about ten minutes later, sat down next to Katharine again, and placed a wadded-up napkin in front of her. Katharine opened it up and looked down at a little pink pill.

"Take it," Suling urged her.

Katharine stared at it, very reluctant to do as they encouraged.

"Trust us, you'll love it," Suling said.

"Yeah, it's even better than sex," Annabella added.

The old Katharine wouldn't even have given it a thought. *Just say no* had always been her motto. But the new and improved Katharine, who had a courageous heart and an adventurous spirit and who wasn't afraid to try new things, felt like she had to take it just out of spite.

"What the hell," she said, quickly snatching the pill from the napkin and popping it into her mouth.

Both girls smiled as they watched her wash it down with her drink.

"That's the spirit," Suling said, patting her on the back.

Then the two got up from their chairs and headed for the dance floor.

"We'll be back to check up on you," Annabella shouted back at her.

Twenty minutes later, Katharine still sipped her margarita through a straw, her head hung low. This time she was feeling a little disappointed. Then all of a sudden a strange smile swept over her face. At that moment, she was facing the bar, but she immediately scooted her chair around so she could peer out into the dance floor. She spotted Annabella and Suling dancing with two other girls. They seemed so happy that she felt compelled to join them. She quickly jumped up and rushed out to the middle of the floor. They all smiled at her as if they'd been expecting her. At first she stood there with a goofy grin on her face, bobbing her head to the hypnotic disco beat. But then she surprised everyone by jumping in between the two couples, throwing her arms into the air and shaking her tush. The girls were so inspired by this that they each took turns getting behind her and rubbing up against her body. She felt so good that it didn't even bother her. After a whole hour of bumping and grinding, they practically had to drag her off the floor, worried that she might get overheated.

"I didn't know you were such a great dancer," Annabella said as they sat her back down at the table.

"I haven't danced in years." Katharine laughed.

She kept trying to get up and go back out there, but they sat her back down again.

"I'm going to get another drink," she said finally as she grabbed her purse, jumped up and rushed over to the bar.

One of the bartenders was a big man with a dark complexion, dark curly hair, broad shoulders, and a large belly. But what really caught her eye was the colorful Hawaiian shirt he wore.

"So what will it be?" he asked when he finally got around to her.

"Another margarita." She grinned. "No. Make it a whiskey this time."

"Jack Daniel's okay?" he asked.

"That'll do." She nodded.

He quickly prepared the drink for her and sat it down in front of her with a wink and a smile.

"Thank you. You're a real sweetheart," she said as she grabbed it and slapped a ten-dollar bill down on the bar. "Keep the change."

"Appreciate it," he replied, putting seven dollars and fifty cents into the cash register and the rest of it into his tip jar. Then he just looked at her.

"What?" She grinned.

"Are you X-ing?" he asked.

"No." She laughed.

"Don't worry, I'm not going to tell anyone," he said. "But you really shouldn't be doing that stuff, a pretty young thing like you."

"I'm not so young," she said.

He winked at her again, suggesting it had been just a joke. "I mean it," he said. "It's very bad for you. And so are those girls you're hangin' out with."

"Those are my new friends." She grinned.

"Well, they're a couple of freaks if you ask me," he said, full of contempt. "They come in here every night lookin' for some poor, innocent victim to sink their teeth into. All they want is sex."

"I like sex," she replied.

"Are you straight?" he asked.

"You mean am I heterosexual?" she said. "Yeah."

"Are you into the real kinky stuff? Human bondage, that sort of thing?" he then asked.

"No." She laughed.

"Then your idea of sex is a lot different than theirs, believe me," he said. "If they offer you any more pills, don't take them. And don't go to any after parties with them either. They're not to be trusted."

"I appreciate your concern," she replied. "But I can take care of myself."

"I'm just trying to be helpful," he said, appearing a little offended.

"I know. You're a knight in shining armor." She smiled and reached up to touch his cheek.

"I'm just a bartender." He blushed.

"And you're that, too," she said.

She walked back to the table with her drink and sat down. Suling smiled at her and slid her another wadded-up napkin. At that point Katharine was feeling too good to say no. She immediately opened it and grabbed the little pink pill that was inside of it.

"Bottoms up," she said as she popped it into her mouth and washed it down with a shot of whiskey.

After the club closed, they all hopped into the Dodge Neon and rushed off to the after party that was being held in someone's studio apartment.

"I wish I had known about this drug a long time ago," Katharine said as she sat in the back seat, still grinning from ear to ear. "I don't want this feeling to ever go away."

Suling turned around in the passenger's seat and smiled at her affectionately.

"Don't worry," Annabella said, sitting behind the steering wheel. "We go out just about every night. And Steve's got whatever we need—coke, smack, crystal meth ..."

"Wonderful." Katharine grinned, thinking that she had just entered into a whole new lifestyle.

As soon as they got to the party, the girls took her into the bathroom and gave her another pill. Plus they spread out several lines of coke on the vanity and had her snort a couple through a rolled-up dollar bill. Afterward they fixed her a drink inside the kitchen. Then they sat her down on the living room couch with a bunch of strangers and started mingling with the crowd. The place was filled with gay couples, Katharine observed, from one end of the enormous smoke-filled room to the other.

Just as her third pill started to kick in, a strange bearded man with a squeeze-bottle in his hand walked up to the couch and started pouring a clear liquid substance into everybody's drink. When he finally came up to Katharine, she instinctively jerked her Styrofoam cup away.

"It's just liquid X," said the young man sitting to her left. "It's even better than the pills."

"Well, in that case." She smiled and held out her cup.

All of a sudden the big bartender from The Diamond stepped through the front door, wearing a brown leather jacket over his Hawaiian shirt and blue jeans. She noticed many people turn their heads and give him strange looks as he walked into the room; they looked at him as if he was a gatecrasher. His eyes locked onto hers almost immediately, and he walked straight up to her.

"Hey, Joey, I always knew you was a big ol' queen," said a man seated on another man's lap at the end of the couch.

"Shut up, Russell," he replied.

"I remember you. You're the bartender." Katharine grinned. Her speech was slurred, and she could barely keep her eyes open.

He nodded and smiled.

"What's your name?" she asked.

"Joseph Milano," he answered. "But my friends call me Joey ... or Big Joe."

"Hey, Big Joe," she said. "I'm Katharine, but my friends call me Kat."

"Are you doin' all right, Katharine?" he asked. His voice was filled with concern.

"Never felt better." She laughed.

He nodded and said, "I guess I'll go into the kitchen, then, and pour myself a drink. See you later."

He slowly walked away. He returned about five minutes later and joined a group of people that she recognized from the club—all bartenders and cocktail waitresses. They stood close enough for her to overhear at least part of their conversation.

"Hey, Big Joe, break anyone's legs lately?" a young man said as he stepped into their little circle.

They all smiled.

"Just kidding," he said and put his arm over the big man's shoulder. "He's really a nice guy … as long as you don't owe his boss any money."

"Very funny," Joe sneered.

He kept glancing over at Katharine through the crowd, and on some of those occasions, their eyes met. Then her friends came back, pulled her off the couch, and quickly escorted her out of the room. They walked through a long crowded hallway and entered the last door on the right. They quickly shut the door behind them and stepped up to a king-sized bed. A young redheaded girl sat in the middle of it in a white negligee; she was snorting lines of cocaine off a silver plate. There were tarot cards on the nightstand and candles burning in every corner of the room. Katharine also happened to notice a whip and a black leather mask hanging on one of the walls. But she thought nothing of it in that moment.

"This is our other friend, Stephanie," Annabella explained to her. "She owns this place."

The girl crawled off the bed and walked straight up to Katharine with a sexy smile.

"Are you doing okay?" she asked.

Katharine nodded.

"If there's anything you need, anything at all, don't hesitate to ask," she said as she began to caress Katharine's cheek. "I hear you're fed up with men."

"Maybe a little." Katharine blushed.

"Has anyone ever told you that you have the most beautiful blue eyes?" she said.

"Not lately."

"Well, you do," she said and kissed Katharine on the lips while the other two unzipped her dress and pulled it down past her shoulders. Then they started kissing her on the back of her neck.

It all happened so fast and she was so out of it that she didn't even bother to put up a fight; she simply let them have their way with her, even though it felt very strange. Joe suddenly burst into the room just as they were kissing her all over and pushing her closer to the bed.

"What the hell!" he exclaimed.

"Get out, Joey!" the redhead shouted. "You know you're not supposed to be in here!"

"You girls should be ashamed of yourselves!" he shouted back at them as he rushed up to Katharine and pulled her away.

"Oh, give me a break. You think you're better than us?" the redhead scoffed. "At least we don't kill people for a living!"

"Yeah, you fuckin' goomba!" Suling shouted.

He just shook his head at them in disgust and zipped up Katharine's dress. Then he lifted her into his arms and carried her out of the room.

"Way to go, big man!" someone shouted as they headed for the front door.

Others clapped and cheered.

"A knight in shining armor … just like I said," Katharine whispered in his ear.

He drove her to his apartment, which was only a few blocks away, and sat her down in a chair.

"I've got a CD here that I think you'll like," he said as he walked over to the stereo, bent down, and turned it on. Then he swiftly walked out of the room.

His place wasn't much larger than hers, but it had nicer furniture. She sat on a gray leather recliner, and a matching loveseat stood next to it. The entertainment center on the wall directly across from her featured a big screen TV and the state-of-the-art hi-fi stereo system right below it. An old Frank Sinatra tune she found very soothing played on the CD player. Joe stepped back into the living room and handed her a glass of ice water. Then he sat down in the loveseat.

"You have excellent taste in music," she complimented him. "So you're a big Sinatra fan, huh?"

"He's the best," Joe said. "Tony Bennett's up there, of course … Dino and Sammy, maybe, but none of them hold a candle to Ol' Blue Eyes."

"I think you and my mom would really hit it off." She laughed. "She loves everyone you just mentioned. How old are you, anyway?"

"Forty-one," he answered.

"Just three years older than me," she said. "Do you go to gay parties very often?"

"No … I don't like to hang out with gay people," he replied bluntly. "They're okay, but I just can't stand that lifestyle. You know what I mean?"

"So what made you decide to go out there tonight?" she asked him with a playful grin. "You weren't following me, were you?"

"No," he answered a bit defensively. "I just had a feeling that you would end up there. You were really wasted at the bar. And like I said, those girls are not to be trusted."

"I was joking," she said. "I know you weren't following me."

"I just felt that I should do something," he continued to explain. "You seem like a very nice lady, and I didn't want them to have their way with you."

"Well, I hate to break it to you, but I'm not such a nice lady." She laughed. "And what makes you think that I wanted to be rescued in the first place?"

"I thought you said you were straight." He gasped.

"I am, but that doesn't mean that I'm opposed to trying new things," she said. "Who knows? I might have enjoyed it."

"Well, I'll just drive you back there then." He scowled.

"No, this is fine," she said. "The music's good, and you look like someone I can trust."

"Damn straight." He nodded. "I don't take advantage of women, especially when they're X-ing."

Suddenly "Strangers in the Night" began to play on the stereo, and it seemed to fit the occasion. Katharine got out of her seat and walked up to him.

"Dance with me, Joe," she said, extending her hand to him.

"Are you still high?" he asked, appearing hesitant.

"Yeah, a little bit," she replied. "It's just dancing. I'm not asking you to fuck me."

He slowly got up and put his arms around her waist. They moved to the center of the room and began to slow dance, almost in place.

"You're a hell of a dancer," she said.

"I've danced with a few women in my day," he replied. "How 'bout you? You dance?"

"Nope," she answered. "Me and my husband usually went bowling on the weekends."

"Oh, so you're married?"

"I left him. He was having an affair."

"Well then, the guy's an idiot if you ask me," he said. "Why would he want to be with someone else when he has you to come home to?"

"My sentiments exactly." She smiled and rested her head on his chest. "I like you. You remind me of the teddy bear I once had."

"I'm flattered." He sighed.

"You should be," she said. "I really loved that bear. It was always there for me, and it was a hell of a good listener. How did you get to be such a nice guy, anyway?"

"Well, I hate to break it to you, but ..." he replied.

She looked up at him and laughed.

"I heard the girls say something about killing people for a living," she said. "What was that all about?"

He suddenly stood still and bitterly shook his head. "Why do they do that?" he asked himself. "Just because you work for a high-profile gangster people automatically assume that you're a monster.

"What?" said Katharine with a puzzled look on her face.

"The truth is I'm not just a bartender," he explained to her. "I work for Louis Bartoli."

"You mean *the* Louis Bartoli ... of the Bartoli crime family?" She gasped.

"Yeah," he answered.

"What is it that you do for him, exactly?" she asked.

"You mean besides killing people?" he scoffed. "Whatever he needs. I collect money for him most of the time. But I'm also his bodyguard, his chauffeur, and right now I'm workin' at The Diamond while there's nuttin' else to do. He owns it. Actually, he owns a lot of things. But this new dance place of his, that's his pride and joy. He loves to watch people dance."

"Wow, I never met a real live gangster before," she said with a nervous laugh. "What's he like? They say that he's the most dangerous man on the planet."

"That's just business, Katharine," he replied. "Say what you will about him, but I happen to love the man. He's been like a father to me."

"Someday I'd like to sit down with him and just listen to him talk," she said as they started dancing in place again. "I bet you guys have the most amazing stories."

"Woman, I could tell you stories that'll make your head spin," he replied.

Once the song had ended, they sat down in the loveseat together, and he told her a yarn or two.

"I once knew this crime boss who shot his rival in the back of the head and cooked him in a pizza oven 'til his skin was a crispy golden brown," he began. "Then he carved him up like a turkey and served him to his subordinates ... just before he killed them all."

"Fuck," she replied.

"All the bosses are like that," he explained to her. "Real psychos. That's how they got to the top. A lot of them like to keep souvenirs from their killings—decapitated heads kept in pickle jars, tongues, fingers …"

Then he told her stories about his own boss as a young lad still making his way up the ladder, like the time when he made over twenty hits in one week.

"They called him the piano man," he said, "because he liked to sneak up behind his victims and strangle them with piano wire. He even killed his own stepbrother that way … over a girl, of all things." He laughed to himself and added, "He's mellowed out a lot since then."

She just shook her head and said, "Wow. Do you mind if I use this stuff for my next book?"

"What?" he exclaimed. "You're a writer?"

"Mmm hmm," she nodded.

"You didn't tell me that!"

"I thought I did."

"No, you didn't."

"Right now I'm finishing up a spy thriller," she explained. "But I always wanted to write a book about the Mafia."

"You can't write any of this stuff down. No way," he said vehemently.

"Why not?" she asked.

"Because if Louis ever reads it he'll kill us both," he said.

"You said he's been like a father to you." She laughed. "I doubt that he'd kill his own son. Oh, wait a minute. He *did* kill his stepbrother."

"It's no joke, Katharine," he said. "There are rules in this business. And the first one is you don't tell your dirty secrets to anyone outside of the family, especially the media. That's how a lot of us wind up dead."

"Don't worry, I'm not the media," she replied. "I'm just a novice storyteller who can't even find a publisher."

He looked at her disapprovingly.

"I promise I will never write anything down that you say to me," she said to him finally and in earnest. "You can trust me."

"Thanks. I appreciate that." He smiled.

She really started to come down at that point, and she became painfully aware of the time.

"Damn. It's seven o'clock already," she said, noticing the digital clock on the stereo. "I've got to be at work in three hours."

"Doesn't look like you're gonna make it," he replied, shaking his head. "Might as well call in sick."

"No way," Katharine said.

"Why not?"

"Because I can't afford to lose my job," she said. "So far I've never been late and haven't missed a day."

"Look at you," he argued. "You've been rollin' all night, and I doubt that you're gonna get any sleep. Is your boss already at work?"

"Yes. He gets there at six-thirty every morning," she answered.

He grabbed the cell phone on the coffee table and handed it to her.

"Call him," he insisted. "Tell him that you're not coming in today."

"I don't know," she muttered.

"Everyone gets sick, Katharine," he said. "Just tell him that you got the flu, one of those twenty-four-hour bugs."

"All right," she said, quickly flipping it open and punching in the phone number.

"Cardenelli's," her employer answered.

"Hey, Sal, it's Katharine," she said. "I'm sorry, but I don't think I can make it to work today. I have a cold." She threw in a fake cough for good measure.

"Please don't do this to me, Katharine. Not today," Sal said. "Annabella and Suling have already called in sick. And I'm short one bartender."

She froze. Joe raised his fist and encouraged her to hang tough.

"All right, I'll come in." She sighed.

"Thanks, Katharine. You're a lifesaver," her boss said and immediately hung up.

"That didn't go exactly as planned," Joe said as she handed the phone back to him.

"What am I suppose to do?" she said. "They need me."

"You're too good for 'em, Katharine." He smiled.

"Can you take me home so I can get ready?" she asked.

"Sure."

When she got back to her apartment, she took a cold shower, put on her uniform and makeup, and walked out again, heading straight for the subway. She made it to work on time, as always, and felt all right for the first hour or so as she helped her two bosses open up the joint. But as the day wore on, she started to feel very tired. To make matters worse, Sal had her working behind the bar for the first time. *Thank God most people don't drink this early,* she kept telling herself. Joe showed up at noon to lend her moral support.

"What's going on here?" he asked as he sat down on the bar stool directly in front of her. "I thought you said you were a waitress."

"Hello, Joe," she said, happy to see him. "We're short one bartender, so Sal hired another waitress this morning and put me here."

"Have you ever tended bar before?" he asked.

"No," she answered. "They gave me a crash course just twenty minutes ago. Plus they gave me this."

She handed him a list of drinks and their ingredients.

"Oh, here," he said as he started to read it and put something in her hand.

"Jesus." She frowned, looking down at a large brown capsule. "Not another pill."

"This one's good for you," he assured her. "It'll give you the strength you need to make it through the rest of the day. Then your pill-popping days will be over, I hope."

She looked at him skeptically.

"They're just energy pills," he said. "And they do the trick, believe me. I take a dozen of them whenever I work a double. But you're much smaller. I think one is all you need."

She put it in her mouth, took a sip of water, and went to check up on her customers while he continued to look at the list.

"I don't see how you can read this," he said when she returned. "It's in small print. And there must be over a hundred drinks on this thing."

"Yeah, well, let me see it," she replied, snatching it from him. "Ol' baldy over there wants a Rusty Nail."

"That's easy," he said. "Just put some ice in a glass, pour in an ounce of scotch and an ounce of Drambuie and stir. Best served with a straw."

She threw down the sheet of paper and did exactly as he said, flashing him a smile as she took the drink over to her customer.

"Thanks," she said after she returned from the cash register.

"No problem," he smiled.

Seconds later, a man sat down at the other end of the bar and shouted, "Black Russian, please!"

"A glass of ice, one point five ounces of vodka, and point seventy-five ounces of coffee liqueur. Stir it a bit and maybe add a swizzle stick," Joe whispered as she reached down to get another glass.

After the transaction was complete, she looked at him and said, "You can't leave 'til my shift's over."

"All right," he agreed.

"I'm joking." She laughed.

"I'm not," he said. "I've got nothin' better to do."

"Oh, shit. Here we go again," she sighed, noticing a young couple walking up to the bar.

She went to get their order and came right back.

"I've got this one," she said to him with a wink.

She leaned over, grabbed two bottles of Heineken from the ice bucket, and twisted off the caps.

"What are you doing Saturday night?" he asked her before she got away.

"Taking a much-needed rest," she answered.

"You can do that Friday night." He laughed. "Let me take you out. It'll be more fun than last night, I promise you."

She gave it a quick thought and said, "Sure. Why not?"

She rushed off again and returned a few minutes later.

"One Bloody Mary, a Cosmopolitan, and a B-52," she said to him as she started putting ice in the glasses. "So where are you taking me?"

"B-52 … that's one part Grand Marnier, one part Kahlua, and one part Bailey's Irish Cream," he responded and added, "You let me worry about that. It's a surprise."

"Please, Joe, nothing fancy," she begged him while mixing the first drink. "McDonald's is fine for a first date. Burger King's even better."

"Bloody Mary," he said. "That's one point twenty-five ounces of vodka, two point five ounces of tomato Juice, a dash of Worcestershire sauce, a dash of Tabasco, and a dash of salt and pepper. And cheeseburgers on a Saturday night? Forget it. I'm taking you out Sinatra-style."

She stopped for a second and studied him closely, feeling a little apprehensive. But she still trusted him.

On Friday morning, Katharine ran into Bree in the laundry room again. She stood directly opposite her, like before, and gave her a quick glance as she shoved her clothes into the washer.

"Don't you just hate doing laundry?" Katharine said to her finally.

Bree looked at her very sternly for a moment, and then she asked, "How's that book coming along?"

"All right, I guess," Katharine answered.

"I'd still like to read it sometime," Bree said.

"Why don't you come up and look at it now?" Katharine suggested. Then she realized that she didn't have it. "Oh wait a minute. I forgot." She blushed. "I gave it to my agent so her daughter could type it."

"How's that workin' out for ya?" Bree asked. "Has she found you a publisher yet?"

"No, not yet," Katharine said with a heavy sigh. "Actually, I'm beginning to wonder. I never hear from her. I'm paying her all this money to type my manuscript, and every time I go to see her, she's wearing fur coats and expensive jewelry. It seems like I'm doing more for her than she is for me."

"I'd be calling her every day if I was you," Bree said, "just to see if she's found out anything. The squeaky wheel gets the grease, as my grandma always said."

"Yeah, you're right," Katharine replied. She suddenly grew excited and added, "You can come over anyway, and I'll show you what I've written lately. Or I could just tell you the whole damn story. I mean, if you're interested and have nowhere else to be."

"Oh all right." Bree laughed. "But just for a minute or two."

They left their clothes in the wash and their empty baskets on the counter and went up to Katharine's apartment.

"That's a pretty couch," Bree said as soon as they walked through the door.

"Thanks," Katharine replied. "But it came with the apartment, like everything else."

"There's no furnished apartments in this building." Bree laughed. Then she gasped. "Wait a minute. Didn't they tell you?"

"Tell me what?"

"The old man who lived here before you died of a heart attack or something," Bree said. "We watched the paramedics come and take his body away."

"You mean this is all his furniture?" Katharine gasped.

Bree nodded.

"Wow, that explains a lot," she said. "Sometimes in the middle of the night when I'm trying to get to sleep, I hear that chair rocking back and forth." She pointed to the old wooden rocking chair next to the living room window. "And when I get up in the morning, it's always facing the window. It wasn't before I went to bed."

"You mean to tell me that …"

"Yeah," Katharine said, and they both looked at each other fearfully. Finally Katharine laughed and shook her head. "No, I don't believe in ghosts," she said. "But it would make a wonderful story … don't you think?"

Bree just gave her a dirty look.

"Well, I'll go make us some tea," Katharine said and rushed into the kitchen.

She returned a couple of minutes later with a glass of iced tea and a notebook and handed them to Bree as they sat down on the couch together. As Bree started to read, Katharine told her the whole story from the very beginning, when Kitty Everhart and Commander Stone were in Nazi Germany, spying on Hitler and his regime.

"It all sounds very interesting," Bree said after Katharine was finished. "I'd pay the ten bucks to see the movie. I'm afraid I ain't much of a reader, though." She put the notebook down on the couch.

"Neither am I," Katharine replied. "I'm too busy writing."

"I really admire what you're doing here," Bree said. "I don't do nothin' all day but sit around watchin' Jerry Springer and whatever else is on the tube. I'm gettin' pretty damn sick of it to tell you the truth."

"Are you married?" Katharine asked her curiously.

"You kiddin' me?" She laughed. "Leon ain't the marrying type. He don't want kids either."

"I have two," Katharine said.

"Excuse me?"

"I have two children—a boy and a girl."

"And you just upped and left them too, huh?" Bree replied, suddenly fixing her with a disapproving look.

Katharine froze.

"My mother left me and my two brothers when we were really young," Bree said. "We don't know where she went. About three months later, my father killed himself, and we were sent to Harlem to live with our grandma. They would've separated us for sure if it wasn't for her. After she died, we were forced to take care of ourselves—stealing food, suckin' dick. We did whatever it took to survive. Then one day, I was caught shoplifting and ended up in the juvie house 'til I was eighteen. I've been in and out of prison ever since. I just spent two years in Albion for possession of narcotics, as a matter of fact. Can't even begin to tell you what a nightmare that was." She laughed to herself and shook her head. "Don't know what happened to my brothers," she said. "Probably ended up dead somewhere."

Katharine remained frozen and was left utterly speechless. "I'm sorry. I didn't know," she somehow managed to blurt out.

"No, I'm sorry," Bree said. "I had no right to lay all that shit on you. It's my screwed-up life. I have to go now." She jumped up from the couch and showed herself to the door.

A few minutes later, Katharine dialed her agent's cell phone number.

"Yes?" Mrs. Levi answered.

"This is Katharine," she said. "I just wondered if there was any word on my novel."

"No, dear," the old woman replied. "I told you I'd call you if there was any news."

"I know," she said, becoming very apologetic all of a sudden. "I didn't mean to bother you. It's just that I haven't heard from you in a while, and I thought maybe you had given up on me."

"Why on earth would you think that?" Mrs. Levi asked, sounding a little offended. "I've been talking to publishers on your behalf all morning. I'm waiting to see one right now, as a matter of fact."

"Oh, I'm sorry," Katharine said, though she still didn't trust her. For all she knew, Mrs. Levi was sitting at home in her pajamas, watching QVC on her brand-new big screen TV.

"It's quite all right, dear," Mrs. Levi said and quickly hung up.

Katharine walked over to the window and flopped down in the chair. She had never felt more lost as she watched the cars zoom past and the people walking up and down the sidewalks, all of them heading *somewhere*. *What the hell am I doing here?* she thought and started to cry. *My life wasn't so bad. And then I had to go and screw it all up, you big baby.*

"I'm going to New York to become a writer," she said, mocking herself.

Chapter 7: Waltzing with Gangsters

On Saturday night, Joe showed up at Katharine's doorstep dressed in a dark blue suit and tie and carrying a dozen long-stemmed roses.

"Damn it, Joe, what's going on?" she said as she opened the door. She wore an orange blouse and blue jeans. "I thought this was supposed to be casual?"

"This *is* casual," he said, looking himself over. "At least it is for me. Frank wore suits all the time. All the rat packers did. You look great, by the way."

He handed her the roses.

"Thanks," she said, taking them inside.

Then she came back with her purse, stepped out, and locked the door behind her. Minutes later, they were sitting in the backseat of a stretch limousine. She glared at him as they headed toward Midtown.

"Where are you taking me?" she asked him.

"You'll see," he smiled.

Finally, they pulled into a parking lot, and she recognized the long rectangular building with the big neon sign on top. It didn't appear to be flashing at the moment.

"The Diamond … Are you shittin' me?" She laughed as he looked at her and smiled.

She noticed that the parking lot was empty except for the Cadillac parked in front of the building.

"It's Saturday night … How come nobody's here?" she asked him curiously.

"It's all ours until midnight," he said.

"You shut the whole place down just for me?" she asked.

"Compliments of Louie Bartoli," he said.

The real surprise was waiting for her inside the building. They walked in, and the man himself stepped up to greet them. She instantly recognized his face from television and the newspapers, but he didn't look quite as scary in person. He was just a frail old man; he had a face like a prune, a shiny bald head, and a thick gray mustache. He was dressed very sharply in a gray pin-striped suit and walked with a wooden cane in one hand. His other hand held on to a big busty blonde who appeared to be in her forties. Even though Mr. Bartoli was of average height, the blonde stood almost a foot taller and was wearing a pretty lavender dress.

"So this is her?" he said to Joe in a crusty old voice while looking Katharine in the eye. "She's even more beautiful than I imagined."

"You're just being kind." She blushed.

"No, I'm not," he assured her. "And what do you think of my boy here? Isn't he handsome?"

"Boss, please." Joe blushed.

"Yes, very," Katharine answered him.

"I keep telling him that he needs to lose some weight," said the old man, poking Joe in the belly with his cane. "But other than that, you won't find a better catch anywhere."

"Jesus, Louis!" Joe exclaimed.

"Okay, okay, I'll stop." The old man laughed. "C'mon in, you two lovebirds. Time to feast."

He and the woman turned, holding hands, and led them to their table. The place seemed a little odd with the lights on and without any customers. It looked like a large empty warehouse with a dance floor in the middle of it. All the tables had been stripped away except for one. A large muscular man stood behind the bar in a white long-sleeved shirt, serving as both bartender and bodyguard, Katharine suspected.

"Before we sit down, I want to introduce you to the love of my life, the apple of my eye, Miss Janice Papp," the old man said as they got to the table.

"Nice to meet you." Katharine smiled.

"Likewise," the woman said in a thick Hungarian accent.

They all sat down at a table, which was covered with a white tablecloth. Candles burned at either end of the table, and four empty wineglasses sat at each place setting. Louis and Miss Janice sat facing the dance floor while Katharine and Joe sat down opposite them. Then a young Italian waiter suddenly appeared. He handed them menus and opened a fresh bottle of red wine.

"I'll give you a shout when we're ready, Federico," Louis said to the waiter after he finished pouring.

The young man nodded and quickly walked away.

"My own personal chef is workin' the kitchen tonight, so everything should be great," the old man said as they buried their heads in their menus. "But I have to recommend the veal parmesan. It is simply outstanding."

"I'll have that," Katharine replied and put down her menu.

"Me too," said Joe.

"Just a salad for me," said the busty blonde.

"All right, Federico. We're ready!" the old man shouted, and the young man rushed back out to take their orders.

While they waited for their food, Louis talked about how he met "Miss Janice" on the Las Vegas Strip.

"She was servin' cocktails at the time," he said. "And when I saw her in that cute little waitress outfit, I decided right then and there that she was the one. So I cashed in my chips, brought her back here, and asked her to marry me. Maybe one of these days she'll say yes."

They all laughed.

"Hell, I'll ask her again," he said, encouraged by their laughter. He turned his chair toward her, put his hand on hers, and said, "Miss Janice …"

"Stop it." She laughed and bopped his hand away. "You're not even doing it right. You're supposed to get down on one knee. And where's the ring?"

"Will you marry me?" he asked, undaunted.

"I'll think about it," she said, followed by more laughter.

The waiter brought out their meals about five minutes later and refilled their wineglasses. As they started eating, Louis turned toward the DJ's booth up in the balcony and shouted, "Kenny, can we get some music down here?"

"Sure thing, Boss," a deep voice said through the loudspeaker. Music began to play—Perry Como singing "It's Impossible," to be exact.

"Thanks, Kenny!" the old man shouted. "I hope you guys don't mind. I like to listen to music when I'm eating."

"Not at all," said Katharine. "I sure don't remember him playing this one the other night."

After they wolfed down their food, he sat back in his chair and pulled two Cuban cigars out of his jacket. He handed one of them to Joe across the table. Katharine watched as they unwrapped them, stuck them in their mouths, and leaned into the candles to light them. Then she asked, "You got one more of those?"

They both looked at her and laughed.

"What's so funny?" she asked, pretending to be offended.

"You're serious?" Louis said.

She nodded.

"Sure, why not?" he said, reaching into his lapel and pulling out another cigar.

He slowly unwrapped it and handed it to her. He grabbed the long candle, reached across the table, and lit it for her as she held it in her lips. She immediately started coughing, and everyone laughed at her again.

"What are you doing, Katharine?" Joe playfully scolded her. "These things are thirty dollars apiece."

"No, no, leave her alone," the old man said. "She'll get the hang of it."

Before long she was puffing and chomping on it like she was George Burns. Louie taught her how to blow smoke rings through it, and he appeared to grow more and more fond of her by the second.

"Where are you from, Katharine?" he finally got around to asking her.

"Oklahoma," she answered.

"Indian territory." He nodded. "They still run around half naked, ridin' bareback and collecting scalps?"

"No, not that I know of," she said.

"So have you lived in New York for very long?" asked the old man.

"Three or four weeks," she answered.

"Hmm," he nodded.

They continued to make small talk while Rosemary Clooney sang "Mambo Italiano." Then Sinatra's "I've Got You Under My Skin" suddenly filled the room, and both men were ecstatic.

"I saw him in Atlantic City just before he died," Louis said. "And his voice sounded better than ever ... like he was still at Capitol Records."

"He was something else," Joe agreed.

"Well, are you just going to sit there?" Louis said to him. "Or are you going to ask the girl to dance?"

Joe quickly turned to Katharine and asked, "What do you think, Katharine? Would you care to dance?"

"Not now, Joey." She sighed and shook her head. "We just ate."

"C'mon, Katharine," Louis begged her with his charming smile and penetrating stare. "Make an old man happy, will ya?"

"Oh all right," she said, putting her cigar out in the ashtray that Federico had provided for them. "If it pleases you, my liege."

"It pleases me." He smiled.

She and her date stood up, walked out to the middle of the floor, and started dancing very slowly.

"Do you realize I'm the only one here that looks like crap?" she scolded him in a low voice.

"You look fine," he assured her.

"I can't believe we're on a double date with Louis Bartoli and his moll ... or mistress ... or whatever," she said.

"His girlfriend," Joe corrected her. "There ain't no wife waitin' at home. In fact, he hasn't been married for years."

"Yeah well, next time warn me before you do something like this," she said. "I don't like surprises."

"I thought you said you wanted to meet him," he replied.

"I believe what I said was I'd like to sit down with him someday and listen to his stories," she informed him. "You know, for my next book."

"That's not going to happen," he said.

"Yeah, I realize that now." Katharine sighed.

"Then again, you might end up hearin' a tale or two before the night's over," he said nervously, glancing over at the table. "Look how he's going through that wine. Just do me a favor and don't tell him you're a writer."

"Sure, Joey," she replied, rolling her eyes at him. She glanced over at the table for a split second. "He's lookin' right at us," she whispered.

"Like I said, he likes to watch people dance," Joe said.

"Well, the man really loves you, that's for sure," she remarked. She looked up at him curiously and added, "How come *you* never asked me where I was from?"

"I just assumed you were from here," he replied.

"What about the accent?" she said.

"What accent?"

She just shook her head at him.

"Look, Katharine," he said. "I don't care where you've been or who you was with. All I care about is the here and now. We're like a couple of newborn pups just startin' out in the world."

"Are you serious?" She laughed. "You actually see us as puppies?"

"Yeah, why not?" he said.

Louis and Miss Janice applauded them before the song was even over. Then he slowly got up from his chair, grabbed his cane that was leaning against the table, and headed straight for the dance floor.

"Mind if I cut in?" he said as he stood before them.

"Not at all," Joe replied and walked back to the table.

"What about your a—" Katharine said, looking down at his cane.

"What, this?" He laughed and immediately tossed it away. "It's just for show."

He walked up very close to her, put his arms around her, and led her across the floor like Fred Astaire. He moved very gracefully and looked directly into her eyes the whole time. He suddenly seemed at least twenty years younger. She was quite impressed, to say the least. Yet she couldn't help but think that he was trying to seduce her with his eyes and his magical feet, and right there in front of the young man who was supposedly so dear to him. *What nerve,* she thought, looking at him as if he was a dirty old man. But then he surprised her by asking, "So tell me, Katharine, what are you runnin' from?"

"What?" she replied.

"You came all the way here from Oklahoma," he said. "You've got to be running from something."

"You're right," she quickly blurted out. "It's those damn Indians."

He continued to smile at her. But she could see he wasn't amused.

"What am I running from?" she said, approaching the question a little more seriously. "A life full of unhappiness and regret, I suppose."

He nodded as if he knew exactly what she was talking about and said, "Sorry, didn't mean to sound like an ass. It's just that my boy over there has been hurt by women more times than I care to mention. They seem okay at first. But they're always hiding something. And it turns out that they're just using him for his money, to make someone jealous, whatever."

Now Katharine realized that the only reason he had gotten her out there all alone and set up the whole date in the first place was to see if she was good enough for Joey. *How sweet*, she thought.

"He might be tough on the outside," the old man continued, "but he has a kind and gentle soul. And he's also a bit of a romantic like me. He doesn't deserve all the crap that these skanks put him through. I think if someone else was to come along and tear another piece of his heart out, I'd just have to deal with her myself."

Though he said it with that same charming smile, the words sent a chill down her spine. She could easily imagine him sneaking up behind her one night with a piece of piano wire stretched out between his hands.

"I assure you, Mr. Bartoli, I'm not like those other … skanks," she swiftly replied. "Joey seems like a great guy, and I honestly enjoy being with him."

"Please, call me Louis." He smiled.

"I guess the only thing I'm using him for is warmth and companionship," she added. "It's been a long time since a man's shown interest in me."

"Now I know you're lying." Louis laughed.

After the song ended, they walked back to the table, and Louis put his hand on Joe's shoulder.

"Treat her good," the old man said to him. "This one's a keeper." Then he walked over to Miss Janice, bopped her on the head, and said, "Come on, let's go. These two want to be alone."

She immediately got up and grabbed her purse while he fetched his cane. They walked out the door together.

"I'm sorry I did this to you," Joe apologized to Katharine after they were gone. "It's just that he insisted on seeing you for some reason, and it's hard to say no to the guy."

"Yeah, I see what you mean," she said, patting him on the back before she sat down.

They talked for a while and then got up and left so the manager could open up the place. As the limousine pulled up in front of Katharine's apartment building, she asked him if he wanted to come up.

"Sure, I'll come up for a bit," Joe said.

They hopped out of the limo and headed up the sidewalk together. Before they reached the front entrance, her husband Frank suddenly popped up out of nowhere and nearly frightened her to death.

"Jesus, Frank!" she exclaimed. "What's gotten into you? Are you stalking me now?"

"Yeah, I guess I am," he said, laughing crazily. "You won't let me come up, so I usually stay out here underneath your window. Tomorrow I might even pick up a guitar and serenade you like I did back in college ... remember? I'll do whatever it takes. I'm your fool." He then looked up at Joe, standing beside her. "Who's this joker, by the way?" he asked.

"This is Joey, my date." She sighed. "Joe, this is Frank."

"Her husband!" Frank quickly butted in and got right up in the big man's face, refusing to shake his hand. "I reckon she told you that she was married."

"Yes, she did." Joe smiled.

"Well then, mister ... you've got a lot of nerve dating another man's wife," he said angrily, raising his fist. "What if I was to knock the shit out of you?"

"Stop it, Frank!" Katharine exclaimed. "When are you gonna get it through your head that I'm not going back with you? It's over! I've got to move forward, not backward!"

"When did you stop loving me, Katharine?" he asked, suddenly looking very sad. "I know it was long before I cheated on you. You just used that as an excuse to finally walk out on me."

"That's not true," she muttered.

"You're really something," he said, shaking his head. "Cleaning up after us for all those years, pretending that you cared. And all the while you were just waiting for me to fuck up. God knows it would happen sooner or later."

"I stayed because I loved you guys," she said. "And I still do. But I'm here now ... and I've made up my mind. I'm not going back. Maybe it's wrong, but I've got to think of myself for once."

"Then I want a divorce," he said as a last resort.

"Of course," she replied. "Just send me the papers, and I'll sign them."

"Nice to meet you," Joe said as she grabbed his hand. They started to walk away.

"You're making a terrible mistake, Katharine!" Frank shouted at her before they reached the front steps of her building. "Soon you're gonna want me back, and it'll be too late!"

"Bye, Frank!" she shouted back at him. "Have a good night!"

Frank showed up bright and early the next morning and banged on Katharine's door until she finally answered with the chain still attached.

"Katharine, can I please come in?" he said frantically.

"Frank, I don't want to argue about it no more," she sighed.

"No, no … it's not about that," he said. "I was mugged."

"You were?" She gasped and undid the chain lock to get a good look at him. His suit was torn, and he had scratches all over his left cheek. "When?"

"Last night after I left your apartment," he said with a nervous laugh. "Can you believe it?"

She quickly let him in, led him into the dining room, and sat him down at the table.

"Who was it?" she asked as she sat down next to him.

"Just a couple of kids … teenagers, even," he answered. "One of them held a knife to my throat while the other one took my wallet. They stole everything—my driver's license, credit cards, and five hundred dollars in cash."

"Wow," Katharine said. "Did you go to the police?"

"I've been there since seven o'clock this morning," he replied. "If you want to report a crime around here, you've got to wait in line. When I finally got out of there, I was starving. But the fleabag hotel that I'm staying at doesn't even serve donuts, and I had no money for the vending machine. I ended up walking into a soup kitchen a couple of blocks from there."

"What?" she said.

"Yeah, a soup kitchen!" he exclaimed. "I can't believe it either." He put his hands over his face and shook his head. "That turned out to be a real nightmare as well," he said. "Two homeless men standing in the line in front me started fighting over a piece of bread. One of them tried to bite the other one's ear off. Then he took him to the ground and pulled his eyeball right out of the socket."

"No." She gasped.

"Yes. It was terrible," he said. "They had to shut the place down."

"You poor guy," she replied and put her hand on his shoulder. "Why didn't you stay at a nicer place like the Holiday Inn or something? You can afford it."

"Because I'm cheap, remember?" he said. "And it was the only place that I could find close to you." He grabbed her hand. Looking deeply concerned, he added, "You really shouldn't stay here. I mean, it's a nice place to visit and all, but I can't see why anybody in their right mind would ever want to live here. These people are nuts."

"I happen to like it here," she said and quickly pulled her hand away.

"You've been lucky so far, but they're gonna get you sooner—"

"Frank!"

"All right," he said, immediately backing off. "The reason I'm here is I was wondering if I could borrow a couple of bucks. I haven't eaten anything since yesterday afternoon."

"Yeah, sure," she replied, quickly getting up and walking out of the kitchen.

She came right back and handed him a twenty dollar bill.

"Here," she said. "Get yourself a decent meal."

"I'm going to call my mom and have her wire me some money," he explained to her. "Then I can pay you back."

"Forget it," she said. "After all the food you bought me over the years, what's twenty bucks?"

"Thanks, Kat. You're a lifesaver." He smiled as he got up from the chair and stuffed the money into his pocket.

"So, do you plan on sticking around for a while?" she asked him as she followed him out of the kitchen.

"Hell no. I've had enough of this town," he said. "I'm takin' the first plane out as soon as I get my money. I've really got to hand it to you, though. I thought you wouldn't last a minute here. And now look at you. Supporting yourself, making new friends. You're a tough old gal."

"Thanks." Katharine laughed.

He stopped and turned around at the front door, looking at her very curiously.

"Norma says that you've written two stories already," he said. "And that you were writing long before you even came here. Why didn't you share that with me and the kids?"

"I don't know." She sighed. "I probably should have."

"I would've loved to see your writing," he said with a warm smile.

"Well, I guess we both had our little secrets," she said, suddenly turning on him.

"Okay," he said, losing the smile. He immediately turned around and let himself out.

Her next day off was on a Monday, and she spent the whole morning trying to put a scene together in her head. Around 11 AM, there was a sudden knock on her door. She slowly got up to answer it, worried that Frank was still around. But it was Bree standing in her doorway, which caught her by complete surprise considering that her last visit had ended very awkwardly.

"Hey. Are you busy?" Bree asked.

"No," Katharine said. She stepped back to let her in.

"Well, *your* air conditioner seems to be workin' fine!" Bree exclaimed as she walked in and flopped down on the living room couch.

"Mmm hmm," Katharine said, sitting down at the other end of it. "I'm actually starting to feel a little chilly."

"It's hot as hell in my place," Bree complained. "What is it … June already?"

"Yep. Summer has officially begun," Katharine declared.

"Mr. Brown keeps tellin' me that he's gonna get the air conditioning fixed, but I don't see it happening in this century,"

Bree said. "So I'm up there sweatin' my ass off. Plus I'm bored as hell. Have you ever been so bored out of your mind that you just wanted to kill yourself?"

"No. Can't say that I have," Katharine said. "I guess that's why I write. But I can see how a person could go mad when there's nothing to fill the time."

"Well, I ain't no writer, that's for sure." Bree laughed.

"Maybe your talents lie elsewhere," Katharine said. "Have you ever considered photography?"

"Girl, even if I *could* afford a camera, I wouldn't have any ambition to use it," Bree replied. "I'm not like you. The way I see it, only some people were meant for greatness. The rest of us were put on this earth to help them get there." She looked at Katharine very sternly. "You believe that, don't you?" she asked. "That we all have a purpose?"

"I guess," Katharine replied.

"Well, that's what my grandma always said," Bree said. "And now I know that she was right. We crossed paths for a reason—you and me."

Katharine just looked at her, wondering what she was driving at.

"I want to help you finish your book," Bree said, "so you can hurry up and get published and go back to those two children who really need you right now."

You mean those two monsters who hate my guts? Katharine thought.

"I know it's none of my business," Bree continued, "but I also think you should give that husband of yours a second chance. Most men are dogs, but I'm sure there's one or two good ones out there who just make a mistake now and then."

"I just don't know what I'd have you do," Katharine said, getting back to the original subject. "I mean, this isn't what you'd call a collaborative effort. Writing is something you usually do on your own."

"I'm not askin' to be a co-writer." She laughed. "You said your agent might be taking advantage of you. Let me type everything you write from now on. I'll do it for less. Let's say a dollar a page?"

"That's more than reasonable and also very tempting," Katharine replied. "But I don't even have a typewriter."

"I can fix that," Bree said. "Do you have some money on you?"

"Yeah," Katharine replied, a bit hesitantly.

"Go get it and come with me." Bree got up and headed for the door.

"All right," Katharine said, growing excited and a little curious.

As they stepped out of the building, Bree grabbed her by the hand and led her to the little pawnshop directly across the street. They quickly walked inside, and Bree pointed to a rusty old typewriter sitting alone on a table in the middle of the room.

"There it is," she said, flashing a big smile, which was very rare.

"That?" Katharine laughed, looking a little flustered from all the excitement. "That's what you brought me here for?"

They stepped up to get a closer look.

"And it's only twenty bucks," Bree said, pointing at the price tag.

"Wow, what a bargain," Katharine said sarcastically. "But I just remembered it has to be a computer."

"They've got plenty of those, too," Bree replied, turning toward the shelf full of computers along the back wall.

Most of them were dinosaurs from the early to midnineties, Katharine observed as they walked to the back of the room and began looking.

"Have you ever used one of these before?" Katharine asked Bree.

"No. Have you?" Bree replied.

"Once or twice … at the local library," Katharine said. "You *do* know how to type though, don't you?"

"Nope."

"What?" Katharine gasped.

"Seriously, how hard can it be?" Bree said. "You just push a little button and out pops the letter on the computer screen."

"Yeah, I guess you're right." Katharine sighed.

"So, what do you say? Can we do this?" Bree asked. "I've got nothin' better to do with my time. Like I said, I just sit around all day watchin' Jerry Springer."

Katharine remained skeptical.

"Use me, Katharine," Bree begged her. "And that way we'd be helping each other."

"All right," Katharine said. They turned to each other, smiled, and shook hands.

Katharine ended up spending a hundred dollars on a twelve-year-old desktop computer with a fifteen-inch monitor, a keyboard, a mouse, and a printer. After they carried the entire system back to her apartment in two large boxes, they set it up on the dinner table and stared at the computer screen like a pair of cavemen seeing fire for the first time.

"How do you turn it on?" Bree asked.

"I think you push this thing here," Katharine said and pushed a little button on the computer tower, which stood over a foot tall.

Suddenly the tower lit up and made a terrible hissing noise and so did the monitor. Katharine used the mouse to open the word processing application. Then she stepped back and looked at Bree.

"It's all yours," she said.

"Very well." Bree nodded. She slowly walked up to the keyboard, placed her forefinger over one of the keys, and gently poked it. A lowercase *h* instantly appeared on the screen. "Perfect," Bree said. They looked at each other and smiled.

Then using the one-finger method, she hit another key and another until the screen read, *hi, i'm brew.*

"Looks like I fucked up on that last letter," she said. They both looked on in disappointment.

"Here, let me see," Katharine said, stepping up to the table again and deleting it with the backspace key.

"There ain't nothin' to this at all," Bree remarked after Katharine corrected the mistake. "Let's see your notebook. I think I'm ready."

"Now?" Katharine replied.

"Yeah. Why not?" Bree said. "Unless there's someplace you gotta be."

"No." Katharine sighed. She stepped out of the dining room for a second and came back with the notebook. She tore out the used pages and handed them to Bree. "Sorry about the messy handwriting," she said.

"It's not that bad," Bree replied, appearing extremely confident as she looked at the first page. "I can work with this."

Katharine taught her to capitalize letters using the shift key. Then she took the notebook into the living room and wrote while Bree began pecking away at the keys, one finger at a time. Around 3:00 PM, they heard Leon shouting Bree's name over and over again out on the stairwell.

"Goddamn it. He's off already?" Bree muttered to herself as she got up from the table and headed for the door.

"What does he do, anyway?" Katharine asked her curiously.

"Oh, he's a pimp," she answered nonchalantly and quickly walked outside, leaving the door open behind her.

Katharine got up from the couch and ran after her. She stopped short and stood just outside her door. Bree stood at the edge of the stairwell, looking up.

"Shut up, Leon! The whole building can hear you!" she shouted back at him.

"I'm not even gonna ask you what the hell you're doing down there!" he exclaimed. "Get your butt up here and fix me something to eat!"

"Fix it yourself!" she shouted. "I'm busy!"

Then she quickly turned around and walked back to Katharine's room.

"Goddamn it, woman!" Leon exclaimed even more furiously. "Don't you walk away from me!" Then he started to whine. "Please, baby doll. You know I can't cook worth a damn. Come and fix me somethin', will ya? I'm hungry."

Katharine could see Bree's resolve weakening before she even made it back to the door. She slowed down a little. Her hard expression suddenly turned soft.

"I guess I better go feed him before he starves to death," Bree said. "What time should I come over tomorrow?"

"I'll be working all day," Katharine said. "Thursday's my next day off."

"I'll see you Thursday then." Bree nodded and walked off again.

Chapter 8: The Beginning of a Beautiful Friendship

Though Katharine was still a little uneasy about the whole arrangement, Bree showed up at Katharine's apartment twice a week on Katharine's days off. Sometimes it seemed like she just wanted to talk, and it was always about the most crude and embarrassing subject matter. She spoke of things such as the homeless person she saw defecating in the park or how the subways always smell like urine, all of it stemming from her deepest fear that the homeless and their unpleasant smells were taking over the city.

"New York is nothing but a giant cesspool," Bree often remarked. "And there's so many damn people that the shit just keeps piling up."

She even made fun of Katharine, who looked at Manhattan like it was the most exciting place on earth, filled with romance and beauty.

"It's a dump, I tell ya," Bree said to her one time. "Maybe if you had gotten here a few years earlier, while it still had some of its charm, but I'm afraid it's on its last leg. And all the Manhattanites have moved out and gone to Brooklyn. I don't see why anyone would want to come here now. All I want to do is get the hell out."

Katharine just laughed and replied, "I guess that's the difference between you and me. You're Ratso Rizzo, and I'm Joe Buck."

"Only you're not a male hooker." Bree smiled. "And I'm not some crippled-up white guy dying of tuberculosis ... or whatever was ailing him."

What Katharine hated more than anything was when Bree interrupted her to criticize her work.

"Tigers?" Bree exclaimed when she finally got to the part of the story where Miles was attacked.

"What?" Katharine said, immediately putting down her pen and rushing over to the computer.

"How can you have tigers on a deserted island?" Bree complained.

"Why not?" Katharine said defensively.

"Because white tigers are mostly found in Asia or India, not on some island in the South Pacific," said Bree. "I might just have a fourth-grade education, but I know that much for sure."

"Bree, in this business," Katharine began as if she was already a bestselling novelist, "it's important to keep the readers on the edge of their seats. And facts are often distorted for dramatic effect. I felt like the story needed a tiger, so I gave it one."

Bree appeared unconvinced.

"Don't worry," Katharine said. "It'll all work out in the end."

"And what about the black guy?" Bree inquired.

"Huh?"

"The black guy, Jonesy," she said. "He comes back and kicks everybody's ass, doesn't he?"

Katharine just smiled at her and went back to her writing.

Morning of April 11

Kitty woke up and heard Dr. Faraday moaning as he sat by the campfire. She walked up to him and noticed he looked extremely pale and had a red rash on his cheeks and forehead.

"What's wrong, Doctor?" She gasped.

"I don't know." His voice was husky and he was breathing very heavily. "It must be from the berries that I picked yesterday. I thought they were harmless blackberries. But now I'm thinking that it was a perennial herbaceous plant, commonly known as Atropa belladonna or deadly nightshade."

"Is that bad?" she asked.

"It's extremely poisonous," he explained to her. "If I don't get to a hospital within the next twenty-four hours, I could be in serious trouble."

"I'm not going to let you die on me, Doctor," she said resolutely and shook her head. "Not you."

"I don't want me to die either." He laughed, which immediately turned into a cough. "But in this case, I'm afraid I don't have a choice."

"Balderdash," she scolded him. "Get up and get your things ready. We're leaving."

She then walked over to the other two castaways, who stood next to a tree, sharpening their spears with sandstones.

"Did either of you eat the blackberries yesterday?" she asked them.

"I did," Omar said.

"Me too," Jenkins said.

"Yeah, and so did I," she confessed and let out a big, heavy sigh. "You two get ready. We're about to head out."

Just as they left the camp, the good doctor started to stagger and lose his balance until he finally fell to the ground. Kitty came to his rescue. She slowly lifted him up, put his arm over her shoulder, and carried him. After the first mile or so, he began to groan painfully and begged her to stop.

"No way," she said, fiercely determined.

Then as they climbed up a steep hill, he shouted, "Goddamn it, Kit … I'm not gonna make it! Please, I'm beggin' you … just let me die."

"No!" she exclaimed angrily and carried him another mile.

Finally Omar and Jenkins turned around and forced her to stop.

"You can't keep this up," Jenkins snapped. "Just look at him. He's dead weight."

She slowly turned to look at the doctor's face and saw he was unconscious and barely breathing.

"Please, miss, put him down," Omar implored her.

She nodded reluctantly and dragged him over to the nearest tree. She had Omar and Jenkins grab a hold of him as she sat down with her back against the tree. They placed him in her lap. He regained consciousness for about thirty seconds while resting in her arms and said to her in a low voice, "Thanks for trying." He died soon after. They buried him in the shade, using their spears to dig the hole. Kitty said a few words over his grave, but her words were actually directed toward God.

"I never asked for your help," she said angrily. "I don't need it. But why must you keep standing in our way? First you take Commander Stone from me … then Miles … and now this dear, sweet man. He didn't deserve to go like this." She glanced at Omar, who stood next to her. She noticed his left cheek starting to break out in a rash. Plus he looked a little pale. "Who else has to die?" she exclaimed as she suddenly gazed up at the clouds. "Just leave us alone, will you? I could get us out of here if you'd just let us be!"

The three of them headed out again with Kitty leading the way, carrying her spear while Jenkins had his spear and the rifle as well. All of a sudden they noticed a big Black-footed Albatross land about twenty feet away from them, which suggested they were close to the shoreline.

"Wait. Don't move," Jenkins whispered loudly as he came to a sudden stop. The other two did the same. He slowly removed the rifle from the back of his shoulder and took aim.

"What do you think you're doing, Jenkins?" Kitty exclaimed.

"If you'll be quiet for a moment, I might be shootin' at some food," he said to her in a low voice. As he spoke, his gaze remained fixed on his prey.

He fired and missed the large bird by a couple of feet. It immediately flew away and so did all the other birds in the surrounding trees. A second later, the earth began to shake and a herd of roaring beasts came stomping through the trees, heading directly for them. They immediately turned and ran. They found a huge rock to jump behind just as twenty elephants stormed right past them.

"Elephants?" Bree shouted as she began typing it a week later. "Now you're giving us elephants?"

"Don't worry. It'll all work out in the end!" Katharine shouted back at her from the living room couch.

At the end of the second week, Katharine handed Bree thirty dollars just as she was leaving. Katharine felt she had earned it even though she had typed less than twenty pages thus far.

"But the deal was a dollar a page," Bree reminded her.

"Please take it," Katharine insisted. "You deserve it."

"All right, thanks," Bree said, stuffing it in her jeans pocket. "But just so you know … I'm not doin' this for the money."

"I know." Katharine nodded.

Bree turned and walked out of the apartment. Katharine didn't see her again for over a week. Afraid that something might have happened to her, Katharine walked up to her room one morning and knocked on the door over a dozen times before Bree finally answered. She looked tired and strung out, as if she hadn't slept in days. She wore smelly old clothes and had what looked like vomit stains on her blouse.

"What do you want, Katharine?" Bree asked very sternly.

"I-I-I just wanted to see if you were okay," Katharine stuttered, feeling like she wasn't welcome all of a sudden.

"I'm fine," Bree said and started to shut the door.

Katharine immediately stuck her foot in front of it.

"Are you sure?" she asked, concerned. "You don't look so good. Mind if I come in for a minute?"

"To tell you the truth, I've been feelin' a little sick lately," Bree said. "I don't want you to catch whatever the hell it is."

"Don't worry, I won't," Katharine assured her. "Please let me come in."

"Okay," Bree said with a sudden devil-may-care look about her. She stepped back to let Katharine in.

The apartment looked similar to Katharine's, except for the furniture. Katharine also noticed the bedroom door was closed. And right there on the living room coffee table for all of the world to see was a crack pipe. Or at least it looked like a crack pipe. Katharine had seen one only a couple of times on TV in her favorite police drama, *Chicago Beat*, and in the television documentary *LA Gangbangers*. Sitting next to it was a cigarette lighter and three empty one-inch bags with a white residue left in each of them. Katharine naturally assumed they were coke bags.

"So what happened to you last week?" she asked, determined to get to the truth.

"Well, it's like I said," Bree began, seeming only too happy to oblige, "I was feeling a little under the weather and needed to be alone for a while."

"I see." Katharine nodded. Then she pointed at the items on the coffee table. "And what's this?" she asked.

"That's a crack pipe, a cigarette lighter, and three empty coke bags," Bree replied bluntly. "And I'm a crackhead. Plus I like to dabble in crystal meth and heroin now and then. Frankly, I don't care what it is—as long as it gets me high."

"I don't believe it," Katharine muttered, feeling betrayed. "And all this time you've been looking down on me and makin' me feel like a piece of shit for abandoning my children."

"Have I?" Bree said. "I didn't mean to. Obviously I'm in no position to judge anybody."

"You can beat this thing, you know," Katharine said. "Have you ever tried to get help?"

"What makes you think I want anybody's help?" Bree snapped.

"You've got a drug problem, Bree!" Katharine exclaimed.

"Now you see, that's the difference between you and me," Bree said. "You see it as a drug problem. To me, it's just a way of coping with an impossible situation."

"Oh, Bree," Katharine muttered, shaking her head in disappointment. "This is all my fault, isn't it? If I hadn't given you that money …"

"Don't blame yourself." Bree laughed. "You had no way of knowing that I would spend it all on dope. Besides, thirty bucks don't buy you much rock these days. It was enough to get me started. Then Leon paid for the rest."

Katharine shook her head again.

"Stop looking at me like that, will ya?" Bree snapped. "Now that you know the truth, why don't you just go away and let me be?"

"I'm not going anywhere," Katharine said resolutely. "I'm going to stay here and help you get through this."

"Through what?" Bree scoffed. "I've been smokin' crack since I was a kid. Who are you to come in here and tell me it's wrong? You just got off the bus five minutes ago."

"What about your grandma, a higher calling, and all of that?" Katharine argued. "Do you think this is why God put you here—to get high all the time and shut everyone out?"

"I don't know what the hell I'm doing here," Bree said, looking extremely frustrated. "All I know is that I was feeling pretty damn good 'til you showed up. Why are *you* acting so high and mighty all of a sudden? You're the one who took six hits of X—all in one night. Or so you say."

"It was probably the stupidest thing I've ever done." Katharine nodded. "If I could take it back, I would. But it was just that one night. And I haven't touched the stuff since."

"It felt really good though, didn't it?" Bree said.

Katharine just looked at her.

"C'mon, be honest," Bree said. "Wasn't it the best you ever felt in your whole miserable life?"

"Yes," Katharine admitted.

"Then why on earth would you stop doing it?" Bree asked, looking totally mystified. "Why aren't you out there on the dance floor every single night of the week getting fucked up out of your gourd?"

"Because if all I cared about was feeling good all the time," Katharine said, "soon, I'd lose my job and my apartment, and the manuscript would never get finished. All I would have managed to do while I was here is develop an expensive drug habit."

"Don't knock it 'til you've tried it," Bree joked.

Suddenly the bedroom door opened and a tough-looking young man with red hair and a goatee stepped outside. He was fair-skinned, had a tattoo across his neck, and wore a gray sweat suit.

"Is everything okay, Bree?" the young man asked her.

"Yeah, I'm fine," she said. "Why don't you go back inside? I'll be right there."

He looked Katharine up and down, but only for a split-second, and said, "No, I think I'll be leavin' now."

"Wait, don't go," she urged him as he headed straight for the door and quickly walked out.

"Catch you later, cheeky mama," he said before he shut it behind him.

"Great. There goes my connection." She sighed.

"He was a drug dealer?" Katharine gasped.

"Mmm hmm," she said.

They could hear him talking to another man out in the hallway. Then Leon burst into the room with two women in his arms. Both were white, and they were dressed like hookers. He had on his flashy yellow suit and pimp hat.

"Hey there, neighbor," he said to Katharine with his evil grin. "What you doin' up here? Wanted to see how the other half lives?"

"Well, I guess I better go," she said to Bree, suddenly very nervous.

She started walking toward the door as Leon and his two prostitutes slowly made their way to the bedroom.

"Ah, why don't you stay awhile, sweetmeat?" he said, pretending to be disappointed. "We'll make room on the bed for you, won't we, girls?" The two women giggled. Then he looked at Bree and said, "Won't we, Bree?"

She simply glared at him while Katharine quickly left the apartment.

A few days later, Bree showed up at Katharine's door with her head hung low, asking to be let in.

"So that's the way it's going to be from now on?" Katharine scolded her. "You go off on a drug binge 'til you've had your fill and then come back here and expect me to let you in as if nothing ever happened?"

"Yeah. Is that going to be a problem?" she asked.

They both smiled, and Katharine let her in. Bree went straight to the dining room table and sat down in front of the computer.

"I used to be a lot worse, you know," she admitted shamefully before she turned the machine on. "I got high almost every day and never came down." She paused for a moment. Then she added, "Just bear with me, Kat ... Will ya?"

"All right," Katharine promised.

Chapter 9: The Killer Emerges

While Katharine worked with Bree during the day, she spent many free evenings hanging out with Joe—a man who wasn't all that attractive except for his thick, wavy hair and puppy dog eyes and who had the reputation of a monster. Yet to her, he was always a perfect gentleman, and she enjoyed being with him, whether they were taking horse and buggy rides through Central Park, playing Scrabble in his apartment, or attending the opera at the Met. Joe loved the opera almost as much as he loved Ol' Blue Eyes. It always made him cry. On Independence Day, they sat in the luxurious Hudson Terrace rooftop bar-lounge overlooking the Hudson River and watched the Macy's fireworks display. Their chairs were almost touching as they sat at a table facing the water. In the midst of all the excitement, he put his arm around her, looked at her, and smiled. She slowly turned her head toward him and leaned in to kiss him. Later that night, he took her back to his apartment and they made love for the first time inside his bed. Afterward, she was shocked to discover that it wasn't just the opera that made him cry. She quickly rolled off him and noticed he had tears in his eyes.

"Are you crying?" She laughed.

"No," he answered, though she detected a whimper in his voice.

She laughed even louder and shook her head.

"I'm not," he snapped.

"Don't worry. I'm not going to tell anyone," she said. "Your reputation's safe with me." As they lay there staring up at the ceiling, she added, "Actually, I think it's kind of cute."

"Oh, really?" he said, scooting closer toward her pillow. "Then maybe I should cry more often."

He tickled her belly, and she laughed like a little girl. They were always playful like that and enjoyed each other's company. It was the most fun she'd had in quite some time, in fact. After four weeks of nonstop laughter, she even thought about moving in with him. Then one night, it all came to a screeching halt.

"Joey, what's wrong?" she asked him as they sat at opposite ends of the dinner table, eating their supper. "You've been moping around all evening. Plus, you've hardly touched the meatloaf, and that's your favorite dish. You're usually on your third helping by now."

He just laughed to himself and continued to pick at it with his fork.

"C'mon, tell me," she begged him.

"I'm sorry, Katharine, but I can't discuss it with you," he said. "Trust me. It's for your own protection."

"Can't you just give me a hint?" she asked, looking deeply frustrated.

"The boss wants me to do something that I have strong objections to," he suddenly blurted out. "That's all I can say."

"Well, that's an easy one. Don't do it," she said.

"This is Louis Bartoli we're talkin' about!" he exclaimed. "How am I supposed to say no to the man?"

"I notice every time he tells you to do something, you jump," she said. "Be a man for once, and tell him you won't do it. He might not like it, but he'll respect your decision."

"No, he won't," Joe scoffed. "He'll have someone put a bullet in my head."

"What?" She laughed and looked at him strangely.

"He's not that sweet, lovable guy you met at the club," he said. "The truth is he's a ruthless, paranoid old fuck just like you read in the papers. And, if you cross him, you're dead. Simple as that."

"So does he want you to whack somebody?" she asked him curiously after a long pause.

"Katharine," he snapped.

"What?"

"Don't you realize that I'm putting your life in danger just by being with you?" he said. "Please, no more questions."

"If you don't like your job, why don't you just quit?" she asked him.

"Just like that, huh?" He laughed.

"Yeah, just like that," she replied. "That's what I would do."

"It's not like I'm moving furniture or selling TVs for a living," he said. "I'm in the Mafia, for Christ's sakes. There's no quitting. You've seen enough gangster movies to know what I'm talking about. It's all true."

"Then we'll run away together, just you and me," she said excitedly.

"Now you're just being silly," he grumbled.

"No, I'm not!" she exclaimed. "I don't know what we've got here. But I know we're way past just being friends. And right now I'm saying I'll do whatever it takes to make this thing work."

He gave her a long, hard look. Then he shoved away his plate of meatloaf and said, "I've killed men before, Katharine. Surely you must have known."

She simply nodded.

"Most of them deserved it. Some didn't," he said. "But they were all soldiers, like me. And we all know that's just part of the business. Sometimes you end up gettin' whacked." He paused for a moment and let out a long, heavy sigh. "Now Louis wants me to kill somebody in the family," he said. "And for no good reason except that he believes him to be weak and untrustworthy. This guy's a real talker, don't get me wrong. And he might actually flip on us someday. But he hasn't yet. Like I said, I've killed innocent men before, and if that's what Louis wants then so be it. Only this time he wants me to kill the wife and kids as well, just because he's afraid they might know something or the kids might grow up and seek revenge." He lowered his head and let out another sigh. "I think the old man's finally lost it," he said. "He's never asked me to kill women and children before. It goes against my nature."

"Can't he get somebody else to do it?" she asked.

"Are you kidding?" he said. "I'm the one who does his dirty work. I'm his Luca Brasi." He looked at her and added, "I understand if you want to leave."

"Leave? Why?" she replied.

"What I just said doesn't frighten you?" he asked.

She simply shrugged her shoulders and said, "You're telling me that you're a cold-blooded killer, but to me it's all hearsay. And quite frankly, I don't see how it could possibly be true. The Joe I know is a very sweet and compassionate man. That's the Joe I've fallen in love with."

He smiled at her affectionately.

"So when is all of this supposed to go down anyway?" she asked him.

"Tonight," he answered.

"You can't go through with it," she said resolutely. "How would either of us be able to live with something like that? We'll have to pack our bags and leave right now."

"I'm not going to let you go on the run with me, goddamn it!" he angrily exclaimed, which caused her to flinch. "I never should've told you in the first place."

"It's too late now," she joked. "I know too much already. So I guess we're off to South America."

He looked at her disapprovingly and shook his head. "It was wrong for me to push myself on you and tell you all my dirty secrets," he said. "It's probably the most selfish thing I've ever done. There's people out there who want me dead for the simple fact that I'm Louis's muscle. They think they could get to him a lot easier with me out of the way. That's why I'm constantly looking over my shoulder. It could happen at any time, Katharine, even when you least expect it. I don't want you to be around me when it does."

Katharine imagined the worst possible scenario: All of a sudden the front door burst open and two large, scary-looking men rushed into the dining room before she and Joe even had time to react. Both men were well-dressed, wore shades, and carried nine millimeters. One of them stood right behind Joe and shot him in the back of the head, while the other one blasted a giant hole through Katharine's forehead; her face fell directly into her plate. After the gruesome scene played out inside her head, she simply laughed it off and said, "I thought you said Louis was the paranoid one."

"You should probably go now." Joe sighed and got up from the table. "I'm feeling a bit tired. Think I'll go take a nap."

"I'll lie down with you," she suggested to him.

"Go home, Katharine," he snapped as he headed for the bedroom.

"Okay," she muttered to herself and sighed bitterly.

She got up and walked out.

When she returned and let herself in the next morning, he was still in bed, and the New York Daily News was spread out on the dining room table. The headlines read, "Brooklyn Family Found Murdered Inside Their Home." Reading on, she discovered that around 1 AM all six family members had been shot to death, including a three-year-old boy. The police suspected it to be mob-related because the family patriarch had been a member of the Louis Bartoli crime family.

"Poor Joe," she mumbled, completely horrified.

He finally rolled out of bed fifteen minutes later and staggered into the dining room in his skivvies and undershirt.

"Oh, it's you." He burped as he caught her sitting at the table with and the newspaper still laid out in front of her. She knew her expression looked grim. "I started reading that earlier this morning and got so damned depressed that I went right back to bed. I should probably cancel the damn thing, with all the negative crap that they put in it."

"It's a beautiful day out," she said to him in a solemn voice. "Do you want to do something?"

"Nah ... better stay in," he replied. "You go have fun."

Then he slowly turned around and walked straight back to his bedroom like a zombie. He even had the audacity to shut the door on her this time.

"Okay," she muttered to herself, just like before.

She got up and headed for the front door, stopping in front of his bedroom along the way to give it one last chance.

"Joey, is there anything I can do?" she asked as she opened the door and poked her head in.

He lay in the middle of the bed with the light off.

"No, Katharine. Please, just go," he urged her.

"Are you sure?"

"Yes."

"Well, if you need me for anything, anything at all, you know where to find me. Or you can just call me at …"

"Oh, leave it alone, why don't you," he snapped, "now that you know who I am and what I'm capable of? Do yourself a favor and find somebody out there who really deserves you—a banker or an insurance salesman, perhaps."

"I want you," she muttered.

"It's not going to work," he said very grimly. "You know it as well as I do. Just go away, will ya?"

She slowly shut the door and slapped the extra key that he gave her down on the coffee table before she left the apartment.

She moped around for days on end, unable to write or focus on her job. *How could he do it?* she asked herself at one point. *How could someone so sensitive and so full of life be capable of such a heinous crime? And to think that I was about to drop everything and run away with him. Boy, I sure know how to pick 'em.*

Oh, don't be such a hypocrite, said her conscience. *You already knew he killed people for a living, and that didn't stop you from seeing him. And you'd still be with him right now if he hadn't shut you out. There's a darkness inside you. The longer you stay here the more it will come to light.*

You should be grateful to him for shutting you out, said her heart. *But how do you get back those four weeks he stole from you? Four whole weeks of lies and false promises. And now here we are at the end of July, a little wiser and far more cynical. Didn't Frank teach you anything? Fifteen years of marriage wasted there. Just stay away from men from now on, and focus on your writing. They're bad news. And they're not worth the heartache.*

Bree continued to type for Katharine while she wrote. But a lot of times, Katharine pulled her away from the typewriter and they fleshed out a scene together. Katharine began to appreciate Bree's creative input, in fact, and even considered making her a co-author. There were also times when they said to hell with the novel and spent the entire day shopping in Times Square. Though they were complete opposites in every way, they enjoyed each other's company. Katharine's positive attitude appeared to both amuse and inspire the troubled Bree. And Katharine admired Bree for her honesty and her ability to cut through the crap. She was like Norma in a lot of ways, Katharine realized, only smaller and with a darker complexion.

Chapter 10: The Wrath of Leon

On the morning of the fifth of August, Bree showed up at Katharine's door with a black eye, which was actually more purplish in color and looked extremely painful.

"Good lord, what happened to you?" Katharine exclaimed as she let Bree in.

"It's nothing. Don't worry about it," Bree said, heading straight for the table.

"If *he* did this to you, you shouldn't let him get away with it this time," Katharine said.

"I didn't," Bree replied as she sat down and turned on the computer. "I gave him a fat lip."

"What I'm saying is maybe you should get him out of your life," Katharine said.

"I believe we've had this conversation before," Bree huffed. "He's my man. I love him."

"How could you love anyone who would do something like that to your beautiful face?" Katharine said.

"He didn't mean to do it," Bree said. "He was drunk."

"Oh, that's a hell of an excuse," Katharine scolded her. "One of these days, he might actually kill you. But he didn't mean anything by it. He was drunk."

"Would you just drop it, Kat?" Bree said, starting to get a little agitated.

"What was the fight about, anyway?" Katharine persisted.

"It was about you, actually," Bree said. "He said that I was spending too much time with you. And he wanted me to stop coming over here because you're a bad influence. Then I told him to go fuck himself, and he popped me in the face."

"*I'm* a bad influence?" Katharine laughed.

"Anyway, that's how it all started," Bree said. "It ended with him lying flat on the floor screaming, 'My mouth is bleeding! Get me a Band-Aid!'"

"So you really let him have it, huh?" Katharine smiled.

"Didn't I tell you that I could take care of myself?" she replied sternly.

That was all that was said on the matter until about 4 PM when they heard Leon walking upstairs and shouting, "Bree, I'm home! Get your butt up here!"

"Oh no. I think he's drunk again," Bree said, her voice filled with dread.

"Then you shouldn't go up there," Katharine replied.

"If I don't, there's no tellin' what he'll do," Bree said, quickly getting up from the table. "It's like defusing a bomb. Somebody's got to do it."

"Well, all right." Katharine nodded. "But be careful. And remember, you can always come down here if he tries to hit you again."

After Bree stepped out of the apartment, Katharine heard her arguing with him in the stairwell. Once they were inside their own apartment, it turned into a fierce shouting match that lasted throughout the evening. Katharine promised herself she would stay out of it this time. But as soon as she heard objects crashing to the floor and Bree yelling, "Stop it!" she jumped up from the couch and rushed outside. Before she made it to the stairwell, she noticed Mrs. Chang sticking her head out her door, as usual.

"You go up there, miss?" the old woman asked fearfully, while the shouting continued to fill the halls.

"Yes," said Katharine with a determined look on her face.

"I go with you," Mrs. Chang said. She stepped back inside for a moment and came out with a Little League baseball bat. "It belongs to my grandson," she said proudly. She quickly shut the door and followed Katharine up the stairs.

The old woman stuck close behind her and held the bat up like a torch as they reached the other hallway and slowly crept up to 411. Katharine turned around for a second to make sure Mrs. Chang was armed and ready. Then she banged on the door. The shouting ceased almost instantly, just like it had before. But this time, Leon jerked the door open and scared them half to death.

"What do you want?" he exclaimed, snorting like an angry bull.

"Where's Bree?" said Katharine. "I have to speak to her."

"She's busy at the moment," he snarled. "Now go away."

Katharine slipped through the door before he could slam it in her face. He immediately grabbed her and pushed her back outside. Mrs. Chang swung her bat at him and struck him across the forearm.

"Ow, that hurt, you old bag!" he cried out, quickly letting go of Katharine and grabbing his own arm. "Hit me with that again, and I'll shove it up your ass!"

Bree came to the door at that point and looked at Katharine harshly.

"Kat, what's going on here?" she asked.

"I could hear you all the way downstairs," said Katharine. "I thought you were in trouble."

"Everything's fine," Bree assured her. "Go home."

Katharine nodded and started to turn away, suddenly feeling a little foolish. But then she looked at Leon and said, "If you hit her again, I'm calling the police."

"Me too," Mrs. Chang said, shaking her bat at him.

"Oooh," he scoffed, pretending to be scared and then flashing his evil grin.

"Come on, Mrs. Chang," Katharine said.

She took the old woman by the hand, and they proudly marched away. When they got back downstairs, they shook hands. "Thank you, Mrs. Chang," Katharine said. "You were a big help."

"Yes, yes, you're welcome." The woman bowed and grinned excitedly. She bowed a couple more times and then swiftly went back into her apartment.

Around midnight, Katharine heard a gentle knock on her door. As she jumped out of bed to answer it, she could hear Bree whispering, "Katharine, please ... open the door. Katharine?"

She quickly opened it, and Bree ran inside.

"Hurry up and lock it," she said frantically. "He's coming this way, and he's got a gun."

Katharine shut and locked the door, and they then scrambled over to the corner of the room, dropped to their knees, and held on to each other very tightly while staring at the door. It was dark, however, and all they could see was the light shining in from below. All of a sudden, Katharine heard large, heavy footsteps in the hallway. Then someone banged on the door as hard as he could, causing them both to shudder.

"Open this goddamn door," Leon shouted angrily, "or I'll fill it full of holes!"

The two remained very still even as he rammed himself into the door repeatedly, and it was about to explode off its hinges. The next thing Katharine heard was a woman shouting, "You go away now! I call the police!"

"It's Mrs. Chang," she whispered to Bree.

"Get away from me, you old bag," Leon snarled. "I'm warning you."

It sounded as if there was a scuffle. Then Katharine heard another woman shouting in a high-pitched voice, "What is this? Leave that poor woman alone."

"Mrs. Poindexter," Katharine and Bree whispered simultaneously.

Katharine started to hear other voices as well. Then seconds later it sounded as if everyone in the building was there—people who rarely ever showed their faces. They seemed to come out of their apartments in droves, creating a sense of community like never before. *All it took was a black man brandishing a firearm and threatening to kick down doors,* she thought and smiled.

Suddenly she heard multiple sirens directly outside the building, followed by a stampede of footsteps pounding their way up the stairwell and a man shouting, "Freeze! Put the gun down!"

"This ain't none you all's business!" Leon shouted.

"Put the gun down!" the man repeated even more sternly.

There was another scuffle, and Leon let out a violent scream. He even shouted Bree's name at one point. She attempted to go to him, but Katharine held her back.

"No, Bree. Are you crazy?" she whispered.

"Do you know who lives here?" someone asked, standing right outside the door.

"That would be the new tenant, Mrs. Beaumont," they heard Mrs. Poindexter tell him.

There was a knock on the door. Katharine immediately stood up and went to answer it. She flipped on the light switch, undid the deadbolt, and turned the knob.

"Are you Mrs. Beaumont?" asked a young chubby policeman who stood in the doorway.

She nodded and glanced over at Leon, who was being held to the floor by three policemen. He, in turn, saw Bree standing in the living room and cried out to her again. She immediately ran to the door and said, "Please let him go. I'm begging you."

"Are you related to him, ma'am?" the chubby police officer asked.

"He's my boyfriend," she said. "We live in the apartment upstairs."

"And what about ..." he began, pointing at Katharine.

"She has nothing to do with this," Bree quickly butted in. "She's just a friend."

"Like hell I don't have nothing to do with it!" Katharine exclaimed. "He tried to break down my door!"

"Katharine ... please," Bree implored her, placing a warm hand on her shoulder.

Katharine reluctantly backed off and didn't say another word.

"What about you, ma'am?" the policeman asked Mrs. Chang, who stood close by and looked a little shook up. "Are you okay? Do you wish to file a complaint?"

"No," she said and shook her head. "Had enough for one night. I go to bed now."

She slowly turned around and headed for her door.

"All right," the policeman sighed, looking at Bree. "We're gonna take you and your boyfriend upstairs and straighten this whole thing out."

He and his fellow officers escorted the couple back to their apartment, while Mrs. Poindexter started breaking up the crowd.

"Sorry for the disturbance, folks," she said. "Now please go back to your rooms."

Katharine hoped to get a good look at the woman this time, but all she could see through the crowd was that big nose of hers. The people scattered and disappeared all at once, leaving Katharine standing there all alone. She immediately closed her door and went back into the living room. She heard Leon and Bree arguing with the police for thirty minutes before they all went outside and headed for the stairwell. She heard Leon cursing them all the way down to the lobby. She rushed over to the living room window and watched as they shoved him into one of the police cars lined up along the curb. Bree stood just a few feet away crying.

When Katharine talked to Bree the following day, she was still very upset.

"I told them that I wasn't going to press charges, but they took him anyway," she said as they sat next to each other at Katharine's dinner table. "They got him for aggravated assault and resisting arrest. Plus the gun wasn't even registered under his name." She laughed to herself and shook her head helplessly. "The stupid jerk was just askin' for it," she muttered. "I did all I could do for him."

"Of course you did," Katharine replied. "Is this the first time he's been arrested? For assault, I mean?"

"Yeah," she answered. "I went to see him at the county jail this morning. He wants me to hock the ring that he gave me for my thirtieth birthday a few months ago … so I can bail him out. I told him I couldn't do it. It means too much to me." She held up her left hand and showed Katharine the large diamond ring on her finger.

"It's beautiful," Katharine said.

"Three stones set in platinum," Bree boasted. "They cost around fifty thousand or more. It's probably the closest thing I'll ever get to an engagement ring."

"I never even noticed it before," said Katharine.

"I usually take it off when I step out of the apartment so no one will try to steal it from me," Bree explained. "But I wanted to show it to you. Now you see why I'm not about to give it up just to bail his sorry ass out of jail, especially when he's got a hundred thousand dollars stashed away somewhere."

"A hundred thousand?" Katharine gasped.

"Runnin' whores can be a very lucrative business," Bree said.

"Well, looks to me like you did the right thing." Katharine nodded. "Spending some time in jail might be the best thing for him."

"His best friend Bubba is bailing him out right now," Bree scoffed. "They'll be here in a couple of hours. And I'm sure he won't be very happy to see me."

"Then don't let him in," Katharine replied.

"Kat." Bree sighed and shook her head.

"I'm sorry, but I think you're making a terrible mistake by not pressing charges," Katharine blurted out. "If you're not willing to cooperate with the prosecution, the case won't even make it to court."

"All he did was wave a gun in my face and pretend like he was gonna kill me." Bree laughed.

"He *did* try to kill you!" Katharine exclaimed.

"He doesn't have the balls," Bree retorted. "Men are like little boys. Their bark's always worse than their bite."

"I saw the look on your face when I let you in last night," Katharine reminded her. "You were scared to death."

Bree looked down at the keyboard and didn't say anything.

"The man is dangerous, Bree," she persisted. "He needs to be locked up for good."

"Obviously you don't know him the way I do," Bree said.

"I think I know him well enough." Katharine laughed.

"Just let it be, Katharine," Bree urged her. "I understand what you're saying, but I can't change the way I feel about him. To you, he's dangerous. But to me, he's just a man—crude, obnoxious, bullheaded. He's also very sexy, and he knows how to make me laugh. More than that, he loves me when most people in this world don't give a shit whether I live or die."

"All right," Katharine nodded and didn't say another word. She slowly got up from the table and went back to her writing.

April 12

Less than two hours after the doctor's untimely death, the trio was forced to a sudden halt again. Now it was the young boy, Omar, who lay in Kitty's arms, gasping for breath beneath a giant oak tree. She, too, was starting to feel very week and dizzy, and her face was extremely pale. The poisonous berries seemed to have no effect on Jenkins, however. He still looked very healthy and appeared to be having a blast shooting at and missing everything in sight, wasting precious ammo. Finally, he gave up and went to check up on Kitty and his young friend.

"Jesus, you look bloody awful," he told her flat out.

"Thanks, Jenkins," she replied, rolling her eyes at him. "I don't think I can go much farther."

"Don't worry. I'll get us out of this mess," he assured her. "We've got to be close to the other side by now. I'll go the rest of the way by myself and bring back help. But before I go, I'll get some wood to make you a fire and then hunt for food."

"Don't waste anymore ammo, Jenkins," Kitty groaned. "We can't keep anything down anyway. Just go. We don't have much time left."

"Don't worry, I'll be back shortly," he promised her, looking very confident.

He quickly stood up and darted off through the trees, with his spear in one hand and his rifle in the other. Five minutes later, Kitty heard his gun go off. A few minutes after that, he came running back to them, minus both weapons and yelling, "Tiger! Tiger!" The roaring beast was right behind him, snapping at his rear. The little man fell, and the white tiger attempted to jump on top of him but was shot in midair. It fell to the ground next to him, part of its head blown off.

"That was way too close!" he shouted frantically as he got up and ran some more.

Kitty turned to where the shot was fired and saw a man rising up from a bush and lowering his hunting rifle. He was tall and slender and dressed like a big game hunter in a white safari suit and hat. He stepped away from the bush along with two other men and started walking toward her. The closer they got to her, the more she began to realize it was him—the man that she was supposed to kill. She recognized his long, thin face; soft, blue eyes; and blond hair from the hundreds of snapshots they had taken of him when she and her commander were in Berlin. He suddenly stood over her and smiled. His face glowed in the sunlight as if he was a heavenly being.

"You don't look so good," he said to her with a thick Swedish accent. "Tell me you didn't eat the blackberries. They're poisonous, you know."

She nodded and tried to smile.

"Well, don't worry," he said. "We'll get you both to the house and fix you right up. I'm Mikael Ljungberg, by the way."

He flashed his beautiful pearly whites at her again. Then he and the two men—his servants, she presumed—carefully placed her and Omar in the back of his jeep and drove the three castaways to his mansion, just a half of a mile away and right next to the ocean. There was also a chapel and a hospital, where Kitty and Omar were taken and treated by his own personal physician and a team of skilled doctors and nurses.

By the second day, after having their stomachs pumped and taking some very powerful emetics, Kitty and Omar looked and felt much better. They were soon released from the hospital and moved to the second floor of the three-story house, directly across from Jenkin's room. Looking outside her bedroom window, Kitty counted at least a dozen German soldiers walking around the premises; some carried rifles, others submachine guns. Plus there was a man up in the gun tower. It made her feel more like a prisoner than a guest. That and the twelve-foot chain-link fence enclosing the entire property. Beyond the fence was the jungle that had almost destroyed her.

On the third day, she and her fellow castaways were given the grand tour of the mansion by their gracious host. The house was more like a luxury hotel; it contained a gym and a game room, eight deluxe bathrooms, and over fifty bedrooms. Ljungberg's elderly mother and younger sister lived in two of the bedrooms. He introduced them to his guests as well.

The last place he showed them was the arsenal down in the basement, which seemed to impress Jenkins the most. Ljungberg had over two hundred and fifty guns in his collection, and Jenkins had his hands on every single one of them. His childlike excitement amused the multi-billionaire to the point that he promised to take him on the next hunting expedition. There were at least thirty different species of wildlife on the island, Ljungberg pointed out to his guests, most of which had been shipped in from the mainland.

"But I'm afraid we're down to just two tigers now," he said. "What can I say? I love to hunt big game. And this way I can enjoy my favorite sport without ever leaving the island."

After he was finished showing off the house, Kitty agreed to take a walk with him outside. It became a daily routine, in fact. One morning as they were taking a leisurely stroll around the mansion, she noticed Omar staring at them through his bedroom window. Around midnight, the boy snuck into her bedroom and knelt down beside her bed.

"So when are we going to do it?" he whispered to her.

"Do what?" she asked.

"You know," he said and pretended to slit his throat with his hand.

She didn't even attempt to answer him, except to say, "We? There's no we."

"I saw you walking with him yesterday over by the garden," he said in his Egyptian accent. "And the day before that ... and the day before that. Are you trying to make him fall in love with you? That's it, isn't it?" He grew excited as he spoke. "Then one night when you're pretending to be asleep inside his bed, you reach over and slit his throat! Yes, yes, very good! He'll never suspect! You are most excellent spy!"

"Be quiet," she whispered to him. "Do you want everyone to hear us?"

"No, no," he whispered. "But what about the armed guards ... and the servants? You'll have to take them out as well. And for that you'll need me ... and Jenkins, perhaps. Three is better than one. We'll break into the arsenal and steal his weapons. And I know where all his ammunition is stored."

"You're very courageous," she said. "But your plan lacks subtlety and finesse. There are many ways you can kill a man and make it look like a complete accident, without anyone ever suspecting foul play."

"Yes, I suppose you're right, miss." He sighed. "I just feel deep in my heart that I must help you fight these evil Nazis."

"I know," she said, patting him on the shoulder. "But I don't need any help on this one. It's strictly a one-man operation."

He nodded as if he understood. But just a couple of days later, Jenkins asked Kitty to meet him inside the greenhouse.

"I just had an interesting talk with Omar," he said to her, looking a little flustered as they stood together behind the hibiscus plants. "He's afraid that you have fallen in love with Mikael and that you've forgotten all about your mission. You don't still plan on killin' him, do you? He saved your life, you know. And I see you with him all the time. So you must know what a swell guy he is. So what if he's workin' with the Nazis? Nobody's perfect."

"Don't worry. I'm not going to kill anyone," she assured him.

"Well, okay then," Jenkins said, looking relieved. "That's all I needed to know. Now all I have to worry about is Omar. Somehow he's got it in his head that Ljungberg must die." He sighed and shook his head. "Barkesdale was right about that kid," he said. "He lives in a fantasy world. I tried to tell him that, and he got all upset. And he ran out of the room shouting, 'I'll show you. I'll show everyone.'"

"I guess I'll have to have a long talk with him," Kitty said.

"Please do," Jenkins said. "I'm supposed to go tiger huntin' tomorrow, and I don't want him to mess it up for me."

"Are you sure you want to do that?" Kitty asked him. "You remember what happened last time."

"The damned thing caught me by surprise," he snapped. "I'll be ready for the next one."

As he walked away, it now seemed perfectly clear to her that she had to get both him and Omar out of the way in order to complete her mission. When she talked to Ljungberg later on in the day, she was her usual cunning self.

"I appreciate everything you've done for us," she began as they sat in the porch swing together, overlooking the beach. He wore his smoking jacket, and she was dressed in a pretty dress that belonged to his sister. "But now that we're back on our feet, isn't it time for us to leave?"

"Leave?" he said, stuffing his pipe. "But you just got here."

"I know," she replied. "But as you can see, we're all better now. And here we are, eating up all your food and overstaying our welcome."

"Nonsense." He laughed.

He just sat there smoking his pipe and staring out at the waves, and she began to show a little concern.

"You are *going to let us leave, aren't you?" she asked him.*

"Of course," he said, appearing offended. "I wouldn't dream of holding you here against your will. I just thought, perhaps you enjoyed being here."

"I do," she replied and cuddled up next to him. "It's the other two that I'm worried about. They miss their families, and they're ready to go home."

"And you?" he inquired.

"I have no family," she said very solemnly. "I was an orphan child."

"Then stay here with me," he begged her. "At least for a little while longer."

"All right," she said. "But what about ..."

"I'll have my pilot fly them out of here first thing tomorrow morning," he assured her.

She smiled and rested her head on his shoulder.

The following morning, she stood in front of the hangar and watched Omar and Jenkins board Ljungberg's private plane—the Lockheed L-12 Electra Junior, which had two engines and two propellers in front and seated up to six passengers. They were reluctant to go at first. Omar wanted to stay and "fight the good fight," while Jenkins was all excited about shooting his first tiger. But in the end, they realized it was time to go. Jenkins promised her he would take the boy with him back to Liverpool and watch over him. The boy had lived aboard ship, and Captain O'Hara had been the closest thing he had to a parent. She waved to them for the last time as the pilot started up the engines and the plane taxied down the runway. It took off and flew into the sunset. She envied them in a way. Their war was over while hers was just beginning.

That night she dressed up for Ljungberg again, this time in a long beautiful gown. He put on his white tuxedo. They stepped out into the courtyard, which was all lit up, and started dancing to Johann Strauss playing on the Victrola.

Jones could see them both perfectly from the other side of the fence. What the hell is she doing, he thought, lying flat on his belly, perfectly camouflaged by the color of his skin. And how the hell did she get here before me?

He pulled out his knife and started digging into the dirt in front of him so he could crawl underneath the fence and save her from her captor, who was obviously insane and most likely had her brainwashed. First, he would have to take out the two guards that kept pacing back and forth just a few yards in front of him, plus the man in the gun tower. But he didn't see that as a problem.

Katharine was jolted back to reality by a sudden tap on the head.

"I guess I'll be going now," Bree said, standing directly behind the couch.

Katharine looked up at the clock on the wall and couldn't believe it was already 4 PM; she had been writing for six solid hours.

"All right," Katharine said, holding her pen in place as she watched Bree leave.

Bree called her up on the phone the very next day while Katharine was at work.

"When I stepped back into my room yesterday, Leon and Bubba were sitting on the couch drinking beer," Bree said to her.

"How did it go?" Katharine asked hesitantly.

"A lot better than I expected," she said. "He walked up to me, and I thought he was going to kill me. 'I couldn't sell the ring, Leon,'

I immediately tried to explain to him. Then he surprised the hell out of me. 'I'm glad you didn't," he said. 'That ring is a symbol of our love, and I never should have asked you to give it up.' After that he threw his arms around me and apologized for the way he's been treating me. 'Things are gonna be a whole lot different around here, I can promise you that,' he said."

"Wow," Katharine replied, finding it all so very hard to believe.

"So you were right, Kat," Bree said ecstatically. "Spending a night in jail was just what he needed. He's like a whole new person."

"Really?" Katharine replied.

"After he threw Bubba out of the apartment, we made love all night long," she continued.

"You did not." Katharine gasped.

"Did too," she said. "And when we woke up this morning, he was ready to go again. I'm tellin' you, the man's a sexual dynamo. Can't say for sure just yet, but I think we're lookin' at a brand new day. Grandma always said that love conquers all in the end."

"I hope she was right," Katharine said, still a bit skeptical.

Chapter 11: A Crime of Passion

It appeared that things were really starting to look up for Bree Withers. Katharine didn't see her for days, and she didn't hear a peep out of them from upstairs except for the bed banging against the floor during their lovemaking. *A brand new day, indeed,* she thought. Then one night as she was about to go to sleep, the two started yelling at each other again.

"I guess Grandma was wrong," she scoffed, grabbing the extra pillow and putting it over her ears.

Two hours later, around midnight, that dreaded knock came on her door. She swiftly got up to answer it. As she suspected, it was Bree, looking very numb and zombielike, the way Joe had looked when she had last seen him. Katharine quickly dragged her inside and shut the door.

"What did he do to you this time?" she said angrily. "Did he hit you? Did he take out his gun?"

"No," Bree replied and shook her head. "I killed him."

"You mean he's ..." Katharine gasped.

Bree nodded. "I'm not sure what happened," she continued. "All of a sudden I just snapped. It all started when he came home late tonight and brought a couple of prostitutes with him, expecting another four-way, I guess. 'Hmm mmm, not this time,' I said to him and threw both of those bitches out. I wasn't all that furious though, at least not yet. I was just layin' down the law for once. 'There will be no more four-ways in this apartment,' I said. 'No more hoes, either.'

Then he started whining like a baby and stomping his feet. 'I wasn't trying to dis you,' he said. 'I just wanted to liven things up a bit. It gets a little old being with the same person night after night.' I guess he didn't realize how much that really hurt me. I chewed him out good ... told him what a no 'count son of a bitch he was. And finally he just turned around and started walking to the door. 'I don't need this shit ... I'm leaving you,' he said. That's when I really lost it. Next thing I know, I was lunging at him with a kitchen knife."

"Are you sure he's dead?" Katharine asked.

"I'm pretty sure." She laughed nervously.

"Well then, we have to call the police," Katharine said. "We'll tell 'em it was self-defense."

"I stabbed him twenty times in the back with a kitchen knife," said Bree. "I don't think they're gonna buy it. And I'm not gonna let them take me back to that prison. I'll kill myself right here and now before I let that happen."

"Then what are you gonna do?" Katharine asked.

"I don't know," said Bree. "I was hopin' you'd have some idea. You've written murder mysteries before."

"That was fiction, Bree," Katharine quickly pointed out to her. "You know, a little lighthearted entertainment for the masses? This here is some serious shit."

"I know," Bree said. "It's my mess. I should've kept you out of it. I'll go if you want me to."

Katharine didn't say anything, hoping that Bree would just turn around and leave. But she didn't. She just stood there and waited for Katharine to make a decision. *If I tell her to go and that I don't ever want to see her again, I'll be a coward, and perhaps I won't be able to live with myself,* Katharine thought. *If I tell her to stay and try to help her, I'll be an accomplice to murder, and perhaps I won't be able to live with myself. God, why did I let this person into my life?*

Because you're a kind and compassionate human being, said her heart. *You can't just throw her out and turn your back on her. It's not in you. Don't worry. Be strong. Now, we'll see what you're really made of.* Seeing how adamant Bree was about not going to the police, Katharine's conscience remained silent.

"All right, I understand," Bree said and started to back off.

"No, stay," Katharine blurted out. "I want to help. After all, what are friends for?"

"Thank you." Bree put her arms around Katharine and rested her head on hers.

"I guess what we need to do then is get rid of the body somehow," Katharine said, suddenly pulling away and taking charge. "Where is he now?"

"Lying about six feet away from the door," Bree answered bluntly.

"Well, we're gonna have to hide him," Katharine said, "in case someone decides to pop in all of a sudden. But I don't think we should go up together. It might look suspicious. You go first. I'll be there in five minutes."

"Okay," Bree replied, doing exactly as Katharine said.

Five minutes later, Katharine walked up to Bree's apartment and let herself in. Sure enough, Leon lay flat on his stomach just six feet away from the door, with multiple stab wounds on his back. His white silk shirt was soaked with blood. She found Bree standing over in a corner next to the living room window, staring down at the wood floor, appearing to be in shock.

"Bree!" Katharine shouted and slapped her across the cheek as hard as she could.

Bree suddenly looked up at her and sternly replied, "Don't ever do that again."

"I'm sorry," Katharine apologized. "I thought you were …"

"I'm fine," she assured her. "Let's just do this thing, shall we?"

They grabbed Leon by the arms and dragged his lifeless corpse across the floor, leaving a trail of blood behind them. They dragged him all the way back to the bathroom door. Once they got him inside, Katharine pulled back the shower curtain, and they lifted him into the tub.

"Now what?" Bree said as they stood over him, trying to catch their breaths.

"We cut him up into a million pieces and take him out with the trash," Katharine said.

"You're kidding, right?" Bree sighed.

"Well, maybe not a million pieces," Katharine said.

"I can't do it," Bree said, suddenly becoming hysterical as she looked down at Leon's face.

Katharine walked up to her and gave her hug. Then *she* looked down at Leon's face and noticed his sinister eyes staring back at her as if he was still alive.

"Don't worry about it," she replied and patted Bree on the shoulder. "I'll get some help. Luckily I know someone who does this sort of thing for a living. I just need to make a call. Can I use your phone?"

"Sure, it's in the kitchen," Bree said.

Katharine went to make the phone call. Then she helped Bree clean the blood off the floor with a bucket of water and a sponge mop. An hour later, Joe arrived. He was accompanied by another man who was tall, lean, and in his early twenties. Katharine recognized him as the waiter from their dinner date at the Diamond, but she didn't say anything as she let them in. Both men wore leather jackets and carried four extremely large suitcases.

"Thanks for coming," she said to Joe and hugged him.

"Glad to help," he said.

They quickly broke away from each other, and he slapped his partner on the back.

"This is Federico," he said. "You might have remembered him from the club."

"Yes, of course," she said and smiled at the young man.

Then she introduced them to Bree, who stood behind her.

"Sorry about your boyfriend," Joe said to her as he shook her hand. "Where is he, by the way?"

"In there," Katharine said, pointing toward the bathroom.

The two men put down their suitcases and quickly headed in that direction. Bree and Katharine stayed behind.

"So why didn't you tell me about him?" Bree whispered.

"I don't know." Katharine laughed, looking a little puzzled herself. "I didn't tell him about you either."

"What, are you ashamed of me?" she asked.

"No," Katharine said. "I guess I didn't feel like sharing you with anyone, if that makes any sense."

"It don't," Bree replied. "But never mind. Do you really think we can trust these guys?"

"Are you kidding? They're gangsters," Katharine said. "Joe would never rat on me. He hates cops."

"Well, you've got him in the right place," Joe said as he and Federico stepped out of the bathroom and headed back into the living room. "Is there some place where we can change and put all of our things?"

"Sure, follow me," Bree said.

The two women led them into the bedroom, which was just to the right of the bathroom. Then they stood back and watched as the men sat the suitcases down on the bed and opened them. Two of the cases were empty, while the other two contained everything they would need—visqueen, plastic drops, duct tape, trash bags, knives, cable cutters, hatchets, sawzalls, and two biohazard suits. First, Joe removed the white suits.

"Mind if we have a little privacy here?" he said to Katharine and Bree. "We gotta strip down to our underwear and put these on."

"Of course," Katharine said.

The ladies quickly left the room and shut the door. Joe and Federico stepped out wearing the white suits a few minutes later. They headed for the bathroom with a row of visqueen, several plastic drops, and duct tape to cover the walls and the tiled floor.

"You guys need some help?" Katharine shouted to them from the living room as they started working.

"Nope, we've got it!" Federico shouted back to her.

It took them about ten minutes to plastic the entire room. Then they went back into the bedroom and came out with their electric sawzalls and other cutting tools.

"We wanted to bring the chainsaw, but we thought it would make too much noise," Joe said as they headed for the bathroom again.

"Oh God … what have I done?" Bree muttered to herself and started crying.

Joe suddenly stopped short in front of the bathroom door and noticed Katharine rushing over to her side and putting her arm around her.

"Is she going to be all right?" he asked.

"Yeah," Katharine said unconvincingly.

After he sat his tools down on the vanity, Joe walked into the bedroom once more and came out with a CD in his hand. He walked up to the two women, patted Bree on the shoulder, and said, "It's okay. You sent him to a better place."

Bree immediately stopped crying and looked at him strangely. "What an asinine thing to say," she bluntly replied. "How could you possibly know that for sure?"

"I don't." He blushed and looked down at the floor. "I was just trying to be helpful." He then turned to Katharine and handed her the CD.

"I noticed the CD player over there next to the television set," he said. "Why don't you put this in and give it a listen. It's Sinatra's *Greatest Hits*."

She looked at the singer's face on the cover and smiled.

"Turn the volume all the way up to seven," he said. "We should be done by the time it's finished playin'.

"Are you sure there's nothing I can do?" Katharine asked him.

"Stay here and look after your friend," he said.

He gave her a quick wink, turned, walked to the bathroom, and quickly shut and locked the door behind him. Katharine placed the disc into the CD player and turned the volume up. She then sat down on the couch next to Bree as the first track began to play. It was the cool and jazzy "Summer Wind," one of Frank's best. Its soothing sounds managed to calm them down a bit. But neither the Chairman of the Board nor Nelson Riddle and his brilliant orchestra could keep their minds off of what was going on behind that closed door. A feeling of déjà vu came over Katharine as they held each other tightly and kept staring at it, completely horrified. Listening very closely, they could hear the saws cutting through flesh and bone.

The next track was "It Was a Very Good Year," a beautiful and nostalgic tune that captured a man's life from beginning to end. But like the song before it, it merely made the occasion seem all the more surreal. At the end of the song, Federico came storming out of the bathroom; he was covered in blood. He immediately shut the door behind him and rushed into the bedroom.

"I'll be right back," Katharine said to Bree and quickly got up from the couch.

She walked up to the bedroom door and found him seated on the edge of the king-sized bed that was now covered in visqueen. He lit a cigarette.

"Are you guys about done in there?" she asked him.

He looked up at her and nodded. "Just taking a break," he said, looking a little peaked. "You never get used to it—all the blood and guts … and the smell." He took a couple of puffs from the cigarette, flicked his ashes onto the plastic, and drew a heavy sigh. "I don't know. Maybe I'm in the wrong business," he said. "I should've been a shoe salesman like my uncle Phil."

They looked at each other and laughed. His face suddenly turned grim.

"I'll be back in there in a minute," he said.

She nodded, turned around, and walked off. As she flopped down on the couch, she watched him go back into the bathroom. Twenty minutes later, both men stepped out just as the music stopped playing. Joe's white suit was also covered in blood.

"Well, we're almost done in there," he said as they carried their tools to the bedroom.

Katharine and Bree kept silent as he and Federico continued walking back and forth from one room to the other, carrying plastic bags full of body parts and bloodied visqueen and cramming them into the suitcases. When they had emptied the bathtub pulled all the plastic from the walls and the floor, Joe walked up to the two women and asked for the murder weapon.

"It's in the kitchen sink," Bree said. "I'll go get it."

She hurriedly walked away and came back with an eight-inch steak knife. She had already rinsed off all of the blood.

"I'll take care of that," Joe said, carefully removing it from her hands. "Now, are there any cleaning products in the house?"

"Yes," she answered.

"Good," he said. "We got most of it. But now it's up to you guys to go in there and give it a thorough cleaning. Don't leave anything for the cops."

"All right, we can handle it," Katharine assured him.

She grabbed Bree's arm, and they marched into the bathroom together while Joe went into the bedroom and helped Federico clean up in there.

Tiny specks of blood flecked the yellow walls and tiled floor of the little six-by-eight room. But the worst of the bloody mess was inside the tub itself. Bree removed the Comet and SOS pads from the bottom cabinet, and they began with the tub, getting down on their hands and knees and scrubbing as hard as they could.

"Damn you, Leon." Bree started to moan to herself as she worked.

"Are you okay, Bree?" Katharine asked.

"Couldn't be better," she scoffed.

"You don't have to help, you know."

"Yes, I do," she said. "This is all my doin'. It's my responsibility."

When they were finally finished about thirty minutes later, Joe came in to inspect their work. He had already changed back into his clothes, as had Federico.

"Well done, ladies," he said, looking very impressed. "It looks like nothing ever happened."

"Except that there's no more Leon," Bree remarked.

Joe nodded respectfully.

"So he's just gonna vanish into thin air?" she then asked him.

"Pretty much," he replied.

"I'd like to know what you're gonna do with him," she said as they all walked into the living room together.

"Forget about it," he replied. "The cops will be snoopin' around here and asking questions once he's reported missing, and the less you know, the better."

He and his partner grabbed the four loaded suitcases that sat in front of the couch and headed toward the door.

"Wait," Katharine said. She rushed over to the stereo and pulled out the CD, which she promptly put back in its case.

She walked up to the two men, who now stood at the door, and tried to hand it to Joe.

"You keep it," he said to her. "Just a little something to remember me by."

She smiled at him and then reached up and gave him a big hug, followed by a kiss on the cheek. He was so affected by it that there were tears in his eyes.

"Really, what *are* you going to do with him?" she asked while she still had him in her arms.

"Really, it's none of your business," he said to her flat out. "All I can say is we're going to put him someplace where no one will ever find him."

"All right," she nodded. "Thanks for doing this for me … both of you." She glanced over at Federico, and he smiled.

"Anytime," said Joe, slowly stepping away from her, suitcases still in hand.

"Is there any reason why you and I can't be friends?" she asked him before he turned away.

"Of course not," he replied.

"Then call me," she said, playfully punching him in the arm.

"I will," he nodded, though she could tell he was lying.

She opened the door for them, and they immediately stepped out. She poked her head out and watched them walk all the way to the stairwell. She knew Mrs. Chang would be eyeballing them as they headed down the stairs, but there was nothing she could do about that except pray. It was completely out of her hands at that point. She stepped back inside and shut the door.

Now that they were alone, Bree and Katharine just stood there looking at each other. For Katharine, it was a very awkward moment after committing such a ghastly crime.

"I can't stay in here tonight," said Bree. "Can I sleep on your couch?"

"All right," Katharine agreed even though she didn't feel like seeing or talking to Bree for a while.

They ended up sleeping on opposite sides of the same bed, with their backs turned to each other. For the first couple of hours, Katharine's eyes were wide open, her mind filled with worry and shame. When she finally did get to sleep, she had a terrible nightmare.

She was in the witness box inside a giant courtroom. Hundreds of angry spectators stared back at her from the gallery. Some of the faces she recognized, including her two children, Billy and Maggie, who sat on the front row with Katharine's elderly mother and dead father. The twelve jurors looked like something straight out of an Edvard Munch painting. They all had white skeletal faces and black holes for eyes. And sitting on the bench way up high was Leon. He wore a black judicial robe, and his eyes were glossed over and bulging out of their sockets as if he was an actual zombie. Katharine's husband, Frank, stood directly in front of her, serving as prosecuting attorney. But he appeared to be incognito; he was dressed like John Adams, with a long white wig, fancy dress suit, and knee-breeches.

"Katharine Beaumont, you have just proved to this court that you are not the person you pretend to be," he said, "that you are, in fact, a cold-hearted bitch. What do you have to say for yourself?"

"Not guilty," she blurted out, causing everyone to laugh. "I didn't kill anyone!" she shouted over them.

"Not yet," he sneered. "But you did abandon your own children … and your husband of fifteen years."

She looked at Billy and Maggie, who sat behind him with sad faces, wearing their Sunday best. She started to cry.

"Why don't you leave them out of this?" she exclaimed. "It has nothing to do with them! You're the one who drove me away! You're a goddamn liar and a cheater!"

Everyone gasped. The twelve jurors had the same look of horror on their identical faces while her husband looked at her sympathetically for once and said, "But it has everything to do with them. They're the unfortunate victims of your little escapade. And now it appears you're helping your friends get away with murder. What's next? Is it true you'd take a life to save your own skin?"

"Of course not!" she exclaimed. "You people got me all wrong! I'm not like that! Just ask anyone. Ask my best friend." She pointed to Norma, who was sitting in the middle of the crowd and giving Katharine dirty looks like everyone else. "She'll tell you what kind of person I am," she said. "I'm actually very sweet." They all started to laugh again. "I am," she blurted out. "I'm sweetmeat." They laughed even harder. Leon joined in with his deep zombie laugh as well. "Why are you all laughing?" she shouted and put her hands over her ears. "Shut up and leave me alone!"

Finally, Big Joe burst through the double doors and ran up to the witness stand.

"Don't worry, I'll save you," he said to her, doing his best Dudley Do-Right impression.

He grabbed her and lifted her into his arms, swiftly carrying her out of the courtroom. After they exited through the doors, he carried her down the steps of a dimly lit basement where all of his mobster friends stood waiting for them. Louis Bartoli stood in the forefront, chomping on his cigar and holding a gun in his hand.

"Finish it, and you'll be one of us," he said to Katharine as Joe put her down in front of him.

He handed her the gun and quickly moved out of the way to expose her target—a human being tied to a chair with duct tape and wearing a potato sack over her head. Despite their attempt to conceal her identity, she knew exactly who it was. But it didn't stop her from raising the pistol and shooting her point-blank in the head.

"Welcome to the family," Louis said and gave Katharine a big hug while Joe patted her on the back. The fifty goons standing behind them cheered and raised their whiskey glasses.

Early the next morning, Katharine woke up to the sound of someone banging on the door upstairs. Bree was already leaning up against the headboard and listening very closely.

"Hello, you guys in there?" a man shouted in a deep voice. "Bree? Bro?"

"Don't worry. It's just Bubba." Bree smirked as Katharine crawled out from under the covers and sat up next to her.

"Come on, you two!" he continued shouting. "Get your butts out of bed and come answer this goddamn door!"

Then he banged on the door even louder to the point that it seemed like he was never going to leave. Finally the noise ceased, and they heard him walk away, cursing aloud.

"It would probably be better if you stayed up there from now on," Katharine said. "Don't you think? I mean, if you're not there to answer the door, people are going to get suspicious awful quick."

"You don't have to worry about Bubba," Bree replied. "I can handle *him*. But I see your point."

"Does Leon have other friends besides Bubba?" Katharine asked.

"Plenty," Bree said, suddenly looking very discouraged.

"What about family?" Katharine asked.

"Just his mother," Bree answered.

"Leon has a mother?" Katharine said just to lighten the mood a little.

Bree responded with a slight laugh. Then she let out a heavy sigh. "I'm screwed, aren't I?" she said. "You can't just murder someone and expect to get away with it. Think of all the work it's going to take to keep it covered up. I might as well quit now and go straight to the police."

"What?" Katharine gasped. "But we're in this thing together— you and me. If you go to the police now, we're both screwed."

"Oh, Kat, I'm sorry," Bree said as she turned and placed her hands on her shoulders. "I would never do that to you. I was just talking out of my ass. You did me a solid. Now I'm gonna do you one by remaining strong. And no more talk about going to the police. I promise." She jumped out of bed in her T-shirt and panties and grabbed her jeans that were on the floor. "I'm going back upstairs," she said as she started to put them on. "And if anyone comes over askin' for Leon, I'm just gonna tell them that I threw him out once and for all. Surely they'll believe *that*. Everyone knows we've been having problems."

Katharine nodded in agreement, but she wasn't quite convinced that Bree would hold up her end of the bargain.

"I really appreciate what you did for me," Bree said before she left the room. "I just hope that I haven't abused our friendship."

Katharine simply shook her head.

"You're the only true friend I ever had," Bree added, smiling at Katharine affectionately. "And I want you to know that if *you* ever have a problem, no matter how big or small, I've got your back."

"If there's someone I need help gettin' rid of, I'll definitely give you a call," Katharine joked.

Chapter 12: Continuing Nightmares and an Air of Distrust

Bubba came back in the middle of the afternoon and started banging on Bree's door again.

"Come on, Bree. Answer it," Katharine muttered to herself as she sat at the dinner table, eating a grapefruit and dabbling in the notebook.

Finally Bree opened the door and exclaimed, "What do you want?"

Katharine suddenly stood up and rushed to her own door; she opened it very slightly and put her ear to the crack.

"Where is he?" asked Bubba.

"Where's who?" said Bree.

"Your boyfriend!" he snapped.

After that, Katharine could only hear bits and pieces as they began to speak in lower tones. They argued with each other for a whole minute. Then he shouted, "Leon, you in there? Leon?" There was no response. "There's something going on here, Bree!" he exclaimed. "I don't know what! But I'll find out! Bubba is on the case!"

Katharine felt very uneasy as she heard him walk away, cursing aloud just like earlier that morning.

That evening, Bree had another unexpected visitor, and Katharine had her ear to the door again, trying to catch every word. This time it sounded like a young woman, but she had such a delicate voice that Katharine couldn't hear a single word that she said. In fact, all Katharine heard was Bree saying, "He ain't here, honey." And later, she said, "Keep it. You earned it."

When Katharine talked to her on the phone a few minutes later, she learned it had been one of Leon's prostitutes; she had come to give him his money because he hadn't been in his office all day.

More women came and went throughout the night, trying to give Leon his money, Katharine presumed. Then on the following day, an older woman came looking for him. Or at least she sounded much older. She had a sharp, gravelly voice and was so direct in her questioning that Katharine assumed that she was a woman of means and was use to having things done her way.

"Have you seen Leon? Is he here?" the woman said very loudly and distinctively as soon as Bree opened the door.

Thirty seconds into the conversation, her voice started to sound a little weak and shaky as if she was about to break down and cry.

"It's not like him, not answering my phone calls," she said. "I've never been so worried. Is it okay if I come in for a minute?"

"Sure," Katharine heard Bree say.

After she heard the door close, Katharine went back to her writing. Fifteen minutes later, she heard the woman step out again.

"If he comes back here, have him call me," the woman demanded before the door closed.

Katharine then heard her clicking all the way down the stairs, wearing high heels, no doubt. She jumped up from the couch, rushed over to the living room window, and watched her come out of the building and walk up to the white limousine that was parked at the curb. She wore a long white robe that appeared to be made of silk and had a light blue scarf wrapped over her head.

"Who does she think she is, Lawrence of Arabia?" Katharine laughed.

The driver opened the door for her, and Katharine caught a glimpse of her face as she turned to acknowledge him before she stepped in. Her skin was black, and she wore dark sunglasses. Suddenly the phone rang. Katharine rushed over to the kitchen counter to answer it.

"Did you catch any of that?" Bree said on the other end.

"Yeah," Katharine said. "Who is she?"

"*That* is Leon's mother," Bree answered very bluntly. "Otherwise known as the Wicked Witch of the East. Well, technically she's a voodoo priestess."

"No, she's not." Katharine laughed.

"Mmm hmm," Bree said. "She's even got the license to prove it."

"So that's Leon's mother," Katharine muttered and shook her head.

"He'd want you to think that he was raised on the streets like me," Bree said, "but to tell you the truth, he was a real mama's boy."

"And I take it she's loaded?" Katharine asked.

"Yep," Bree said. "But she never gave us a dime, and I doubt that I'm in her will. She doesn't care too much for me, you see. She always thought that he could do better."

They both laughed.

"She also didn't care for the idea of us livin' together and not being married," Bree continued. "Plus I haven't given her any grandchildren. I'm surprised she hasn't put a hex on me already."

"You don't really believe in that stuff, do you?" Katharine asked.

"What, voodoo?" Bree said. "It's real, believe me. She's had three ex-husbands, and they all died unexpectedly of some strange illness. There's no tellin' what she'll do to me if she even has the slightest notion that I did something to her baby."

"Don't worry about it, Bree," Katharine quickly butted in. "We'll get through this."

"She says she's going to hire a private detective," Bree said. "And she's already reported him missing to the police. So they'll be here soon enough." She laughed to herself. "Did I happen to mention that her and the police commissioner are old friends?" she said. "I bet she used one of her spells to get him that position."

"Leave it alone, Bree," Katharine urged her. "You're worrying too much."

"I'm not worried; I'm scared to death," Bree replied. "And this place is giving me the creeps. I don't know how much longer I can stay here. I can still feel his presence. Plus I've been having these weird dreams where he crawls into my bed and he's choking me to death. How 'bout you? Has he been in *your* dreams?"

"No," Katharine lied, afraid to upset Bree even more.

"That old man who died in your apartment, do you still hear him creepin' around at night?" Bree asked.

"That was all a joke," Katharine replied. "I thought you knew that."

"Well, *I'm* definitely hearing things," she said. "I really need to get out of this place."

"Just hang on," Katharine urged her. "Things will get better, I assure you."

"I think it might be better if I go away," she said.

"Don't you dare skip out on me, Bree," Katharine snapped. "Don't leave me here with all of this."

"I'd be doing you a favor." Bree laughed. "You'd be rid of me for good and you could put it all behind you."

"The police will definitely be looking for you once they realize that you've skipped town," Katharine pointed out to her. "We've got to stick together. That's your only chance."

"Then come with me," Bree said. "We'll go somewhere like Russia or China—places they won't even bother to look. Would you do that?"

"Sure, why not?" Katharine replied, only partially bluffing.

"Oh, what the hell am I saying?" Bree sighed. "I'm not going anywhere. I'm stuck here, afraid to stay but even more afraid to leave. Maybe I should just go ahead and turn myself in."

"You promised me that you wouldn't talk like that anymore," Katharine said.

"Sorry. I forgot," Bree replied.

"Do yourself a favor and stop worrying, will ya?" Katharine begged her for the last time. "I'll get us through this somehow. Just don't go crazy on me, and don't go to the police."

"I won't," she said. "You have my word."

Bree hung up. Katharine stood there wondering if she could really trust her not to do them both in. The only thing she knew for sure was that she'd have to keep both eyes on her from now on and be strong enough for the two of them.

That night when she finally got to sleep, she had another terrible nightmare.

Bree sat in an interrogation room, being bullied by two homicide detectives. Katharine stood close by but appeared to be invisible.

"We know you did it," said one of the detectives as he bent down over the table and got right in their suspect's face. "Just tell us where you hid the body."

Bree sat there with tears in her eyes and looking tired and miserable as if she had been there for hours.

"All right, all right! I'll tell you!" she exclaimed. "We buried him out in the woods!"

"No, we didn't," Katharine scoffed. "She doesn't know."

But no one could see or hear her.

"Show us," the detective snarled.

Suddenly they were all walking through the woods in the dead of night along with a dozen other policemen carrying flashlights and shovels. Bree led the way. She came to a sudden halt and pointed down at the ground just a few feet in front of her.

"There he is!" she exclaimed.

"She's lying!" Katharine shouted as she rushed over to that very spot and stood before the entire group.

She remained invisible to them, however, and they all came rushing toward her with their shovels.

"I'm tellin' you, he's not here," she said. "He's somewhere at the bottom of the ocean, wearing cement shoes!"

And just as she spoke, a large black hand shot up from the ground directly beneath her feet, grabbed onto her ankle, and pulled her down.

"No, no," she muttered in her sleep, while the earth continued to swallow her whole.

Next she heard Leon's mother chanting some strange incantation in her creepy, piercing voice.

"*Vini do nan lavi, mwen mouri gason,*" she said over and over again, followed by a gurgling sound at the foot of Katharine's bed.

Katharine immediately opened her eyes and sat up and was shocked to see Leon's body parts piled up on the floor along with his blood, which was starting to boil. Then all of a sudden, his head reattached itself to his torso, his arms found their way back to their shoulder sockets, and his hands crawled out of the heap to rejoin his wrists. With the upper half of him properly restored and brought back to life by the witch's spell, he crawled onto the bed and slowly crept toward Katharine. His hideous eyes bulged from their sockets.

"Hello, sweetmeat," he said to her in a faint voice. "You've been a very bad girl, and now you must be punished."

As he started to crawl up her legs, she let out a terrifying scream and woke up for real this time.

"Jesus, that was the worst one yet," she said to herself as she lay there in a cold sweat.

Though it was only 5 AM according to her alarm clock, she immediately hopped out of bed to avoid another nightmare. Around 9 AM she received a surprise visit from Bree. They had not seen each other for nearly two days.

"Hey, what's up?" Katharine said a bit awkwardly as Bree walked in and headed straight for the dining room table.

"Have you been working on your story lately?" she asked.

"Not really," Katharine replied. "I've been having trouble concentrating, if you know what I mean."

"Well, let's finish it," Bree said. "What do you say?"

"Oh to hell with the story, Bree," Katharine huffed.

"No. We have to finish it," she quickly butted in. "It's your only ticket out of here."

Then she sat down at the table, turned on the computer, and grabbed the wrinkled pages from the notebook. Katharine stood there and scowled as Bree began typing. She admired Bree's dedication. But she, herself, wasn't quite ready to get back to the "grind," as she now referred to it. She eventually sat down on the couch and listened to Bree type for about an hour before she finally decided to pick up the pen and write a fitting climax for her young heroine.

April 12

After the two lovers were finished dancing, Ljungberg declared, "I have a surprise for you." He went to the other end of the house to get it, allowing Kitty just enough time to sneak into the arsenal and steal a German Luger along with several cartridges. She was busy loading it when Ljungberg knocked on her bedroom door.

"Kitty, can I come in?" he asked.

"Yes," she answered, quickly stuffing the weapon underneath her pillow.

He slowly stepped in and sat down on the bed next to her.

"I'm so glad that you decided to stay," he said and started running his fingers through her hair. "And now I have just one last favor to ask you." He reached into the inner pocket of his white tuxedo and pulled out a tiny wooden box. He quickly opened it and showed her a large diamond ring, all shiny and new. "Will you be my wife?" he said.

"It's beautiful," she replied, her voice filled with awe. "But—"

"No buts," he interrupted her and placed his fingers over her lips. "Would you at least think about it?"

She grabbed his hand and slowly pulled it away to reveal an affectionate smile, deeply moved by his proposal.

"All right," she said. "I'll think about it."

"Good. You've got five minutes," he replied. They both laughed.

All of a sudden, they heard machine gun fire outside. Someone shouted, "Die, you Nazi bastards!" in a rough masculine voice. Oh no ... not Jones, Kitty thought to herself.

"What the hell's going on out there?" Ljungberg said as he sprang to his feet and rushed over to the window.

"No, Mikael ... don't!" Kitty exclaimed, genuinely concerned for his safety.

He didn't appear to be listening to her, however. As he was looking out the open window, a bullet shot through the glass, missing his head by less than an inch. He immediately dropped to the floor and crawled back over to the bed. He pulled Kitty down into his lap and threw himself over her as more stray bullets ripped through the window. He suddenly *rose to his feet again as they heard the intruder kick open the front door and make his way up the stairs.*

"Please, Mikael," she begged him and held onto his arm.

"I have to face him," he said. "If it's just me he wants—then so be it."

He jerked away from her and quickly left the room. She reached under the pillow and pulled out the Luger. She quickly got up and rushed after him.

"What is it you want?" Ljungberg asked Jonesy as he stood at the foot of the stairs.

Jones came to a sudden halt about midway up and aimed his machine gun at Ljungberg's chest. It was the German MG 42, Kitty observed, which he had apparently stolen from one of his victims. Jones held his fire while Kitty snuck up behind Ljungberg and raised her pistol to the back of his head. Yet she hesitated to pull the trigger.

"Shoot him," Jones snarled.

Ljungberg turned around to face her, which made it even more difficult for her. He looked so shocked and undeserving. That's when she realized she was head over heels in love with the man. All her other victims had had that same look, and it hadn't stopped her from killing them.

"Goddamn it, woman. Finish the job and let's get the hell out of here," Jones said.

"I can't," she muttered and slowly lowered the barrel.

"All right then," Jones said, putting his finger on the trigger.

But just as he was about to fire, she lifted her gun and shot him straight through the heart.

"What the hell was that?" were his dying words as he fell and started to roll down the steps.

She and Ljungberg stood perfectly still, both bewildered and wondering what had just happened. Then finally, Ljungberg walked up to her and took the gun out of her hand.

"My God, what have I done?" she muttered.

"You did what you had to," he said and put his arms around her.

"Done," Katharine muttered to herself, breathing a sigh of relief and putting the pen down on the coffee table.

Bree remained glued to the computer screen the whole time, appearing determined to finish as well. She finally stopped typing when Katharine handed her the final pages from the notebook.

"I think I'll read them, first," Bree said, looking very excited. "I want to see how this thing ends."

Katharine noticed a huge smile on her face as she began reading. But it gradually disappeared. When she finally got to the last page, she simply looked at Katharine and shook her head.

"Well, you had to do it, didn't you?" she said. "You killed the black man. And all he was trying to do was save her sorry ass. Somehow it don't seem right—choosing the Nazi sympathizer over *him.*"

"That's love for ya," said Katharine, "often very cruel and unjust. But you should know that more than anyone."

"So, *I* inspired you to write this ridiculous ending?" Bree snapped.

"I don't know," Katharine said bitterly and walked away from the table.

"Of course I did," Bree muttered. "What the hell do *you* know about love?"

"What's that?" Katharine shouted from across the room.

"You heard me," said Bree. "Correct me if I'm wrong, but in most spy novels, doesn't the hero usually complete his mission in the end? That's what keeps the readers coming back for more, isn't it?"

"This ain't your typical spy novel," Katharine argued. "I want to do more than just entertain people. I want to blow their minds ... give them something to think about. In fact, I think I'm through with murder mysteries and spy novels altogether. I want to write something more meaningful from now on, something closer to real life."

"Oh, that's a bunch of crap, and you know it," Bree said. "You wrote that ending out of spite."

Katharine just laughed and shook her head.

"I understand," Bree said. "You're still a little shook up over the other night. So am I. Plus you're angry and upset, and you're taking it all out on the story."

"It's *my* story," Katharine reminded her. "And I happen to like the ending. I felt it needed a little twist. If you don't like it, write your own damn novel."

"Maybe I will," Bree said.

Katharine flopped down on the edge of the couch and buried her face in her hands, feeling exhausted.

"I don't want to do this anymore," she sighed. "Maybe you should just go."

"So you're mad at me," said Bree.

"No, I'm not," Katharine said. "I just need a little more time by myself."

"All right," Bree said very sternly. She quickly rose from the chair and headed toward the door.

Before she stepped out, she turned around and said, "Please don't shut me out, Katharine. I need you. And we have to stick together, just like you said."

"I know," Katharine replied. "Don't worry about it. Everything's fine. I just need a little time, that's all."

Chapter 13: Enter the Cops

Mrs. Tidwell and the police arrived at precisely 7 AM the next morning and started banging on people's doors, beginning with Bree. Katharine waited for forty minutes before they finally got to her, which gave her plenty of time to get her story straight. She quickly answered the door and was surprised to see a handsome young man standing before her in plain clothes—blue jeans, a white turtleneck, and a tan sports jacket. He looked like Steve McQueen in *Bullitt*, especially with his short-cropped blonde hair and deep blue eyes.

"Mrs. Beaumont … I'm Lieutenant Jacobs, head of the NYPD Missing Persons Squad," he said and showed her his badge. "May I come in?"

"Sure," she said.

He turned to the two uniformed policemen standing behind him and said, "I've got this one," before he stepped inside. He headed straight for the living room and began looking around.

"What's this about, Lieutenant?" she asked him.

"I understand you're friends with Bree Withers, who lives directly above you," he said.

"Yes, I am," she swiftly replied.

"And what about the boyfriend, Leon Tidwell? Are you friends with him as well?" he inquired.

"No, he frightens me," she said to him flat out.

"All the other tenants that I've talked to say he's a hard man"—he nodded—"and that the two are constantly fighting. Yet you're the only one who faced him and tried to put an end to it."

"What should I have done? Just sit here and do nothing?" she asked.

"Of course not," he said. "What you did was highly commendable. You're a very brave woman, Mrs. Beaumont." He wandered into the dining room and noticed the computer on the table. "Where were you on August the tenth at two o'clock in the morning?" he asked. "That was on a Tuesday, I believe."

"I'm pretty sure I was here," she answered. "Where else would I be?"

"Did you happen to notice two swarthy-looking men walking down the stairs, both wearing leather jackets and carrying four large suitcases?" he asked.

"No," she answered.

"One was a very large man in his late thirties or early forties," he said. "And the other one was much younger—tall and slender."

"I didn't see them."

"Well, your neighbor, Mrs. Chang, did," he said. "She said they came out of room four-eleven. Then she saw you and Bree coming downstairs about ten minutes later and enter your apartment."

"Bree was really upset because she hadn't heard from Leon in days, and she needed a shoulder to cry on," Katharine explained to him. "There was no one else in her apartment that night. How could Mrs. Chang know for sure that those two men came out of her place?"

"I guess she just assumed that they did," he said. "Everyone I've talked to says that there's always something goin' on in there during the wee hours."

"What is it you're trying to prove here exactly?" she asked.

"I'm just trying to get all the facts," he replied. "Do you think Bree had something to do with her boyfriend's disappearance?"

"You mean, did she kill him?" she said very sharply. "Of course not. She loves him, even after he beats the crap out of her."

"Then what do you suppose happened to him?" he asked.

"I don't know," she replied. "Maybe a drug deal went sour ... or another pimp shot him."

"You're probably right," he smiled while thumbing through the stack of printed pages next to the computer, the sum total of Bree's handiwork. "So what's this?"

"That's my novel," she answered.

"Oh, you're a writer?" he said. "Have you been published?"

"Not yet," she replied. "That's why I'm here."

"Yeah, I heard that you haven't been here all that long." He smiled. "How are you likin' it so far?"

"I'm having the time of my life," she replied. "I feel like I was born for this place."

"You probably wouldn't know it by lookin' at me, but I like to read novels in my spare time," he said.

"What, crime fiction?" she asked. "I bet you read a lot of James Ellroy and Joseph Wambaugh."

"Nope. I get enough of that shit at work," he said. "I like sci-fi. I grew up reading Robert Heinlein, Philip K. Dick—guys like that. But now I'll read just about anything if it's got a good story to it." He picked up the hundred or so pages and weighed them in his hands. "What's this one about, if you don't mind me asking?"

"It has to do with British spies and Nazi Germany," she answered.

"Ah, there you go," he said excitedly. "I've read all the James Bond novels as well." He put the manuscript back down on the table and got it all neat and square. "I'd like to read it when it's published," he said.

"I'll be sure to send you a copy," she replied.

"Signed, I hope." He smiled. He started to head for the front door. "Well, it was a pleasure," he said as he stood in front of it. "I've never met a real writer before."

"I've never met a real detective before," she retorted.

"So long, Katharine," he said and shook her hand. "It *is* Katharine, right?"

"Yes," she answered. "What's yours?"

"Delbert," he sighed. "But just call me Del."

"Delbert—that's an odd name for a tough, New York policeman," she playfully remarked.

"Well, you've got to be tough with a name like that," he said, "especially growing up in these parts."

He opened the door and quickly stepped outside. She stepped out with him and looked down the hallway. The two policemen waited for him by the stairwell, along with Mrs. Tidwell and three other plainclothes detectives. Suddenly the old woman rushed toward him, dressed in one of her long silk garbs and wearing a purple scarf over her head.

"What did she say?" she asked him in her harsh, gravelly voice.

Seeing her up close for the first time, Katharine thought that she looked like a panther with her slick dark skin and bright green eyes.

"She doesn't know anything, Mrs. Tidwell," said Lieutenant Jacobs, trying to stop her.

"She's lying. They both are," the woman snarled and started pushing and clawing to get to Katharine. "Where's my boy? What did you do to him?"

The men in blue rushed down the hallway and came to the lieutenant's rescue, forcefully grabbing hold of the woman and pushing her back while Katharine stood very still and looked at her with fearful eyes.

"I'll get you for this," the woman snarled. "You and your little friend, too."

After they got her down the stairwell and out of the building, Katharine rushed upstairs and knocked on Bree's door. There was no answer. She turned the knob and saw that it was unlocked. She opened it and let herself in. Though it was dark, she noticed Bree sitting over in the corner of the room.

"Are you all right, Bree?" she asked her.

"Don't worry. I didn't tell them anything," Bree numbly replied.

"I wasn't worried about that," Katharine said.

"Well, she did it," Bree said. "The old hag put a spell on me."

"No, she didn't."

"Yes, she did," she said. "After they were through asking me questions, she placed her hand on my forehead, looked right through me with those hideous eyes of hers, and chanted some old African curse before I managed to push her away."

"It isn't real," Katharine said.

"Is too," Bree insisted.

"No it isn't," she snapped. "She can't hurt you unless you let her get inside your head. If you sit around all day, thinking that you're gonna get sick and die, chances are it's gonna happen."

"You're so naïve," Bree said. "If only I was more like you."

"I think you've been spending too much time in here by yourself," Katharine said, concerned. "We should get out of here. Maybe spend the day in the park or go see the Statue of Liberty."

"I've seen the Statue of Liberty." Bree smirked.

"We'll go see a movie then," Katharine said. "Something light and funny for a change."

"To hell with that," she replied. "I want Leon."

"Leon's dead," Katharine reminded her. "You killed him."

"He might be dead, but he hasn't left this place," she said in a creepy, deadpan voice. "I'm gonna stay here with *him*."

It was so creepy, in fact, that Katharine started to back off very slowly. Then she turned around and quickly headed out the door. She received a call from Bree about four hours later.

"Katharine?" Bree said as soon as Katharine picked up the phone. "The private investigator was just here—a very peculiar-looking little man."

"You mean he was a midget?" Katharine asked.

"No, but close," she said. "He couldn't be more than five feet tall. He was bug-eyed and talked in a whispery voice like he was Clint Eastwood or something. Plus I think he might have been bald. I couldn't tell because of that stupid hat that he was wearing."

Katharine laughed.

"He knows what we did," she said very grimly.

"No he doesn't," Katharine said. "No one will ever know unless they discover the body or one of us ... You didn't ..."

"No, of course not," she said. "I was about to, though ... after the way he kept hounding me with questions. He's like a little pit bull; he goes straight for the jugular and doesn't let up. Plus he's really smart. He knows I did it. He knows how I did it. And he knows that we tried to cover it all up and disposed of the body. He just wants to know what we did with him."

"At least that's the one thing we can't tell him," Katharine said. "We have no idea where he's at."

"Just the same, if he comes to your door, don't let him in," she said vehemently. "'Cause once he's inside, he won't ever leave until he gets what he wants. I practically had to throw him out on his ear."

"You don't have to worry about me," Katharine assured her. "I'm not gonna tell him a damn thing."

"Promise me you won't let him in, Katharine," she insisted. "Don't give the bitch the satisfaction. She has a lot of nerve sending him here to snoop around."

"I promise, Bree," Katharine said just to put her at ease.

It was 8:00 PM when he finally came knocking. Even the way he did that seemed a bit odd to Katharine—four gentle taps, a slight pause, and then another four taps over and over again, as if he was playing some sick game. She tiptoed up to the door and looked at him through the peephole. He was so short that she could barely see his face, and he appeared to be whistling some little tune. She couldn't tell for sure, but it sounded like the love theme from *The Phantom of the Opera*. She put her hand on the knob and considered opening the door; she wasn't the least bit afraid of him. But she had promised Bree that she wouldn't. So she just stood there and looked at him 'til he finally gave up and walked off.

He returned the next morning around 9:00 AM and tried again—four gentle taps, a slight pause, and then another four taps. She slowly walked up to the door and stared at him through the peephole again. This time she wasn't about to let him in since she was trying to get ready for work and was only half dressed in her slip and pantyhose. But he was very persistent. After knocking about thirty times, he stepped up to the door, stood on his tiptoes and stuck his eyeball over the peephole. She immediately jumped back, half-startled.

"I know you're in there," he said in a low, scary voice.

Then she heard him laughing to himself.

"Go away, you freak," she muttered under her breath.

He finally *did* go away about a minute later, whistling another show tune.

Things slowed down quite a bit at Cardenelli's after the noon rush. Sal stood behind the bar with Katharine, keeping her company while the stools were empty. He told her all about the church singles group he had attended the night before. Meanwhile, Manny was breaking in the new girl he had just hired—a beautiful young blonde. Annabella and Suling were busy clearing tables because the restaurant was short a couple of busboys. Suddenly Joe walked in and grabbed a seat at the bar.

"What's up?" Katharine said as she walked up to him.

"We need to talk," he said. "Is there someplace private?"

Minutes later they stood out back by the dumpsters and a large stack of empty pallets, all of which were enclosed by a stockade fence. Both dumpsters were filled with rotting food, and the smell of it was almost unbearable.

"We might have a problem," Joe said. "There was a private investigator snoopin' around the club last night—an odd little, fat man who talks like Clint Eastwood and whistles show tunes. You know anything about him?"

"Yeah. Leon's mother hired him," Katharine replied.

"Well, he knows about you and me." He sighed.

"How could he?" She gasped.

"I don't know," he said, "unless he's been talkin' to those two freaks that you work with."

"You mean Annabella and Suling?"

"They must have told him about that night at the after party."

"Okay, so he knows about us," she said. "Do you really think it'll hurt us?"

"Did anybody see us going in or coming out of Bree's apartment the other night?" he asked.

"No," she said. "But Mrs. Chang who lives three doors down from me saw you and Federico going down the stairs."

"Well, that's it then." He sighed. "If Mrs. Chang recognizes me and my partner's face in a lineup or from our mug shots, they're gonna think that the mob had something to do with Leon's disappearance. And they're gonna turn up the heat on us … me and Federico in particular. You don't have to worry about me. I can take it. But Federico? I don't know. He's young, and he's been showin' signs of weakness lately. I might have to whack him." After a brief pause, he added, "Of course all of that could be avoided if we were to get Mrs. Chang out of the picture."

Katharine thought about it for a second and then shook her head.

"Uh-uh, no way," she said with a sudden look of disgust. "Helping a friend cover up a murder is as far as I go. I'm not going to have someone killed just to save my own skin."

"Who said it has to be murder?" he asked. "We could simply have her relocated to Ecuador … or Finland maybe."

She shook her head again and said, "Forget it. My criminal days are over."

"Well, I think we'll be all right"—he sighed—"as long as nobody talks. How's Bree doing?"

"Bree's fine," she swiftly replied.

"You think she can be trusted not to say anything?" he asked, his voice filled with concern. "In my line of business, the guy you have to worry about the most is the one who pulled the trigger. It eats at your conscience 'til all you want to do is come clean."

"I said she's fine," Katharine muttered, becoming agitated.

"And it doesn't necessarily have to be a cop that they confess to," he continued. "It could be a close friend or a priest. Is she Catholic? Does she have any other friends besides you?"

"No. Would you stop worrying about her?" she snapped. "Bree's tougher than all of us."

"All right. If you say so," he said.

The stench from the dumpsters got so bad that they finally had to step outside the gate and stand in the parking lot. As they hugged each other and said their goodbyes, they heard the sound of someone whistling nearby.

"What's that?" Joe said, appearing alarmed.

"It sounds like the closing number from *A Chorus Line*," Katharine said.

They stepped away from each other and started looking around, at which point a little man rushed right past them, smiling and waving. He stood about five feet tall, had a shiny bald head, and wore a long gray trench coat. Katharine also noticed a camera in his left hand.

"What nerve," she said, filled with disgust.

"I'm gonna kill the little fucker!" Joe exclaimed furiously and took off after him.

"No, Joey. Don't," Katharine said a second too late.

She suddenly felt like she was in an old *Laurel and Hardy* movie as she watched the big man chase the little one through the parking lot, one in a leather jacket and the other one in a trench coat that went all the way down to his feet. Joe was unable to catch up with the little man, and the latter quickly vanished into a sea of empty cars. Joe looked all around for him. Then he looked at Katharine and shrugged his shoulders.

"Just forget it!" she shouted and motioned him to come back.

All of a sudden she heard an engine starting up and a shiny red Porsche peeled out of its parking space just a few spaces behind Joe.

"Look out!" she shouted just as the vehicle shot right past him, grazing his belly and barely missing his toes.

"Hey!" Joe furiously exclaimed and flipped off the driver as he swiftly sped away.

Once he was well out of reach, the driver slammed on the breaks and poked his head out the window. It was the little baldheaded man. He looked back at Joe and cackled like a vicious fiend. Then he took off again as Joe reached into his jacket and pulled out his gun.

"Joey, let him go!" Katharine yelled at him fearfully as he took aim.

He looked at her, lowered his weapon, and immediately put it away.

"Sorry. Lost my head for a second," he said, walking back to her. "I doubt that's the last we'll see of him."

Katharine had to close the restaurant that night, so she didn't get home until very late. She quickly stepped inside the apartment, shut and locked the door, and turned on the lights.

"*Ah!*" she shrieked as she noticed the little private detective sitting in the wooden rocking chair by the window.

His chubby little face and big dark eyes reminded Katharine of Peter Lorre. This time he was wearing a brown fedora along with his gray overcoat; it was almost as if he was living in his own film noir.

"How did you get in here?" she snapped as she tossed her purse on the couch and swiftly walked up to him.

"I have my ways," he said in a sly, whispery voice. "Did you think a bolted door would keep us apart? The name's Krendel, by the way."

"Breaking and entering is a serious offense," she sneered. "What if I was to call the police?"

"That's what I was about to ask you," he said and pointed at the sealed envelope in his lap. "I'm sure you already know what's inside."

She shook her head.

"Don't play dumb with me, Mrs. Beaumont," he said. "You know very well what I was doing out in that parking lot. It's pictures of you gettin' all chummy with that ruthless thug that you call your boyfriend."

"He's not my boyfriend," she said nervously.

"Pictures don't lie." He grinned. "Or maybe they do ... but that won't help you much. Don't worry. I have no intention of going to the police. I hate working with them. And I'd rather solve this one on my own."

"What do you want from me?" she asked.

"First I want you to admit that Bree Withers killed Leon Tidwell," he said. "Not that I have any doubts. It's just that it would be so refreshing to hear the truth for once." He sat back in the chair and starting to rock back and forth, seeming very full of himself. "Then I want to know what you and your friends did with his body."

Not knowing what to say or do, she simply froze.

"My client doesn't want to see you go to jail, Mrs. Beaumont," he said. "You were just helping your friend dig a deeper hole for herself. All she wants is to find her son, either dead or alive, and for justice to be served."

As he spoke, she noticed one of her black spiders slowly descending from the ceiling on its web. *Get the son of a bitch,* she encouraged it, thinking that it was about to land on his head. But it continued on its descent just inches away from his face instead. He kept looking at her and talking, appearing not to notice.

"You can't save Bree Withers," he said to her very sternly. "But you *can* save yourself."

He suddenly snatched the spider off its web with lightning-swift Ninja reflexes and crushed it in his hand, keeping his eyes on her the whole time.

"I've noticed that you have a bug infestation, Mrs. Beaumont," he said as he shook the spider's remains off his hand and onto the floor.

"I most certainly do," she snarled and kicked the chair over as he rocked backward.

He fell straight to the floor, snatched up his hat and the envelope, and quickly scrambled away on all fours, yelping like a whipped dog. Katharine stayed on his tail and kept kicking him all the way to the door.

"You're lucky I don't take my gun out and shoot you," she said even though she didn't actually possess one.

As she reached the couch, she removed a can of Mace from her purse and sprayed him with it. He finally managed to get to his feet and quickly unlocked and opened the door.

"You're making a big mistake. You'll live to regret it," he sniveled, blinking fiercely from the Mace. Then he hurried out of her apartment.

Chapter 14: An Unthinkable Solution

Katharine went to check up on Bree a couple of days later, but Bree wouldn't answer the door. Afraid that she might have done something drastic, Katharine got Mr. Brown to unlock it for her. They both walked in and found her in bed with the sheets over her. She appeared to be unconscious.

"Bree?" Katharine exclaimed and rushed into the bedroom while Mr. Brown stood in the doorway.

Katharine grabbed her arm and shook her until she finally woke up.

"What's going on?" Bree said in a faint voice.

"I was worried about you," Katharine replied. "You didn't answer the door."

"I'm just feelin' a little out of it this morning," she said, yawning and rubbing her eyes.

"It's three o'clock in the afternoon," Katharine informed her.

"Is she gonna be all right?" Mr. Brown asked.

"Yeah, she's fine," Katharine said. "Thanks, Mr. Brown."

"Glad I could help." He smiled. Then he turned and headed for the front door, rattling his keys. "You girls have a nice day!" he shouted as he walked out.

"Oh shit, not again," Bree groaned, suddenly leaning over the side of the bed and throwing up into a large metal pan that was on the floor.

"Have you been doing that a lot?" Katharine asked with concern.

"Since yesterday," she replied and started coughing up mucus. "Plus I've got this nasty cough."

"You should probably go to the doctor," Katharine said.

"No, no doctors," she groaned.

"All right. I'm going downstairs to make you some chicken soup," Katharine said and started to walk out.

"Please, don't bother," Bree said.

"It's no bother," Katharine replied. "You've got to eat something, Bree, and drink plenty of liquids."

She returned about fifteen minutes later with a hot bowl of Lipton's soup and a glass of ice water, sat Bree up in the bed, and began to feed her.

"Did you finish the manuscript and send it in to your agent?" Bree asked as she took the bowl and spoon away from Katharine and started feeding herself.

"Yep," she answered.

"Did you change the ending?"

"Nope," she said. "That wasn't how it ended though. That was just the climax."

"So how does it end?" Bree asked.

"They got married there on the island," she said. "Then she gets pregnant and has triplet boys, all of them blond and blue-eyed like their father."

"So you fucked her over." Bree laughed. "You took this cool, amazingly independent woman and turned her into a dull everyday housewife like you used to be. That's funny."

Katharine laughed and imagined her main character being twenty pounds heavier and looking totally exhausted, her children screaming in her ear and throwing baby food at her from their highchairs. In a moment of sheer anguish and desperation, the character looked at her creator and said, "Why?"

"So do they all end up becoming Nazis?" Bree asked.

"No," Katharine said. "She's able to talk her husband out of doing that whole Hitler thing."

"How in the hell does she do that?" Bree asked.

"She uses her womanly wiles on him like she always does," Katharine said. "He's sittin' there at his desk, writing the man a check for fifty million dollars, and she walks up behind him, puts her arms around him, and says, 'If you really love me, you won't do this.' Of course, he argues that it's just business and that this Hitler fellow promises so much in return. So she has him read *Mein Kampf*, which she borrows from one of the guards. And halfway through it, he begins to realize what a crazy asshole this Nazi dictator really is and breaks all ties with him." She drew a heavy sigh. "Unfortunately, there are plenty of other wealthy businessmen out there who believe in the cause and are ready to take his place, which leads us into World War II and the extermination of six million Jews. She *does* manage to save her husband from making the worst mistake of his life, however. Mission accomplished."

"And they all lived happily ever after," Bree scoffed. "Except for Jones, of course."

"He gets *his* reward in heaven." Katharine smiled.

Bree suddenly leaned over the side of the bed and threw up again.

"You really need to go to the doctor," Katharine said.

"I done told you, no doctors," she grumbled. "Can't afford it."

"What about the hundred thousand you said Leon had stashed away somewhere?" Katharine asked her.

"I couldn't find it." She sighed. "Maybe he has it hidden in his office. I'll have to go down there and look when I'm feelin' better."

"Do you have any money at all?" Katharine asked.

"Just the three hundred dollars I took from his wallet," she replied. "When that's gone, my ass is gonna have to go back to work."

"I could probably get you on at the restaurant," Katharine said. "They're always needing help."

"Shit, I ain't no waitress." She laughed. "I meant going back to sellin' crack."

"Bree, no." Katharine gasped. "I wish I would hurry up and get published so I can get you out of here and away from all of this crap.

We'll move somewhere upstate where there ain't so many people ... or Florida, perhaps."

"Florida," Bree muttered to herself and grinned excitedly. Then she let out a painful moan and sunk down into the sheets. "Who are you kiddin'?" she said. "I'm not going anywhere. I'm cursed."

"No, you're not," Katharine said with fierce determination. "I'm gonna get you well. I promise."

Since it was her day off, Katharine stayed and cleaned Bree's kitchen, changed her sheets, and laid out some clean clothes for her to put on when she felt up to it. Then she fixed her lunch. She left soon after but returned around suppertime with another bowl of soup. She fed Bree breakfast the next morning before she went to work. And when she came back in the evening with her dinner, she was surprised to see that Bree had guests—six people in all, most of them African American. They were all sitting on the bed around Bree, who was sitting up against the headboard with a crack pipe in her mouth and a plate of rock in her lap. Her dealer, the young man with the red hair and goatee, sat next to her, twirling the cigarette lighter in his fingers.

"Get out!" Katharine shouted in a sudden fit of rage.

They all just turned and looked at her, appearing wasted.

"Get out," she shouted even more furiously, "or I'll call the cops!"

They all jumped up and quickly headed out the door; Bree just sat there and looked at Katharine, completely stunned.

"What was that all about?" she asked her after everyone had left.

"You're sick, Bree," Katharine snapped, snatching the plate and the pipe from her lap. "You shouldn't be doing this crap."

"Look, I appreciate everything you're doing for me," Bree said very sternly. "But it's my life, and I'll live it how I damn well please."

"Fine," Katharine said and tried to hand the plate back to her.

Bree immediately shoved it away.

"You didn't say anything to them, did you?" Katharine asked her.

"Oh, now I see." Bree smiled. "No, Katharine. I didn't. How stupid do you think I am?"

"I don't think you're stupid," Katharine said. "It's just that when you're high, things tend to leak out."

"I'd have to be pretty damn high to incriminate myself in front of Leon's friends," she sternly replied.

"All right, whatever." Katharine sighed. She put the plate down on the nightstand and grabbed the bowl of soup. "Here, eat your soup," she said, sticking it in her face.

Bree just gave her a dirty look, so Katharine picked up the spoon and started force-feeding her.

"You expect me to stop talking to people altogether?" Bree asked. "I can't even have friends over anymore?"

"You can do whatever you want, Bree," Katharine said. "Now open your mouth."

She continued taking care of Bree throughout the week, but her symptoms seemed to get worse—frequent chills, nausea, more vomiting, and a persistent cough. One morning she was shivering and sweating profusely when Katharine stepped into the room.

"We need to get you to a hospital," Katharine whispered in her ear.

"Forget it. I'm not doing it," Bree sternly replied. "They'll end up stickin' me with a huge bill. I'll never be able to pay it off."

"What else can we do?" Katharine asked, looking totally confounded. "The chicken soup doesn't seem to be working."

"I think I'm startin' to go through withdrawals," she groaned. "I need a hit."

"No," Katharine said.

"If I don't get my fix soon, I'm gonna be climbin' the walls and pullin' my hair out," Bree warned her.

"Oh, all right." Katharine sighed. "Where is it?"

"There's nothin' in the house," she said. "I did it all." Then Bree just looked at her.

"No way," Katharine said, shaking her head. "I'm not going after your drugs for you."

Bree continued to look at her.

"I'm not doin' it," Katharine said, resolute in the matter.

"Then give me the phone," Bree huffed. "I'll see if I can get him to come over."

Katharine grabbed the cell phone that was on top of the dresser and handed it to her.

"He might not want to do it since you threw him out and threatened to call the cops on him," Bree said as she punched in the number and put the phone to her ear.

They both looked at each other while she waited for a response.

"He's not answering," she said and continued waiting. Finally she gave up.

"Well, I guess that's that," Katharine said, shrugging her shoulders.

"Please, Kat," Bree begged her. "It won't be so hard. Just go down to the beer joint that he owns, apologize to the man, and tell him I'm in really bad shape and that I need my fix."

"What if I get arrested?" Katharine asked.

"That's not going to happen," she assured her. "This guy's really careful. He knows his business."

"I can't," Katharine said.

"Fuck it. I'll do it myself," she huffed and started to get out of the bed.

"No, Bree!" Katharine exclaimed and rushed over to stop her. "Have you lost your mind?"

"I need my fix," she groaned.

"Okay, where's the place at?" Katharine sighed.

"Thanks, Katharine." She smiled. "It's called Donovan's, and it's on the Lower East Side. The taxi driver will know where it's at. When you get there ask for Murphy—that's his name. Take a hundred dollars out of my purse. That should cover everything, including cab fare."

The cabbie dropped Katharine off in front of the pub, and she boldly walked in. There was a scary-looking bald man tending bar and a heavyset man sitting at the end of it. Another heavyset man was putting quarters into the jukebox in the corner of the room. She walked straight up to the bartender and asked for Murphy.

"Murph!" he shouted toward the back of the room.

All of a sudden the young redheaded man walked out of the hallway, looking very buff in his Gold's Gym T-shirt. He gave Katharine a quick glance and then motioned her to come back. She quickly headed in that direction and followed him all the way to his office at the end of the hall. She walked in. He immediately shut the door.

"I'm sorry about the other day," she said to him as he stood over her and gave her a dirty look. "Bree's really sick. I didn't think she should be partying. But I guess I might have overreacted. Again, I'm sorry."

He continued to glare at her.

"Look, you have every reason to hate me," she said. "But don't take it out on Bree. She's in really bad shape, and she needs her fix. Oh, and she wanted me to give you this."

She pulled ninety-two dollars out of her purse and handed it to him. He counted it and then walked over to the desk. He put the money into the desk drawer and took out a large bag of rock. He walked back up to her with the same scornful look, unzipped her purse, and dropped the bag into it. Her hands trembled as he zipped it back up.

"Don't be nervous," he said with a slight laugh. "The cops would never suspect a nice-lookin' gal like you."

"Now, ain't you a doll." She smiled as she reached up and patted him on the cheek.

She turned to walk out, and he went to open the door for her.

"Tell Bree there's more where that came from," he said as she started to walk down the hall. "Oh, and watch out for the guy at the end of the bar. We think he's Five-O."

She stopped for a split second before she realized he was probably fucking with her. She held her chin up, put on a bold face, and continued walking. She kept looking straight ahead and passed both customers very swiftly, quickly heading for the exit and walking several blocks away from the joint before she finally hailed a cab.

She was still shaking when she walked back into Bree's bedroom and handed her the bag.

"I really appreciate this," said Bree as she frantically tried to open it. "Get me a plate, will you?"

Katharine stepped out and came back with the plate. "This is the last time," she said as she handed it to her. "I'm not doing it again for you."

"Sure, whatever you say," Bree replied. "The crack pipe and the lighter's in the top drawer where I left it last."

Katharine fetched the two items while Bree leaned over the nightstand and crushed the rock up on the plate using the end of her brush. After she took a couple of hits, she lay back against the headboard with a huge smile on her face and closed her eyes. Katharine felt relieved that she was feeling better, no matter what the cure. She slowly turned and started to walk out of the room.

"Don't go," said Bree. "Why don't you crawl in here and get high with me?"

"No thanks." Katharine laughed, remembering how crazy she had gotten the last time she did drugs.

"Please?" Bree begged her. "I hate getting fucked up by myself."

"Okay, but I'm just gonna do it once," Katharine said, having no objection to feeling good. Plus she thought, *Why not? At this point, I've done just about everything else to liberate myself from the old Katharine.*

She crawled in from the other side of the bed. Bree filled the pipe with the crumbled up pieces of rock and handed it to her. She had Katharine put it in her mouth and lit it for her.

"Inhale. Keep inhaling, keep inhaling," Bree said, guiding Katharine through it. "Now let it out."

Katharine took the pipe out of her mouth and released a stream of gray smoke. Then she lay her head back and smiled, feeling a very intense euphoria.

"As good as the X?" Bree asked.

"Oh yeah." She smiled.

"Now you're a crackhead." Bree laughed.

"I'm not that weak," she said. "Set me up another one, will ya?"

The next morning she went back to Donovan's Pub to get more of the stuff. Murphy even offered her a job as one of his drug mules while she was there. She told him she would think about it. Later on in the day, she received an unexpected phone call from Lieutenant Jacobs from the NYPD Missing Persons Squad.

"Mrs. Beaumont," he began, "I was wondering if we could get together tomorrow for lunch? I have a few questions I need to ask you, and I'd rather not discuss it over the phone."

She suddenly grew very nervous. "I'm not in trouble, am I?" she joked.

"There's just something I need to clear up," he said. "Don't worry. It won't take long."

"Sure," she replied even though she was strongly opposed to the whole idea.

"Great," he said. "There's this place right next to you called the All Night Diner. They make an awesome cheeseburger."

"Sounds good," she muttered with a nervous laugh.

"So meet you there at twelve?" he asked.

"All right," she said and continued listening as he hung up the phone.

She told Bree about it, and she also became extremely worried.

"Don't go," she begged Katharine.

"I have to," Katharine said. "I don't know, maybe I can use my charm and good looks to get us out of this mess." She laughed to herself. "I'll give it my best shot anyway."

She met Lieutenant Jacobs inside the diner; they sat across from each other in a booth and waited for their cheeseburgers.

"Do you know this man?" Jacobs asked, pulling something out of the inside pocket of his sports jacket and sliding it across the table.

It was Joe's mug shot, Katharine observed, only he looked mean and even a little scary. *Krendel must have showed him the pictures of us,* she thought to herself, trying not to panic.

"Yeah," she answered truthfully. "That's my friend Joey."

"Joey?" he said with a surprised look on his face.

"Well, most people refer to him as Big Joe," she replied. "But I like Joey."

"So you admit to being friends with Joseph Milano." He nodded. "Do you know what they call him in Long Island where he grew up?"

She shook her head.

"Joe the Butcher or Two-Faced Joe," he said, "meaning he's Dr. Jekyll and Mr. Hyde. The man's a psycho, Katharine. May I call you Katharine?"

"Yes," she answered nervously.

"He's killed over fifty people in his lifetime," he said. "None of it can be proved, of course. And we're pretty sure he's responsible for the Lo Bianco killings just a few weeks ago. He murdered an entire family in that one. You're just lucky that you kept on his good side."

"The Joe I know is a very kind and gentle man," she replied.

"But you're aware that he's in the Mafia," he said.

"Yes," she replied. "And he works for Louis Bartoli."

"Another psycho," he nodded. "We've been trying to nail both of those guys for years."

He looked at her long and hard and then laughed.

"What?" she said.

"You're really something else," he remarked. "You've been here for what, two or three months? And already you're making friends with the most notorious gangsters in the city. How did you two meet anyway?"

"At the club where he works," she answered.

"I see," he nodded. "And what were you both doing at Bree's apartment on August the tenth?"

She suddenly felt embarrassed, having lied to him before about that night and with him knowing that she had.

"We were playing poker," she swiftly answered him with another lie.

"You were playing poker," he muttered to himself, looking very puzzled.

"Yes, seven-card stud, I believe," she answered. "I won the first hand and then Bree won the second one with a pair of aces. I remember Leon got terribly drunk that night, and he started slapping her around. Then he took out his gun and threatened to shoot everybody with it. Joe finally had to kick him out."

"So he was looking for trouble when he left," Jacobs said. "And I reckon he found it." He looked at her long and hard again and said, "You know, the more I learn about the man, the less I'm interested in the whole damn case. Here he was, sellin' drugs to minors, runnin' an illegal prostitution ring, and beatin' up on women in his spare time. If you ask me, the world's better off without him. Seems like the only person who's really missing him is his mother, and what a nut job she turned out to be."

They both laughed.

"I think I'll put this case on the back burner for now," he said. "Unless we find something … like his mutilated body in a dark alley, perhaps. I've got over twelve missing children cases goin' on right now. I should be focusing on that. Usually they end badly or go unsolved for decades."

"How horrible." She winced. "It must be a real nightmare."

"Well, sometimes we get lucky," he said. "And seeing that look on the parents' faces when we return their child to them unharmed makes it all worthwhile."

She gazed at him admiringly. *My God, the man's a saint,* she thought, which made her even more uncomfortable.

"At least they ain't got me workin' Homicide, where it's all doom and gloom a hundred percent of the time," he added. He smiled at her and winked at the waitress as she walked up to the table with their food and drinks. "So how's the book comin' along?" he asked as they started eating.

"I finished it and sent it in to my agent," she said.

"It's just a matter of time then, huh?" He smiled. "I'm startin' to read Catherine Asaro now. She's supposed to be the next best thing in science fiction."

"I hear she's pretty good," Katharine said.

"Can I see you again?" he asked. "I promise you there won't be any more questions next time."

She laughed. And even though she'd rather be rid of him for good, just for peace of mind, she shrugged her shoulders and said, "Sure, why not?"

She couldn't wait to tell Bree the news when she got back to the apartment.

"It's over!" she exclaimed as she rushed up to her bed. "The police aren't going to bug us anymore!"

The room was dark, and Bree lay very still and quiet.

"Did you hear me?" said Katharine, grabbing her cold hand. "It's all over."

"That's great," Bree numbly replied. "I saw Leon again. He came to me in a dream. He's finally forgiven me, and now he's worried about his mother. He says I should come clean, let everyone know what happened to him."

"Oh, sure. Why not?" Katharine scoffed. "Now that we're out of the woods."

"Are we?" Bree said. "Why are *you* stickin' around here for? You did nothing wrong. Go on, get out of here. You have a bright future ahead of you."

"So do you," Katharine said.

"No." She laughed. "All I have is Leon."

"Leon's dead, sweetie," Katharine said. "You have to let him go and move forward."

"Goddamn it, can't you see?" Bree exclaimed. "There's nothing left for me here! All my hope died with him!"

"What about friendship, Bree?" Katharine said, deeply offended. "Isn't that worth stickin' around for?"

"No, it's not enough," she replied.

"Okay, drugs then," Katharine snapped.

"Not enough," she said, shaking her head. "They grow tiresome in the end, just like everything else."

"You're full of shit, Bree," Katharine said. "I'm not buying any of it."

"I don't expect you to understand." She laughed. "You've forgotten how good it feels just to hold a man in your arms."

"It's only been a few months since I left my husband," Katharine replied. "And we were married for fifteen years before that. How could I have forgotten?"

"You told me that you weren't in love with him the way you used to be," Bree reminded her. "Were you just lying to yourself? Which is it, Katharine? Do you love the man or not?"

"Fuck you, Bree," Katharine replied.

"Let me tell you something," Bree said as she reached up and grabbed Katharine's blouse. "Love is the only thing worth living and dying for. The rest is bullshit. So if you still love your husband, I suggest that you go back to him before it's too late."

"How is this about me all of a sudden?" Katharine snapped. "If you think I'm just gonna go away and let you do this to yourself, forget it. You're going to be all right. All you need is a quick fix."

Bree laughed crazily as Katharine walked out of the room, grabbed her new cell phone from her purse, and called Murphy at the bar.

"Can you bring some stuff over?" Katharine asked him. "All right, I'll come down and get it then." She hung up and then called a cab.

She stepped into Murphy's office twenty minutes later, and he pulled his goods out of the drawer.

"I'm fresh out of rock, but I've got something better," he said as he lined three large bags of white powder tied with bread wrappers on the desk.

"What is it, coke?" she asked, stepping up to get a closer look.

"Nope. Heroin," he answered. "It's Grade A stuff, too. I'll sell it to you for about the same price as the other. But you've got to watch her. She tends to go crazy on it."

Katharine laughed.

"I mean it," he said, looking deadly serious all of a sudden. "The girl doesn't know when to stop. That's why I don't sell it to her very often."

"Don't worry, I'll take good care of her," she replied and pulled a huge wad of money out of her purse, mostly from tips and working extra hours. "Give me all of it."

She handed him the money, and he stuffed the bags into the purse.

"Pleasure doing business with you again," he smiled and winked.

She smiled back at him, and then she turned and headed for the door.

"If she ODs on the stuff, you don't know me," he said before she walked out.

Bree appeared to be even more depressed when Katharine stepped up to the bed.

"Okay, I'm back, and I've got the goods," Katharine smiled and shook the large bag in her hand like it was a Christmas bell.

"I don't want it," Bree sighed.

"Are you sure?" said Katharine, maintaining a perfect smile. "It's H. I hear it's your favorite."

"The syringes are in the bottom drawer." She sighed. "And you'll have to cook it. I'll tell you how to do it."

"Can't we just smoke it?" Katharine asked as she walked over to the dresser.

"I like to chase the dragon every once in a while," Bree said. "But there's nothing like the rush you get from shootin' up."

Bree told Katharine how to cook up the heroin and even wrote the instructions down for her on a sheet of notepaper. Ten minutes later, Katharine was slaving away in the kitchen just like old times. First she poured half a bag of heroin into a large spoon, mixed in a little tap water and some lemon juice, and then held it over the front burner and watched it cook. Within seconds it turned into a golden liquid. She dropped a piece of a cotton ball on it. Then she grabbed the syringe, placed the tip of the needle into the cotton, and drew up the liquid substance. Once the barrel of the syringe was completely full, she held it up and gently tapped on it to get all the air bubbles to the top.

Meanwhile, Bree was busy strapping a tourniquet around her arm to bring up the vein. When Katharine finally stepped into the room, Bree was ready for her; she quickly grabbed the syringe from Katharine and stuck the needle into her arm. Then she shot it all into her vein, threw the syringe on the nightstand, and lay back down again, smiling and looking extremely relaxed.

"I'd forgotten how good it feels," she muttered to herself. She slowly removed the tourniquet from her arm, looked up at Katharine and said, "Do you wanna try it?"

"No thanks," Katharine replied, finding the whole procedure a little unsettling.

"Have you heard from your agent yet?" Bree then asked after the initial rush.

"No." Katharine sighed.

"Don't worry, you will," she said. "You were meant for this world, Kat. And you're going to be successful at whatever you do."

"How do you know?" Katharine asked her skeptically.

"Because you're the strongest and most courageous person I've ever met," she said. "You'll do whatever it takes to survive, and you're white. That's how I know. Just promise me one thing—that you'll quit runnin' and go back to your family."

"I can't promise you that," Katharine replied.

"All right," she nodded and smiled. "Then go cook me up another one, will ya?"

She kept doing a bump every five minutes until she was barely able to move or keep her eyes open. When Katharine walked in with another syringe full, she could see that she'd had enough and started to back off.

"Please," Bree whispered and lifted up her arm, suggesting that she wanted Katharine to administer it this time.

Katharine shook her head and started to cry.

"C'mon, you'll be doin' a friend a favor," Bree said.

Katharine dried her eyes and slowly walked up to the bed. Then she strapped the tourniquet around Bree's arm very tightly and shot the lethal dose into her vein. Bree smiled and closed her eyes.

"I see him, Kat," she whispered. "My beautiful, sweet man, all in one piece." Then she turned her head toward the pillow and quickly slipped away.

Katharine flopped down next to her and started to cry again. Afterward she just sat there, wondering what to do next. She seriously thought about going to the police and telling them everything and paying for what she had done. But then she imagined being asked, "Why did you do it? Why did you keep giving her the stuff when you could see that she had too much already?"

Because she asked me to, she imagined herself telling them. *It's what she wanted. She was never happy here.*

She could picture them all looking at her like she was Dr. Kevorkian, and she suddenly looking very foolish. *Forget it. Some things are best kept secret,* she thought. She desperately tried to wipe her fingerprints off of everything with a clean rag—the tourniquet, the syringe, the nightstand, both doorknobs, et cetera, et cetera. She left the syringe and tourniquet on the nightstand to make it look like an accidental death or an unassisted suicide.

Stepping back into her apartment, she headed straight for the bathroom and splashed cold water on her face because she felt a little faint. She then looked into the mirror. As usual, she didn't like what she saw. But it was only because she could no longer recognize herself. She was the young and sexy Kitty Everhart, killer of men and whatever else stood in her way. It was the one person she had always aspired to be. But now that she had become her, she was filled with repulsion.

She walked back into the living room and flopped down on the couch, feeling completely drained. Suddenly her cell phone rang. She slowly reached into her purse, which was sitting next to her, and grabbed the phone. Then she flipped it open and put it to her ear without saying a word.

"Katharine, this is Mrs. Levi from the Miriam Levi Literary Agency," the old woman said in a cheerful voice. "I have some really good news. I found somebody who wants to publish your book. Congratulations."

"Thanks," she numbly replied.

"You and I need to huddle up sometime and come up with a good plan of attack," Mrs. Levi said. "Say, tomorrow at three o'clock?"

"Sure," Katharine answered and quickly hung up on her.

"Did you hear that, Bree?" she said, still feeling completely numb. "You were right. I guess we *both* got what we wanted. I'm just not so sure if I want it anymore ... or if I even deserve it."

Chapter 15: Then Comes Fame and Fortune

Now Katharine was the one lying in bed all day, hating herself and feeling completely miserable. It was as if she had suddenly become Bree. The latter had been dead for three days already, and her body still hadn't been discovered. Katharine was worried that it would be weeks before someone found her, after the stench of death and decay had permeated the whole building.

On Tuesday morning, August 24, Katharine had an appointment to see Mrs. Marsden, assistant editor at Femme Fatale Publishing, though she clearly wasn't in the mood for it. She was very depressed and hardly spoke a word while she sat in the waiting area with Mrs. Levi.

"Cheer up. It isn't a funeral," said Mrs. Levi, who looked like a Munchkin sitting next to Katharine.

The old woman wore a gold cashmere dress that looked like it just came off the rack and large diamond earrings. And it appeared that she'd had a couple of facelifts since Katharine had last seen her.

"Mrs. Marsden will see you now," said a beautiful young woman seated at the front desk.

In fact, the place was filled with beautiful female employees sitting in their offices or walking about.

"When we get in there, just keep quiet like you're doing now, and let me do all the talking," Mrs. Levi said as they stood up and headed toward the woman's office.

Mrs. Marsden was about Katharine's age, with short blonde hair and spectacles. She wore a gray pantsuit. She introduced herself to Katharine and had them sit down in the two chairs in front of her desk while she sat down and began to tell them all about Femme Fatale Publishing.

"We have over three hundred thousand readers," she said, "ninety-nine percent of which are female."

Then she talked about the different types of books they published, all from a woman's perspective, of course, and told them how many printing presses they had and where they were all located. At that point, Katharine started to tune her out; she thought of Bree slowly rotting away in her bed.

"I hope I'm not boring you, Katharine," Mrs. Marsden said finally, noticing her staring at the wallpaper. "May I call you Katharine?"

"Sure." Katharine blushed.

"I wanted to see you in person before we made a final offer," she said. "I hope you don't mind."

"No, not at all."

"We really like your story, and we want to publish it," she said. "This whole idea of a female spy is very intriguing to us. But there are a couple of conditions. First of all, the ending has to go. Having your main character get fat and have a bunch of kids just doesn't make sense. Somehow she's going to have to kill the Ljungberg character and escape from the island. Then we want you to write a series of books involving her as a secret agent traveling all over the globe and killing men for a living."

"I'm sorry, but I'm gonna have to say no," Katharine finally blurted out. Mrs. Levi cleared her throat and kicked her in the ankle. Katharine did her best to ignore it. "I just don't see how I could keep writing this fluff with all that's goin' on in the world," she said to Mrs. Marsden. "There's millions of people out there living on the street. Plus you've got kids high on crack all the time and jealous lovers beating up on their spouses. That's the kind of stuff that I want to write about from now on—stories about real people, especially the poor and downtrodden who live right here in the nation's melting pot. I feel like I really know these people now, having lived among them for the past few months. I consider myself one of them, in fact." She smiled proudly and held her chin up. "I've become a cynical, hard-boiled New Yorker," she said. "And our stories must be told."

"What kind of stories are we talking about exactly?" Mrs. Marsden asked. "Fiction? Nonfiction?"

"Fiction based on fact and with factual characters," Katharine answered.

"Oh, you mean like a Truman Capote, *In Cold Blood* sort of thing." The woman nodded.

"Yeah," said Katharine, growing excited. "My first story will be about two women living in the same apartment building, who are complete opposites in every way, and they start out disliking each other. But gradually they begin to accept one another, eventually becoming good friends and helping each other through the hardships of everyday life."

"Kinda sounds like *The Odd Couple*." The woman smiled.

"It's not," Katharine assured her. "It's very dark and tragic … like me."

"Well, there certainly is a place for that kind of writing," Mrs. Marsden said. "But there's also a place for good, old-fashioned entertainment, I believe, especially with all that's going on in the world. You have a gift for storytelling, Katharine. And by that I mean real imaginative storytelling, set in another place and time and filled with larger-than-life characters. I'd hate to see that talent go to waste for the sake of reality, which I think is sorely overrated." She wrote something down on a sheet of notepaper. "Hopefully this will help you change your mind," she said and slid it across her desk. "It's what we're prepared to offer you if you choose us."

Katharine picked up the piece of paper and was surprised to see a very large number on it—lots of zeros. She laughed excitedly and then showed it to Mrs. Levi, who did the same.

"That's how much we believe in your work, Katharine," Mrs. Marsden said. "We feel that this could be a very lucrative deal for all of us. So are you in?"

Both women nodded their heads simultaneously.

"Go ahead, change whatever you want." Katharine laughed. "And I'll start on that sequel first thing in the morning."

They went over the contract, and she signed it. Then she and her agent promptly left the building.

"Want to share a cab?" Mrs. Levi asked as they stepped out on the sidewalk.

"Nah, I think I'll walk a bit, get some fresh air," Katharine said.

"All right, dear." Mrs. Levi nodded and patted her on the back. "You made an old woman very happy, you know." Then she laughed excitedly again. "With twenty percent of a million dollars I could by myself a new house and my daughter a brand new car," she said.

"I thought it was fifteen percent," Katharine said as she watched the woman walk away.

She turned and walked down Sixth Avenue with a big smile on her face, suddenly feeling very happy and surer of herself. Then she crossed West Third Street and headed east through Greenwich Village and Washington Square Park—her favorite part of Manhattan. She loved the quaint little shops and beautiful townhouses. And she enjoyed the carnival-like atmosphere inside the park itself. Yet on this particular sunny day, there wasn't a street performer to be found, and there appeared to be more homeless people than usual, sleeping in doorways or propped up against storefront windows. One homeless man dressed in dirty old rags stood in the middle of the sidewalk and cursed at the crowd. She had seen him doing it before in *her* part of town.

"Cocksuckers," he snapped at them angrily in his gruff voice. "Look at me, why don't you? Look at what you created."

Of course, no one looked at him. They all walked right past him as if he wasn't even there, no doubt wishing that he'd just go away and stop being a nuisance. But Katharine wasn't like them. She understood his pain and didn't think for one second that she was better than him. And this time, she wasn't afraid to confront him.

"Cocksuckers!" he exclaimed once more as she walked straight up to him, raised her hand, and gently placed it on his shoulder.

The old bearded man looked at her with fiery eyes and an evil grin that seemed vaguely familiar to her, though she had never actually got a good look at his face until now.

"Well, hello neighbor," he said. "Come to see how the other half lives?"

His words chilled her to the bone. She suddenly felt like she was looking at a ghost.

My God, it's Leon, she thought. *But how?* She slowly stepped back and started to walk off. A bag lady who had dirt all over her face and looked about a hundred years old came hobbling toward her with a warm smile and even tried to hand her a pretty yellow rose. Katharine showed her no kindness, however. She frantically plowed right over her and blended in with the other pedestrians.

"You can run, but you can't hide!" the old homeless man shouted at her with a wicked laugh. "We'll always be with you, Katharine! Always!"

She looked straight ahead and continued walking as fast as she could. Now everyone was looking at her as if she was the bad guy—homeless and "regular" folk alike. It felt like the whole city had turned against her.

She stepped back into her apartment thirty minutes later; it felt like walking into a dark tomb. No matter how hard she tried, she couldn't stop looking up at the ceiling as she sat on the couch and watched TV. Suddenly her cell phone rang and she quickly grabbed it from the coffee table, anxious to hear a friendly voice.

"Hello?" she answered.

"It's me, Del," he said. "I hope you don't mind me calling this early."

"No, not at all," she cheerfully replied.

"*You* seem awful chipper this morning." He laughed. "Did you win the lottery or something?"

"Yeah." She grinned. "I mean, no. I just got back from a publishing house. Looks like they're gonna publish my book."

"That's great," he said. "I told you it was just a matter of time."

"Oh you did, huh?" She laughed.

"Hell, ya," he said. "I knew from the first moment I saw you that you were a special lady. Now the whole world will see just how beautiful and talented you are."

His words touched her very deeply, though it was obvious that he didn't really know her at all. *And God forbid that he ever will,* she thought.

"So that's it. Might as well lay my cards out on the table," he said. "I find you extremely attractive, and I want to get to know you a little better."

"No you don't," she muttered. "I'm damn near forty years old. Plus I'm …"

"What?" he asked curiously.

But she couldn't say it.

"I don't care how old you are," he said. "I actually prefer older women. The last girl I was with was a twenty-two-year-old supermodel. You might have heard of her. Her name's Lindy Marconi."

"Sorry, I'm not into fashion," she replied.

"We were together for almost five years and even talked about marriage," he said, "until she dumped me for Reece Bentley. I'm sure you heard of *him.*"

"Reece Bentley the movie star?" she replied with an involuntary laugh. "You poor guy. It must have been awful."

"I don't know … I guess it's better than being dumped for an average Joe such as myself," he sighed. "At least I can understand why she did it. It's Reece Bentley for Christ's sake."

"You're anything but average," she quickly pointed out to him. "I've always admired guys like you, guys who actually care about people and are willing to lay their lives on the line every single day. You're a real hero, not the fake one that you see on the movie screen. I'd choose you over Reece Bentley in a heartbeat."

"You certainly know how to cheer a guy up," he joked. "Where have you been my whole life?" Then after an uncomfortable silence, he added, "Do you like jazz?"

"Yeah, I like jazz." She laughed. "Why?"

"Ray Vega's playing at the Blue Note tonight," he said. "I was calling to see if you wanted to come."

"Sure." She smiled.

"Good. I'll pick you up at eight, then," he said. "How's Bree doin', by the way?"

"Huh?" she replied, caught completely off guard and suddenly losing her smile. "Oh, Bree? She's all right."

"I was plannin' on seeing her tomorrow," he said, "to keep her up-to-date on the Leon situation. So far we don't have a clue. But he'll turn up sooner or later. They always do. Maybe I can see her tonight instead."

"Yeah, that'll be good," she blankly replied.

"Alrighty then, I'll see you at eight o'clock," he said and quickly hung up.

"See ya," she muttered to herself and drew a heavy sigh, for she found herself falling for him. Yet she had no other choice but to let him go. She just didn't see how it could possibly work—a relationship built on lies and dirty secrets. And she knew that as long as she was with him, there would be no end to all of her lying and scheming, especially now that a body was about to be discovered. Then there was Frank, who had popped up in her head quite unexpectedly throughout the conversation. For once, she wasn't dead set on getting back at him by plunging straight into an affair with another man. It seemed quite ludicrous, in fact, while the future of their marriage remained uncertain. She saw it as a sign of maturity on her part, since everything she did was just to get back at him—whether it was taking Ecstasy for the first time, getting involved in murder, or allowing herself to fall in love with Joe.

Suddenly, she felt the walls closing in on her; she just had to get out of there. She quickly shut off her phone and jumped to her feet. Rushing into the bedroom, she started to pack her suitcase. After she was finished packing, she called a cab, grabbed the suitcase and her purse, and swiftly left the apartment. She noticed Mrs. Chang crack open her door as she rushed through the hallway.

"Goodbye, Mrs. Chang," Katharine said to her before she passed her by.

The old woman opened the door a little farther to show her face.

"Goodbye," she said, looking puzzled. "Where you going?"

"I don't know!" Katharine exclaimed as she swiftly rushed past and reached the stairs. "I just got to get far away from *here!*"

"Good luck!" the old woman shouted. "Have safe journey!"

Katharine then ran into Mr. Brown in the lobby. He had just stepped into the building, carrying a hot dog in one hand and a cup of coffee in the other.

"Well, hello there, Mrs. Beaumont," he said to her cheerfully.

"Hi. Got to go." She smiled and continued on her way.

"Sure, I understand!" he shouted. "By the way, how's that book comin' along? I'd like to take a look at it sometime if you don't mind!"

She simply ignored him and hurriedly walked out the doors. The taxi arrived within minutes. She opened the back door, threw her suitcase in, and stepped inside.

"Where to, lady?" the cab driver asked.

She stared at him blankly through the rearview mirror. *That's a good question,* she thought to herself. Then finally she laughed, shrugged her shoulders, and said, "Take me to the bus station."

Why not? she thought. *My work is done here. I achieved everything that I set out to accomplish. Besides, I'm tired of running. And Oklahoma's the only home I know.*

"So long, Bree," she whispered, staring at the Greystone for the last time as the driver slowly pulled away from the curb.

For the most part, she felt relieved to leave it all behind. It was like stepping out from under a dark cloud and becoming pure again.

Two days later, on a Friday evening, she was back in Oklahoma City and walking up her driveway with her suitcase in hand, ready to reassume the role of the everyday housewife. *At least it was one I can easily fall back into,* she thought. *And it's safe.* She had also come to realize that she was still in love with her husband, despite his shortcomings. She was ready to give him and the children another go. *But will they be willing to give me a second chance?* she wondered. She stepped up to the front porch and tapped on the door as if she was a total stranger. Frank immediately answered and just stood there with a look of surprise and wonder. She sensed he was afraid to say or do anything that might scare her off.

"We were just eating dinner," he finally managed to blurt out and slowly stepped back to let her in. Then he shouted, "Kids, come see who's here!"

They both immediately ran into the entryway.

"Mama, you're back!" Maggie exclaimed, running up and throwing her arms around Katharine while Billy stopped short and stood at a distance. "Have you come home to stay?"

"Yes," Katharine said as she held her daughter tightly and shed tears of joy.

"I really missed you, Mama," Maggie said very excitedly. "Oh, and guess what?"

"What?"

"I joined an aerobics class, and I've already lost five pounds," Maggie said.

"That's great," Katharine replied. "You look beautiful. But it's not just about looks. It's about feeling good and being healthy. I should have stressed that more." She glanced over at Billy, who just kept gawking at her with wide eyes.

"Billy, aren't you gonna say hello to your mother?" Frank asked him.

Billy simply shook his head.

"Hello, Billy," Katharine said and smiled at him.

He didn't answer.

"I didn't know you were a writer, Mama," Maggie said as she continued to hold onto to her and looked up at her face.

Katharine nodded and said, "I never should've kept that from you guys. I'm sorry."

"I like to write, too," said Maggie. "I got an A on the short story I wrote for my English class."

"I want to read it," Katharine said.

"So how did it go?" Frank asked her. "I mean, with the writing and all. Did you find a publisher?"

"Yep," Katharine answered. "And not only that, I've got a wonderful surprise for you all. We're about to become millionaires."

"Really?" Maggie exclaimed.

"Mmm hmm," said Katharine. "And the book's not even published yet. I haven't sold a single copy."

"Now you can have the kitchen redone like you've always wanted," Frank smiled.

Katharine laughed. "This whole house is gettin' a makeover," she said. "We might even buy a new one."

"We're gettin' a new house!" Maggie exclaimed. "All right!"

"What do you think about that, Billy?" his father asked him. "Your mother's about to become rich and famous."

"Fuck it," Billy muttered under his breath and looked down at the floor.

"Billy!" Frank snapped.

Katharine slowly broke away from her daughter and walked straight up to the young man, since he refused to come to her.

"I think you grew another inch since I saw you last." She smiled, noticing that she was only a head taller than him.

Then she stepped up even closer to him and tried to give him a hug. He immediately jumped back and said, "No."

"All right, Billy. That's enough," Frank snapped, taking a step toward him.

"It's okay," Katharine said to Frank very calmly and gestured him to stay back.

She stepped up and managed to get her arms around Billy this time. She felt him place his hands on her ribs to try to push her away. But she held onto him very tightly and wasn't about to let go.

"You're not supposed to leave!" he shouted angrily, struggling in vain to jerk away from her.

"I know, I know," she said.

"Why did you?" he shouted.

"I can't explain it, Billy," she said. "I just had to get away for a while to try to find myself. But I'm here now, and that's all that matters."

"Bullshit!" he exclaimed. "It's not fair that you get to walk out anytime you want to! How do we know that you won't do it again?"

"I won't, Billy," she said as the tears began to flow again. "You have my word on that."

"I don't believe you!" he exclaimed. "You're lying!"

"No, I'm not," she said. "I never stopped thinking about you and your sister while I was gone. How could I? It's like asking a mother to forget the day her children were born. Those were the happiest days of my life … when you two were born. And now I want to see you grow up and have kids of your own."

"You're lying!" he shouted a second time and tried even harder to get away from her.

But she was stronger and more determined.

"You don't care about us!" he continued shouting with all his might. "I hate you! I hate you!" He suddenly broke down and started crying.

"Shhh, it's okay, baby," she said to him in a low, soothing voice and gently rocked him in her arms.

She felt him put his hands on her back and was filled with elation, for it seemed she had finally torn down the wall between them, allowing the healing process to begin.

"I'm sorry, Mama," he cried.

"So am I," she replied.

"I really fucked up," he added.

"I know," she said. "Don't worry about it. I did some things that I'm not so proud of, too. The important thing is to learn from our mistakes and move on."

He stopped crying suddenly, sniffling. "How could you know?" he asked her very curiously.

"Your father told me when he came to visit," she replied.

"But *he* doesn't even know about it," said Billy.

"Know about what?" she asked as her eyes suddenly popped open.

"I got a girl pregnant," he said. "I didn't mean to do it, honest."

"Who is she, Billy?" Katharine asked, trying to keep calm. "Who did you get pregnant?"

"Her name's Cindy Byson," he said. "She was in my math class last semester, and I've been seeing her all summer."

Katharine glanced over at Frank, who looked almost as surprised as she was. He shrugged his shoulders and shook his head, suggesting that he had no idea.

"She just found out about it yesterday," Billy added. "And she says she gonna tell her parents tonight."

"So we should be gettin' a call anytime soon," Katharine sighed. "Looks like I got home just in time for it."

"I'm sorry," said Billy and started crying again.

"It's all right, son," she said very confidently as she continued holding him in her arms. "I'm here, now. Everything's going to be all right."

Ordinarily, she would've been devastated by the news. But now, teen pregnancy seemed like a minor catastrophe compared to what she had just been through. She was perfectly willing, even eager, to tackle the problem head-on. As far as the last three and a half months were concerned, she had forgotten them already. It was as if she had just awakened from a terrible nightmare.

"Welcome home," Frank said as he and Maggie stepped up to join Katharine and Billy.

"Thanks." She laughed.

Epilogue

Later that same evening, Katharine asked Billy if he had forced himself on Cindy. His exact response was, "No. She wanted it more than I did." Katharine then asked him if he and the girl were the same age, to which he replied, "No. I think she's older. She started kindergarten a year later than all the other kids."

"Hmm," Katharine said, wondering who had actually seduced whom.

They received a phone call from the girl's father shortly thereafter. Katharine didn't know who it was at first since her husband had the misfortune to answer it. Yet she could tell by his frown and his inability to get a word in edgewise that the caller was furious.

"Hold on there, Mr. Byson," Frank said finally. "We're just as shocked and appalled as you are. But all this shouting and name-calling isn't going to help the situation one bit. Furthermore, if you plan on taking us to court, you're in for one hell of a fight because as far as we're concerned it was *your* daughter who corrupted our underage son."

Katharine nodded and smiled as she stood firmly by his side. She had never felt more proud to be his wife. Frank then offered to pay for half of the man's expenses—whether his daughter decided to keep the child or not. Mr. Byson accepted the offer and immediately hung up. The next day, Katharine and Frank drove their son to the abortion clinic and stayed with him and the other family while young Cindy Byson underwent the procedure. She and Billy remained good friends afterward, despite her father's objections, and Katharine always treated her like one of the family whenever she came to the house.

After Katharine received her book advance, the first thing she did was buy a computer and placed it in the den for the whole family to use. Then she and her husband began looking for a contractor to redo their kitchen. She had already changed the ending to her first novel and was currently at work on the second one, titled *Kitty Goes to Moscow*. This time, she had her heroine facing off against the Russians during the onset of the Cold War. Though she was learning how to type, she let Maggie do most of the typing for her when the youngster wasn't busy with her homework. Maggie was an excellent typist, having taken an entire semester of it the year before. The two started dieting together, as well, and Katharine even joined her daughter's aerobics class. Maggie lost another five pounds while Katharine lost only a couple.

Katharine also began to take an interest in her son's movies and music. They often sat together in front of the television and watched old slasher movies from the '70s and '80s—the gorier the better. And she became a huge fan of his favorite rock group, Radiohead. She loved to listen to "Fake Plastic Trees" over and over again on his iPod while he was away at school. Billy made Bs and Cs on his next report card and managed to stay out of trouble during the whole semester. Plus, he stopped spending so much time alone inside his bedroom. He seemed to enjoy hanging out with the family after the evening meal.

Katharine and Frank started having sex more often and even added foreplay to the routine to spice things up a bit. They also started going out more. They went to the movies at least once a week. And on Friday or Saturday nights, Frank took her ballroom dancing. Life was good again and Katharine knew she had Bree to thank for it. She had constantly reminded Katharine of her family, making her realize how much she still loved them—while teaching her a valuable lesson on tolerance and forgiveness. Katharine often thought of Bree and always felt her presence in the room. She was now a firm believer in ghosts and human possession. She believed Bree to be a good spirit, however, who was simply watching over her.

Six months flew by very rapidly. One evening, as the whole family sat on the living room carpet, playing Monopoly, the telephone rang. Katharine immediately got up and went into the kitchen to answer it.

"Beaumont residence," she answered.

"Hello, stranger. Remember me?" said a familiar voice, though she had not heard it in quite some time.

She stood there stunned and speechless as if it was another ghost from her past. "Joe?" she muttered. "How did you find me?"

"I'm in the Mafia," he replied. "That's what we do best—find people." He laughed. "Actually, all I did was look you up in the phone book," he said. "Have you heard from the police yet?"

"No. Why?" Katharine gasped.

"They found Leon's body parts," he answered bluntly.

"I thought you put him someplace where no one would ever find him," she said in a low voice. Frank and the kids laughed and shouted in the background.

"We did," said Joe. "We buried him over six feet deep in the Catskill Mountains. That should've been the end of it. But then some idiot came along and decided to build a giant strip mall right there in that very spot. They're bulldozing the entire area. And yesterday afternoon, they dug up one of the plastic bags containing Leon's severed head and his intestines. The police have already been over here asking questions. Do you know a Lieutenant Jacobs?"

"Yes," Katharine nervously replied.

"Well, he's lookin' for ya," Joe said. "I just thought you should know that. He discovered Bree's body the night you disappeared. He was lookin' for you then, too. But I guess he gave up the search after the coroner ruled her death a suicide. They found a large amount of heroin in her system." He paused. "I don't think he's gonna have any problem finding you if all he has to do is look you up in the phone book." He then pointed out to her, "Or maybe he's found you *already*. You know how the police are. They make you think that they're not watching. Then all of a sudden, they pounce on you ... like a snake on a June bug. Damn coppers."

Katharine suddenly felt very uneasy and stared out the kitchen window, wondering if she was being watched at that very moment.

"You know, I'm probably going to get whacked over this," Joe continued. "Louis is very upset with me right now. They've been hounding him all day, along with those damn reporters. And he blames me for it. He says that I've caused him a great deal of embarrassment, dragging him back into the spotlight like this ... for something he doesn't know a damn thing about. But don't worry. I ain't saying nothin' to nobody."

"What about Federico?" asked Katharine.

"Federico is no longer with us," Joe said. "I'm afraid he met with an unfortunate accident. He drove his Lamborghini off a cliff."

Katharine gasped.

"I kept telling him that he needed to slow down," Joe added. "But you know how kids are." Then he exclaimed in a low voice, "Oh, wait! Here comes somebody! It's the boss. I have to go."

"Joey?" Katharine blurted out, afraid that something terrible was about to happen to him.

"Don't worry, you're secret's safe with me," he said and hung up.

"Joey?" she repeated as the line went dead.

She could still hear her children laughing in the other room. Suddenly Frank shouted, "Honey, who is it? Better get back in here! Your son's cleanin' up ... and you're about to go bankrupt!"

But she remained frozen and was filled with dread as she continued listening to an empty dial tone, for she could see her past swiftly catching up with her. She seriously considered telling her husband everything, while she still had the chance. *Maybe I'll wake him up in the middle of the night and tell him,* she mused. *And in the morning, he'll be serving me my last breakfast. Nope. I was right the first time. Some things are best kept secret. What happens in New York City should stay in New York City.* She decided not to worry about it anymore and quickly hung up the phone. *Joe's a big boy; he can take care of himself,* she thought. *If the police come after me, I'll just have to forget about the kitchen and hire the best criminal lawyer I can find. Plus, I'll sic Kitty on them.*

"Who was it?" asked Frank as she stepped back into the living room and sat down on the floor.

"Oh, it was just Mrs. Levi," Katharine sighed. "She wanted to know how the next book was comin' along." She paused for a moment and then added, "I'm tired of all these interruptions. How do you guys feel about movin' to another country?"

"Really?" shouted the kids simultaneously, seeming thrilled with the whole idea.

"You're kidding, right?" Frank said.

"Just a thought," she replied as she grabbed her dice, gave them a quick shake, and let them roll across the board.